Butterfly: A Lancaster Novel

Book 3

Stacy Goforth

Stacy Goforth

Library of Congress Control Number: 2025919629

Paperback ISBN: 979-8-9985002-5-1

eBook ISBN: 979-8-9985002-6-8

Book Design: by Stacy Goforth

First edition 2025

Praise for the Lancaster Series: Dragonfly: Book 1

Reviewed by Mimie Odigwe for Readers' Favorite

With small-town shenanigans, a tight-knit, albeit meddling family, spiteful exes, and a tender and warming love declaration at the end, I can picture Dragonfly by Stacy Goforth as a Hallmark movie. It's like Goforth knew how engrossing her book was, so there will be other books featuring the whole clan. Yay! The side characters are supportive, humorous, and have believable development. My favorites have to be Jax, Sam's perceptive and wry eldest brother, and the sassy, unfiltered Kelley, Blake's younger sister. Dragonfly isn't all fluff and flirtations; it explores how different families react to grief, the sacrifices made for family, and with just the right amount of romantic tension to keep pages turning well past bedtime. Dragonfly is for lovers of heart and heat, and anyone who has never really gotten over their crush.

Praise for the Lancaster Series: Firefly: Book 2

Reviewed by Mimie Odigwe for Readers' Favorite

Stacy Goforth's Firefly is addictive. One more page turns into five, then ten, and then... whoops, you've finished it. And the characters? Jax is a man after my own heart, with wry quips, fierce protectiveness, and healing from a motorcycle accident that shook his confidence. Jax and Allison are fire and gasoline, but for a blaze to warm yourself over. Firefly contains more of this endearing and exasperating small town, a lovable family, banter, and sultry romance that readers of the first book in the Lancaster series will love. As always, Goforth never sacrifices the story for spice; steamy content has been indicated for readers who may want to skip it.

STACY GOFORTH

Dedicated to the Lancasters, who have occupied my every thought for the past year. Thanks for the lack of sleep, the constant anxiety, and endless presence in my life. May we both rest in peace now!

"Do you really want to look back on your life and see how wonderful it could have been had you not been afraid to live it?"

Caroline Myss

Bad Luck — Noah Kahn	3:12
Lucy in the Sky with Diamonds — The Beatles	3:28
Feels Like Home — Caamp	5:11
False Confidence — Noah Kahn	3:43
Espresso — Sabrina Carpenter	2:55
Walk of Shame — Pink	2:42
Fancy — Iggy Azalea, Charli xcx	3:20
I Think We're Alone Now — Tiffany	3:49
Fallin' For You — Colbie Caillat	3:36
Sour Candy — Lady Gaga, BLACKPINK	2:38
Crazier Things — Chelsea Cutler, Noah Kahn	4:25
Beautiful Things — Benson Boone	3:00
Don't Give Up on Me — Andy Grammer	3:16
Lose Control — Teddy Swims	3:31
Ghosts That we Know — Mumford & Sons	5:40
No Complaints — Noah Kahn	3:25

<u>Dicktionary</u>

Here for the smut? Skip this page and read on...

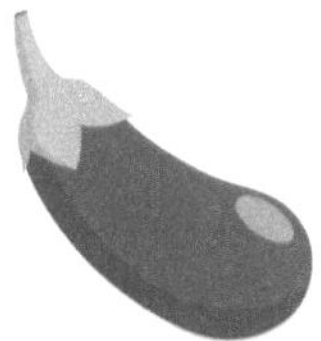

Feeling shy? Feel the need to skip through the more steamy scenes? Below is a list of chapters with sexual content so you are aware ahead of time:

Chapter 14

Chapter 18

Chapter 20

Chapter 22

Chapter 23

Chapter 25

Chapter 26

Happy reading...

Chapter One

Dylan

Love was a four-letter word Dylan Lancaster despised.

Oh sure, love seemed to work out just splendidly for his sister Samantha and his best friend Blake Forrester. They'd been living in an absolute bubble of euphoria for almost a year now. And his older brother Jackson's new relationship with Allison Hanover was benefiting from a big ole case of love hysteria. But in his own life, well, Dylan Lancaster was pretty determined that love just wasn't in the cards for him.

Not that he'd been looking very hard for it. After all, he'd spent the last year falling in and out of bed with Donna Draper, Blake's ex-girlfriend. While she was hot to look at, being compared to your best friend all night long wasn't exactly on anyone's top ten list. But when you come from a small town like Titusville, you take what you can get, and for Dylan, he just wanted to fill the void sitting like a pit in the bottom of his stomach. Which made for a really unhappy and dissatisfying existence.

And he truly was unhappy. Which was how Dylan got to where he was today—sitting at his mother's gravesite, preparing for the first time in his life to leave Titusville and head to New York City.

"Well, Mom, I guess this is gonna be the last Friday visit for a while." A few overhead leaves were turning orange and falling to the ground as he looked around the cemetery.

This spot under the tree had become a place of solitude for him. Ever since Dylan graduated high school, he had been coming up here on Fridays to visit his mom. Sometimes he would just sit on the stone bench, letting his thoughts drift idly. Other times, he would draw in his sketchbook, letting his pen distract him from the disorganized anxiety mulling about in his brain. Then there were moments like today when he would just talk. Like she was still here.

He wasn't crazy. It wasn't like he ever got a response or anything. Talking to his mom was like free therapy, if he believed in that kind of crap.

"I gotta go check on Sam, just to make sure she's doing alright in the big city." So maybe that was a bit of a fib. Sam was fine. Hell, she was probably the most adjusted of all the Lancaster siblings. He closed his eyes and inhaled. "Alright, fine, you win, Mom. I'm not doing alright. This last year has been bad. All the stuff with Blake, the crap I've been doing with Donna. I'm numb. I don't even feel like myself most days, though that might be because I'm drunk most of the time," he sighed. "Who am I kidding? You probably know all of this already." Biting back his emotions, he whispered, "Somehow you still know everything, don't you?"

A breeze caused the leaves to lift off the ground and swirl across the lot. "I've got this dark pit of sadness inside of me. I can't explain it, but something's just missing, and I don't know how to find it, or if it's even out there." He leaned back on the bench and stared up at the sky. "Sam has Blake, and Jax has Allison, and I'm happy for them, really I am. You'd love how freaking happy they both are. It's sickening, honestly. I've never seen Jax smile this much before. It's gross. I'm not gonna miss that for a few months." That was a lie. He would miss his brother and his goofy ass mood more than any thing.

He looked down at the time on his phone and realized that he needed to get going if he wanted to say goodbye to Jax and Allison and make it to his cab on time. "I'm gonna go to the city and figure out my shi—crap, Mom. I promise. I'm gonna make you proud of me." He placed his hand on the stone in front of him and stood, sticking his earbuds in his ears. "Bye, Mom, I promise I'll come back when I'm better."

He walked back to his bicycle, humming along to Noah Kahn's "Bad Luck" as the music came to life in his earbuds. Behind him, the small blue and green dragonfly still fluttered away at the bottom of the tree where he left it.

Dylan sat on the bench, waiting for his cab to take him to the bus station. He stared into the brown paper bag that Allison had given him before he left the house. Dylan was happy to find a granola bar with chocolate chips, a bag of Doritos, some candy, and a can of Dr. Pepper. He had been worried that Allison would try to toss in a few healthy treats like she was always trying to pass off to Jax, but maybe he was her favorite Lancaster after all. Even though they hadn't started out on the best terms, Jackson's girlfriend had turned out to be a pretty sweet addition to the family.

He felt better leaving Jax alone in Titusville with the shop, knowing that he had Allison by his side. He knew Jax hated everyone worrying about him after his accident last year, but Dylan couldn't help it. And he felt pretty guilty leaving him with all the work at the shop. His replacement, Will, was turning out to be a promising mechanic, but the kid was still a noob. It would take him months to figure out how to do half the jobs required to assist Jax in the shop.

Not that Dylan was a master mechanic, he was pretty shit at the job, to be honest. That was half the reason he was sitting on this bench, anxious as hell to get out of Titusville. But then, Dylan hadn't really ever been good at anything except drawing. And he'd never really figured out what good a few pen marks on scratch paper could do for him?

He glanced down at the sketchbook in his lap, pencil marks he'd drawn on the page of the old building across the street from his bench. He started drawing when he was thirteen years old. Back then it was mostly cartoons, silly drawings of little round creatures that mostly vomited or farted. Nothing Dylan ever did was serious. But it made him laugh, and that wasn't something he did often.

Most of Dylan's life was depressing. He lost his mother when he was only eight years old. Cancer sure was a bitch. His dad didn't know how to cope with it, so he told them all to move on. And yeah, Sam was only six, so she just grew up thinking that was normal. And Jax, well, Jax just learned that moving on was what you did. The Lancasters didn't form attachments to anything.

No one wanted to visit the cemetery, so Dylan went on his own. Every Friday, he would bike up to that spot under the tree and sit for hours just talking to her. It became their secret, something he never even told his best friend, Blake. After a while, it just made him angry. Why was he the only one who still cared? Why didn't anyone else miss her?

Communication wasn't exactly a Lancaster trait. But last year had fixed a lot of that. Sam seemed to have resolved her emotional constipation, and Jax stopped running long enough to find something worth settling down for. Which just left him. And damn if that wasn't depressing.

The only Lancaster who could draw stupid things, attracted women who were still in love with his best friend, twenty-nine-years-old and still lived in a one-room apartment over his dad's garage, could survive a whole week on ramen cooked in the microwave (winning!), and had so far messed up everything in his life. Yeah, he was a real prize! He was sure the women would fall all over him in New York.

A cab appeared in the distance, and Dylan stood from the bench, gathering his suitcase from his feet. He exhaled and looked around the town he had lived in his entire life. Once he got in this cab, everything was going to change.

Tentatively, he lifted his suitcase and paused. "You gonna get in or are ya just sightseeing?" The older woman sitting at the wheel of the cab was glaring at him as she impatiently waited with her hands on the steering wheel.

"Oh, um, yeah, I'm just..." He stared back at the bench he had just vacated. "I've never left Titusville before."

The woman groaned. "I'm not a therapist; I just drive the cab."

He walked around the back of the car and shoved his suitcases inside, snorting a small laugh. It was comforting to know that there was someone in the world with a worse attitude than his.

He settled into the back seat of the car and stared out the window as the scenery blurred by and the town he had called home his entire life slowly disappeared from view. He wasn't sure what to expect in New York City—more traffic, thicker pollution, 8.258 million irritating people milling about. Perhaps this was an awful idea, he thought as he cursed under his breath.

"I charge extra for foul language." The woman scowled.

"Sorry." He closed his eyes and laid his head back on the bench behind him. "I just realized that I really hate people."

"You and me both." The woman stared at him through the rearview mirror. "You gonna be staying in Pittsburgh?"

"Catching a bus to New York City."

"Ah heck, you ain't gonna get away from people there." She shook her head and frowned. "They pack em' in, butt to nuts there."

Dylan snorted and shook his head. "I'm visiting my sister and my best friend. They live in the East Village." He didn't know why he was sharing information with the woman; after all, she wasn't exactly friendly. But then again, neither was he.

"I had a cousin who lived in the village, got murdered a couple of years back," she grunted. Dylan's eyes grew wide. "Knife attack." The woman caught his reaction in the mirror. "Oh, she wasn't at home when it happened. It was on that subway thing. Dangerous places, those underground cesspools. You stay out of there." Dylan shook his head rapidly.

"I probably won't go out much, you know, on account of the people hating." He shrugged, smirking back at her in the mirror.

"You know what I say. When you can't go out, go up." Dylan's brow furrowed, and he nodded his head.

"Uh yeah, sure."

"I got a cat." Her voice sounded as if it were scraping on gravel. He figured she was the type that smoked three packs of cigarettes a day. "Her name's Tuna, on account of that's all she'll eat." The woman tugged her visor down, and an array of photos of a gray tabby cat appeared above her head. "I built her an outdoor sanctuary on my roof, and we hide out there, away from that busybody June next door." She made a sound that he wasn't sure was a laugh or a choking noise. He hoped it was a laugh. He didn't want to have to perform the Heimlich maneuver before he got to the bus station, but then she resumed her story and he relaxed into his seat. "Most meddlesome woman I've ever met. Had to get away from her somehow, you know."

"I'll be sure to find somewhere to hide once I get there." He stared out the window, wondering if he would miss the trees once he got to the city. The leaves were turning color, one of his favorite parts of fall. The city might feel sterile without the creek or the forest. He wondered if Sam ever missed that.

"This is your stop." He looked up to see the bus stop in front of them. He gathered his things and walked toward the buses when he heard the woman call out to him. "Hey, don't hide too long. It's hard to get back out there once you do."

Dylan nodded and returned a quaint smile to the woman before she rolled up her window and drove away.

He walked into the station, hoping that six hours on a Greyhound bus would give him plenty of time to reflect and prepare himself for his upcoming visit with his sister and Blake.

But six hours later, the raging headache, miserable attitude, and ache in his back were further signs that the only thing he had reflected on was his complete and utter hatred of people.

Take, for example, the man sitting in front of him. It would be easy to say that he kept to himself for the entire six hours, except he snored for five of them. And not the kind of snoring that could simply be ignored. No, at one point during the trip, Dylan was certain that an ostrich was going to come out of the man's nostrils and lay an egg right there in the middle of the aisle. He was honestly disappointed that it never happened because, if it had, maybe they could have at least made an omelet. He was starving, and he'd already eaten all his snacks Allison had packed for him.

Then there were Reginald and Sarah. He knew their names not because he had met them and become friends with them. He was familiar with these names because their mother had screamed them over one hundred and fifty times during the six-hour drive. "*Reginald*, do not sit on that man's lap. *Sarah*, do not spit on the nice woman. *Reginald*, do not run. *Sarah*, do not..." At one point, Dylan offered to play hide and seek with the kids, only to be rebuffed when he suggested they start by hiding outside on the road.

By the time the bus pulled into the station in New York City, his nerves were frayed and his manners were no longer even in the realm of friendly.

He shuffled down the aisle of the bus, nearly tripping Reginald as the drowsy child stumbled toward the exit. Sarah was sleeping soundly in her mother's arms in front of him. How nice of her to sleep now that the trip was over. "I think she wore herself out," the woman said, glancing back at him. Dylan grunted and glanced away, uninterested in making conversation with the woman whose children had kept him up for the last six hours, begging for a drink to calm his nerves. "She'll sleep the rest of the day now."

Dylan lifted his chin as the line in front of them moved. "I'm sure she will," he grunted.

Reginald tripped as he climbed down the stairs, scraping his knee at the bottom and wailing up at his mother. Sarah woke up at the wretched sound and started crying as well. Dylan's eyes fluttered shut in annoyance. He was never getting off this bus. The bus driver pushed past him, rushing to help the mother with her children. He shook his head and picked the boy off the ground, handing him to the woman as he helped them off the bus. Dylan was grateful to see his moment finally and rushed past the mess of crying children, away from the scene of terror.

"Dilly Bear!" His sister's voice echoed across the parking lot, and he turned just in time to see her running toward him, launching into his arms. He gasped as she leapt, her legs wrapping around his waist. A smile broke across his face for the first time that day.

"You act like I haven't seen you in forever," he said, pulling on the strands of her hair.

"It's been almost a year." She slapped his hand away from her hair, dropping her feet to the ground. "Am I not allowed to miss my big brother?"

He looked up as Blake approached, shaking his head at the two of them. "Sorry, I tried to hold her back, but you're all she's talked about for the last week." Dylan fist-bumped his best friend, and Sam hung onto Dylan's side like she was afraid he would disappear if she let go.

"I don't remember her being this clingy. What's up with that?" he asked, staring at Blake with a raised brow.

Blake smirked and ran a hand through his hair. "What can I say? I'm irresistible. She likes to cuddle now."

"Gross! Is this what I'm going to be subjected to now? You don't know what I've been through with Jax and Allison." Dylan shook his head. "Those two are next level."

His sister squealed. "I want to hear all about it, because Jax is terrible with details. Tell me everything! I want to know how they met. And not the story Jax told, I want the real story." He followed behind her as she practically skipped beside Blake. "I want to know what Allison is like. Was Jackson *really* an asshole to her? And what exactly was Operation Free Firefly?" Sam was rattling off questions as they walked back to the car and, for the first time in months, Dylan finally felt himself relax.

Chapter Two

Lucy

Beatles' music played across the rooftop of the apartment building in the East Village. "Lucy in the Sky with Diamonds" bounced through the flowers and zipped around the walls of the greenhouse as Lucy Patel danced to the music while she watered her plants.

It was the first thing she did every morning after getting out of bed and before going to work at the bookstore. Water the plants, care for the butterflies, make sure her sister had a healthy lunch, and then head to work.

Lucy and her older sister Amber moved to New York City from California three years ago after NY Model Management signed Amber to a contract. It had been Amber's dream to be signed by a New York modeling agency. Lucy was sad to leave her family back in San Francisco, but Amber didn't want to move alone, and Lucy hated to disappoint her sister. Living in New York meant moving away from the only friends she had back home, and dropping out of college, but at least she would be with Amber.

The best thing that had happened to her was finding the job at a nearby bookstore, which turned out to be pretty cool. She'd been working there for the last two years, and her co-workers made work entertaining and welcoming to be around, which was more than she could say about Amber's co-workers.

Models weren't exactly her type of people. At least, not the ones that Amber hung out with. For one, they never ate pizza, and that was a cardinal sin in *Lucy's Guidebook of Rules to Live By*. Second, they looked down their noses at everyone. It's possible she felt that way because most of them were over six feet tall, and Lucy was barely five foot three. But these were the type of girls who looked down on people for having the wrong hair color, or the wrong last name.

That was the first rule in her guidebook. *Rule #1: Always treat people the way you want to be treated.* It was really important to Lucy that everyone feel like they mattered, because what was the point of life if you didn't matter to someone?

Lucy closed the door to her butterfly greenhouse and turned off her music. "I'll be back later, beauties." She looked around hopefully at the greenery on the roof. She only hoped the winter would be kind this year and that most of the plants would survive. Lucy had worked really hard last year to save all her money from the bookstore to build the greenhouse for the butterflies so that they could survive the winter. Amber even chipped in at Christmas the last bit of money she needed to secure the costs the apartment manager asked for to allow her to finish the project.

She was thankful that she had supportive neighbors too, like Blake Forrester, who had moved in last year and rallied behind her to keep the initiative alive. Without him, her butterflies might not be around next year.

She pushed her key into the lock and stepped into her apartment. She could hear the shower running in the bathroom. Amber had an important photoshoot this morning, and Lucy hoped she would finish soon so that she wouldn't be late this time.

She packed Amber's lunch—a grilled chicken salad she had prepared last night for her—with a bottle of that fancy water she liked so much, chilled exactly how she preferred it. She prepped her yogurt, setting it aside in the to-go bowl on the side of the counter ready for her sister to grab as soon as she stepped out of the bathroom.

Looking up at the clock, she realized she needed to get moving if she wanted to get herself ready for work. She rushed to her room and dug through her clothes strewn about on the floor. She had run out of time to do her own laundry this weekend. Lucy was usually too busy preparing Amber for a photoshoot or brand party. By the time she was done with all the prep work, she would fall asleep instead of making the trek to the basement to wash her own clothes. Holding her denim overalls to her nose, she sniffed and shrugged.

Rule #25: If it doesn't smell foul, it's wearable, but always spritz with one pump of body mist, just in case.

Lucy rummaged around in her dresser for the bottle she was looking for, tossing things to the floor until she located it. She spritzed the denim fabric until she felt satisfied no one would be any the wiser and quickly got dressed. She ran a brush through the messy strands on her head and pressed a barrette into her hair. Her reflection stared back at her from the mirror. "Good morning, Lucy!" She curtsied before heading out the door.

The moment she was in the hall, her sister was stepping out of the bathroom. Her tall, toned legs looked perfect in her black six-inch heels. Lucy whistled. "Look at you, sexy woman."

"Morning, Luce. Did you..." She paused at the counter. "Of course you did." She reached for her yogurt. "Thanks for the breakfast. Are you heading out?"

"Yup, off to work. Good luck on your shoot. Call me if you need anything." Her sister kissed her forehead.

"You take such good care of me, Luce."

"That's what sisters are for." She smiled and bounced toward the door.

Rule #2: Sisters are friends for life.

Lucy stepped into the hallway and skipped to the end of the wall until she reached the elevator. She watched the lights dancing toward her floor.

"Lucy!" Blake's voice drifted from the other end of the hall. Her neighbor waved and joined her by the elevator. Blake Forrestor had moved in with his girlfriend, Sam Lancaster, a year ago, and they had become friends almost immediately. Lucy wasn't used to people wanting to be friends with her, but Blake had been an exception. Blake attended cooking school at the Culinary Institute on the other side of the city, and he seemed genuinely interested in providing home-cooked meals for the potlucks that Lucy enjoyed hosting for the apartment residents.

She smiled brightly as he stood next to her, right as the elevator dinged and the doors creaked open. "Good morning, Blake. Off to school?"

"Sure am. Anything exciting happening at the bookstore this week?"

"Oh, we have a new release of a cookbook I think you would like." Lucy always kept her eye out for any new books on cooking that Blake might appreciate reading.

He bumped his shoulder against her. "I'll have to have Sam stop by and grab it." He paused. "Her brother is visiting, we're picking him up from the bus station after I get out of school."

"That's exciting." She had heard a lot about Sam's older brothers—Jackson and Dylan. "Motorcycle brother or?" she asked, hoping her slight grin didn't give her away. She always wondered about the hot older brother who rode a motorcycle. She figured he must be sexy.

"Afraid not, Luce, just the boring one." He laughed.

"Darn." She giggled and looked away, hiding her blush. "We'll have to do a potluck so he can meet everyone in the building." Her voice got higher than she wanted it to. She hated how she got so excited about the community potlucks, but it was fun to plan something and then reap the rewards while everyone got together and had a good time.

Blake bit his lip and held back a laugh. "Yeah, Dylan would sure love that." From the tone in his voice, it didn't sound like Dylan was going to love her potluck idea. "But I think we should do it, anyway."

"Yeah?" Her eyes lit up as the elevator arrived at the ground floor.

"My best friend deserves the finest *welcome to New York bash* we can throw this weekend." She followed him out of the elevator as they walked toward the exit of their building. "I'll bring the food; you bring the Patel pizazz?"

"I won't let you down, B."

"You never do, Luce."

They went their separate ways, as Lucy started her walk toward the bookstore. Lucy loved living in the city. There was always something new to see or do. Every morning, she would pass by the Botanical Garden on 6th Street on her way to work. The garden was one of her favorite places to stop when she had time, which she rarely ever had.

Today was one of those days when time was getting away from her. She cut through Avenue B, picking up the pace as she looked down at her phone. 8:55 AM. She groaned internally. She was going to be late again.

Turning the corner, she smiled the moment she saw Jared opening the shop door. Jared had worked at the Book Club Bar for five years now. He was one of her closest friends. "Cutting it close again, aren't you, Luce?"

"Close is not late," she said with a raised brow. "I made it with a minute to spare." Holding up her phone, she grinned. "That's a record, wouldn't you say?"

He shoved the door open, metal squealing against the old wooden floor. "Are you excited?"

She bit her lip and stared at him. "I don't have a single clue what you are talking about, Jared." His eyes narrowed as he flipped the lights on and the bar ignited in a warm glow.

"You aren't fooling me. You've been waiting six months for this book to come in."

She squeaked and bounced on her feet. "Alright fine, is it in the back?"

He nodded. "Came in right after you left yesterday. I sat one aside for you." Lucy rushed past him to the back room, knocking the door open with her shoulder as she jumped over the boxes by the desk. "Would you slow down before you get hurt?" Jared hollered behind her.

"I just want to touch the cover."

"Top drawer," he instructed. Lucy opened the drawer, and there it was, staring back at her. She swore she heard music playing overhead as she took in the bright blue cover, a cluster of yellow flowers and a small bird sitting in the top right-hand corner.

She ran her fingers along the spine. "Little Bird," she whispered.

"Is that the third or fourth one in the series?" Jared asked as the office lights came on over her head.

"Third. This one is about the youngest sister." She cracked the spine, and the smell of the cream-colored paper wafted to her nose. Oh, how she loved the smell of new books. Her fingers danced along the pages, lightly touching each word. She couldn't wait to get home and rush to the roof to devour each chapter.

"How long is it going to take you to read this one?"

"Depends on how long it takes Amber to find me this time." She laughed. "I just want to know if she ends up with Joel or Karl."

"No one should end up with a man named Karl." Jared frowned. "I dated a Karl once; he was a real ass."

"That's because you have a type, Jared. They're all...jerks!" Lucy frowned.

Jared laughed. "You know it won't kill you to say the word, ass, Lucy. You aren't going combust into flames."

"Hey, don't make her cuss." A tall girl with long dark hair walked into the office.

"Morning, Josephine," Lucy greeted the girl with a smile. "Look what came in." She held up her book triumphantly.

"Ooh! Will it be Karl or Joel?" She reached for the book, and Lucy yanked it away.

"You can't read the ending first, Jo. That's cheating."

"To hell with that. I always start at the end first. That helps me decide if it's worth reading."

Lucy shook her head, tucking the book under her arm as she walked back into the store to get ready for customers. The store was a combination of coffee shop and bookstore, but after 5:00 PM, it became a full-fledged bar. Lucy didn't really drink alcohol herself. It never really seemed like something she would enjoy, but it was a popular concept because loads of people came in after hours to drink, interact with friends and read a book.

And there was nothing Lucy loved more than reading a book. Getting lost in a fantasy world was something she looked forward to every night. As soon as she got off work, she would sneak off to the rooftop, snuggle into her cozy chair, and dive into whatever book she was currently reading. And today was really special because she was going to get to read "Little Bird" after work, which she had been waiting six months to read. Finally, she would know which man the youngest daughter, Lilibeth, had chosen. Karl or Joe l.

Secretly, she was hoping it would be Joel, the dashing but brooding mystery man who had come into Lilibeth's life last year, but it was possible she would choose Karl, the man she had dated on and off for years since she was a girl.

It wasn't as if Lucy had much experience with men to know which one was better for Lilibeth; the only men that Lucy had dated were on the pages of the novels she read. But it didn't stop her from fantasizing about it.

She'd actually fantasized more than once about a striking, mysterious Joel appearing in her life—a man utterly captivated by her. She imagined his voice, low and filled with longing, his touch a spark against her skin. He'd be unable to resist her beauty, his eyes devouring her, until finally, he would sweep her off her feet and carry her into the sunset.

"Someone puked in the bathroom. Can you clean it up, Luce?" She blinked and shook her head. The romantic fairytale would have to wait.

Chapter Three

Dylan

"I still can't believe you take the elevator up to your apartment every day." Dylan stood at the back of the small metal box and stared at the lights as they moved along the numbers to the twelfth floor.

Sam laughed and leaned on Blake's shoulder. "You get used to it."

"I'm just happy we don't have to take the stairs. We looked at this place over in Hell's Kitchen on the fifth floor that didn't have an elevator." The doors opened, and they shuffled out. "There was no way I was carrying groceries up five flights of stairs after a long day at school."

Blake wrapped an arm around Sam, and Dylan followed them down the checkered hallway. He found the familiar smile reappearing on his face at how happy and settled his sister and best friend appeared, ignoring the pit in his stomach that had settled there on the ride over. They were still Blake and Sam, but as the conversation had progressed, he was slowly realizing how much their lives had moved on without him. And with each new revelation about their blended life—Blake was a Yankees fan now (traitor!) and Sam took yoga classes—the more disconnected he felt.

Just as they approached the end of the hall, a door opened to their right and a goddess in heels walked out. The woman must have been over six feet tall without the fuck-me heels. Her long calves appeared to extend for miles on bronzed skin that disappeared under the lamest excuse for a dress he had ever seen. There was barely enough fabric to cover the bits of flesh exposed that otherwise would have made it inappropriate to wear in public.

"Sammy girl, have you seen my sister?" The goddess in glitter floated across the hall toward them. "I've been looking everywhere, but you know how she disappears after work. I swear she blends with the furniture." There were two of them? Dylan had just left the "Donna Drapers" of the world behind, and already he had run into another one by only stepping into his sister's apartment building.

"Afraid not. We just got home." Sam paused and turned to face him. "My brother is going to be staying with us for a while." All eyes focused on him, and for a split second, Dylan wished he had invisibility superpowers.

"Oh! One of the infamous Lancaster brothers! How exciting!" the woman squealed and stepped closer to him. "I'm Amber. Are you the motorcycle brother or the one who punched Casey?"

Sam snorted. "Please don't make him famous for that."

"Hey, he had help with that fight." Blake pouted. "I don't know why Dylan gets all the glory."

"Ah, so the fighter." She bit her lip and smiled, and Dylan straightened himself a little taller. He supposed if he was going to get credit for something in his life, punching the hell out of that asshole Casey Anderson should at least earn him a medal.

"Yeah, well, he had it coming," he nodded, "but, uh, I'm afraid my fighting days are over."

"Getting up there in age." Blake laughed. "Thirty is coming right around the corner, old man." He rubbed his shoulder where Blake had punched him. The pain was yet another reminder that life was moving too fast, and he was getting too old to not know what the hell he was doing with his life.

"I wouldn't talk. You're still older than me." Dylan lifted his chin and narrowed his eyes.

Blake shook his head and smirked. "Only by a month."

"Is this what the next few months are going to be like?" Sam asked, her eyes crinkling as she looked at Amber with a slight frown on her face. "I'm not sure I'm ready for the two of you behaving like children all day long."

Dylan discreetly held his middle finger toward his best friend behind his back. "Don't worry, Sam, I'll find something else to do besides take the piss out of your boy toy all day long."

Amber giggled, her eyes washing over him as she appeared to trail them down his torso and back up to his eyes. "If you get bored, I know the city pretty well."

"All I want is a decent place to get a slice of New York pizza." Dylan patted his growling stomach. He'd been dreaming about a slice of pizza since he got off the bus.

Amber crinkled her nose and cleared her throat. "Oh, um, yeah. Sure, I know a place."

"Oh, yeah?" Dylan wasn't going to turn down food. "Well, you know where to find me."

"I sure do." She bit her lip and looked down at the other end of the hall. "I gotta get to my photo shoot. But you better believe I'll be in touch." She winked and walked past him, her hips swaying back and forth as he watched her head to the elevator.

"Stop drooling in my hallway, loser." Dylan followed Blake into the apartment, growling his disapproval at his teasing. The last thing he needed was another hot chick chasing after his dick.

Blake and Sam's apartment was modest, but very different from what he was prepared for, though he supposed expecting to see clothing on the floor and Blake's old football trophies lining the bookshelves should have been improbable. Instead, he found the apartment to be very...boring.

The bookshelves were lined with cookbooks and photography manuals. There were pictures of Blake and Sam in frames on the walls and a few scattered about of himself and Jackson from when they were younger. He recognized the yearbook sitting on the table in the living room from their senior year in high school. Only Blake would make that a coffee table piece.

The apartment was bright. There were no curtains lining the windows. Sunlight beamed in through the large openings in the walls. It was quaint, not exactly large, but it felt lived in. Loved.

There was a blanket he recognized on the couch. His sister had carried it around since she was a teenager. A photo of Bruce Springsteen spanned the entire fabric. He remembered she used to curl up and watch television while she waited for him to come home from parties. She would pretend she wasn't waiting up for him, but he always knew she was. They would sit on the couch and talk for hours after he got home about who brought whom to the party, which person got too drunk to go home, and who vomited that night.

There were moments recently he wished he could go back to times like that. Back when things seemed so simple.

"I have to go out tonight." He looked up as his sister came into the room. "It's a work thing. I couldn't change it."

"And I..." Blake walked in behind her, wrapping his arms around her waist and dropping his head to her shoulder. "Have a culinary event." Sam kissed Blake's cheek and then looked back at him and frowned.

"We feel awful."

"Hey, don't worry about it." Dylan shrugged. "I don't need a babysitter. I'll find stuff to do."

"You sure?" Blake asked. He could see it on their faces—that quick flash of pity or perhaps anxiety wrapped up in a layer of well meant concern. He could recognize it quickly after seeing it on his brother's face for the last year. But he didn't come to New York to trade Jax's ugly mug of worry for his sister's.

"Yeah, really, I don't want you guys to change your lives for me. I'm here to work myself out. New York is a big place."

Sam sighed. "Well, make yourself at home. What's ours is yours." She smiled and walked over to hug him. "I gotta go get ready, but I promise we'll catch up. Besides, this weekend will be a lot of fun." Before he could clarify what she meant by that, she ran off down the hallway and disappeared.

Dylan narrowed his eyes at his best friend. "Weekend?"

Blake ran a hand across the back of his neck. "Yeah, man. Loads." He hurried off into the kitchen and started putting away the dishes. It was a chore Dylan had watched Blake do for years at the diner, but the task felt so different watching him do it in his own home.

"Loads of what?"

"Fun. Like she said." Blake continued cleaning up without looking at him.

"Blake, why is the weekend going to be loads of fun?" Dylan had specifically asked them not to do anything special for his arrival. He wasn't sure he had the capacity for fun.

Blake sighed, his shoulders sagging as he rested the towel against the counter. "Okay, look, don't make a big deal about it. I know you said you didn't want any big parties or anything."

"Blake..."

"But your dad is stopping by this weekend, and we thought we'd do a potluck on the roof." Blake glanced at him and smiled with that traitorous smirk Dylan used to appreciate. It was a smile that they used to use on their enemies, you know, other people you were about to do something terrible to, yet you knew it was going to be good for them, eventually.

"A potluck? Why?" He hated potlucks. Why on earth would he want to sit around and eat food that other people made? People he didn't even know.

"It will be fun. We have the best potlucks here. You can even try my cooking."

"I've been eating your cooking for years." He tossed himself down on the couch and blew out a breath. "Or did I just imagine you working at the diner all those years?"

"This is different. I'm a chef now. Or a chef in training, at least. But I've gotten so much better. Trust me. You'll enjoy yourself."

Dylan stared at his friend. *Traitor.* "I somehow doubt that."

"Amber will be there," Blake sang with a grin.

He sighed. The last thing he needed was a new Donna, but he also didn't want to start off this trip by disappointing his best friend and sister. "Fine." Blake continued cleaning and then grabbed a basket off the floor, dropping it onto the couch next to him. Dylan's eyes grew bigger as he watched his best friend fold his sister's laundry. "Does it hurt being this domesticated?"

Blake chuckled. "The benefits outweigh everything else."

"Don't you dare start talking to me about any benefits you get from my sister, asshole."

"I'm not just talking about sex. What are you, five?" Blake shook his head and frowned. "I'm talking about having someone around to talk to, someone who understands everything you're going through, even the really shitty stuff you don't tell anyone else."

"Thought that's what best friends were for." Dylan didn't mean to shoot below the belt, but it just sort of came out that way.

Blake dropped the shirt he was folding. "You mean like telling me you were sleeping with Donna for the last year?" *Ouch.* "Is that the stuff you tell your best friend or was it all the other stuff you failed to talk to me about? Sorry, I guess your phone must have been dead all year. You left me in the dark about a lot of shit, Dylan. So why don't you spare me the lecture?"

Dylan stared at his shoes, examining the holes in the fabric of his Converse. He had expected this conversation, just not in the first hour of arriving. "I...I didn't know how to tell you."

"You didn't know how, or you knew how I would react if you did?"

Dylan rolled his eyes and sighed. "Probably a little of both, honestly." Blake stared at him. "What do you want me to say?"

What could he say? Sorry for sleeping with your ex-girlfriend after you moved away for no other reason than being drunk and bored. Sorry that I drank away half the year acting like an asshole because I still don't have any idea what the hell I'm supposed to do with my life now that everyone else is getting their shit together and I'm still just Dylan the screw-up?

"Maybe you could start by telling me what's going on in that head of yours?"

Dylan flinched, then grunted out a laugh. "Ain't nothing going on in my head. That's the point. Don't worry about it, I'm fine."

Blake's eyes narrowed. "Seriously, the Donna thing—it was...alcohol. Stupidity. I don't know. I fucked up. But I'm fine, really." So, it turns out that lying to your best friend gets easier to do the more often you do it.

"Blake, do you know where my..." Sam walked into the room and stopped as soon as she saw the way the two of them were staring at each other. "Sorry, did I—"

"All good. Where's the bathroom?" Dylan asked, standing up, searching for an exit as quickly as he could.

"Down the hall. First door on the right." Sam pointed behind her. He escaped before she could stop him, closing the door and leaning against it. At least he would get to be alone after they both left tonight. He closed his eyes and remembered the cab driver's advice.

"When you can't go out, go up."

Perhaps that was the answer to his problems today. He needed an escape.

An hour later, Blake and Sam were gone, and Dylan abandoned the apartment to explore his options for escape. He had slipped past the elevator to the stairwell at the end of the hall and climbed to the top of the building. It was a pleasant surprise to find the rooftop door not only open, but the area on the other side maintained and inviting.

The patio was covered in plants, with a greenhouse at the other end of the roof. Nestled in between was a sitting area where he could snuggle into a seat with a table. His sketchbook was lying on the table where he was currently scribbling little fat aliens arriving in New York City, the soothing sounds of Caamp, "Feels Like Home" played in his earbuds, allowing him to lose himself to another world on the rooftop as if he was the only person in the city.

The talk with Blake earlier had unsettled him. While he had expected the subject of his reckless year to come up, he didn't expect to have to discuss it this soon during the visit. He had hoped for a few days of catching up, maybe some fun stories from the past; instead, he was already getting confronted with judgemental questions.

Apparently, it had been weighing on Blake's mind. After all, he had been ignoring his best friend for the last year. When he texted or called, it was always to Sam. Rarely did he reach out to Blake on his own. He suspected that was because of his own guilt. Being with Donna was stupid. He knew Blake wouldn't approve, and telling him about it would have gotten him an earful. So, he avoided the topic altogether.

Obviously, Jax had mentioned it, which was unfortunate because Dylan would have preferred keeping that little tidbit locked in a steel box forever.

Apparently, his family was doing a lot of talking behind his back that he was unaware of. He looked down at his page as the scratch marks got wilder. He tossed the marker onto the table and groaned, yanking his buds out of his ears.

"Oh."

He looked up at the intrusive voice and saw a girl with dark hair holding a book staring back at him with a surprised look on her face. "Can I help you?" he grunted.

"Um, no. Or, yes. I mean, I don't know you." Her lips pinched together, and her eyes got smaller as she stared at him suspiciously.

"Do you need to know everyone?" He put his palm over his sketchbook as soon as she looked at it, pulling it closer toward him.

Her hands clutched her book to her chest. It appeared to be some ridiculous romance novel that all the girls were reading. "I know everyone in the building."

"Are you the building police?"

She shook her head and frowned. "That's not a thing." She rocked back on her heels the moment he moved. "What are you doing?" She looked alarmed, her eyes roaming over him wildly as if examining his features and trying to decide if he was an intruder about to attack.

He paused and stared at her. "I'm just turning off my music." He leaned over and paused the music on his phone, holding it up to her so she could see for herself. "Am I allowed to move, or are you going to call security?"

She had the nerve to appear offended by his remark. "Why are you up here? No one comes up here but me."

"Do you own the roof?" He chuckled.

"No one owns the roof." She rolled her eyes and walked toward the greenhouse. "But this is mine."

"You live in a greenhouse?" he asked, raising an eyebrow at her.

She blushed, spinning back to face him. "What? No...no, I don't live in it, but my butterflies do."

How very odd. "Well, I promise you, I was not doing anything to your butterflies. I just came up here to..." He looked down at his sketchbook and noticed that she was looking at his drawings. He shut the book and caught her eye once more. "I'm visiting my sister," he said instead.

"Oh, does your brother ride a motorcycle?" She smiled so widely he almost laughed. What was everyone's obsession with Jackson and his stupid motorcycle?

He exhaled. "That would be my brother, Jackson."

"So, you must be the other one." She examined him, and Dylan nodded. Of course he would get to be known as 'the other one.' The unremarkable Lancaster. "In that case, you can use the roof whenever you want. I come up here to read all the time." She held up her romance novel, something with a lot of flowers and a small bird on the cover. "I just got this one today." Her voice was full of excitement. Dylan just nodded silently. "But I'm happy to share my sanctuary with you, if you want somewhere to hide out." Dylan imagined that hiding out with this girl would end up with her talking his ear off all day. "Not that I would be here all the time. I mean, I work during the day, so, you know, unfortunately, we couldn't hang out when I'm working."

He nodded again, unable to get a word in as she continued talking. "Yeah, that's..."

"But maybe I'll run into you again, you know, when I'm not working."

Dylan frowned. Perhaps finding solitude was going to be harder than he thought. Would it be rude to ask her what her schedule was? "Yeah, sure."

"Cool, I mean, obviously I would be reading, so we wouldn't really be talking or hanging out." She frowned and turned away. "Stupid, Lucy." She shook her head, talking mostly to herself. "I'm talking a lot. I do that when I get nervous around people I don't k now."

He chuckled. "I'm Dylan."

"Oh." She paused. "I'm Lucy."

"Now we know each other, so you can stop talking so much." He didn't mean for it to appear rude, but the way the smile slipped off her face, he supposed it must have come out in that 'Dylan' tone everyone warned him he had.

"I'll, uh, I'll leave you to whatever you were doing," she said, rushing toward the door.

He jumped up from his seat. "Hey, Lucy. You can stay. I was just heading back downstairs." She spun around to face him, her cheeks r ed.

"You don't have to do that."

"No, really, I was heading down anyway." He smiled as she passed him and walked over to the sitting area. "Anyway, it was nice meeting you, Lucy. I'm sure I'll see you around." He turned around as he reached the door and found her staring at him, a look of bewilderment on her face. He waved and closed the door behind him. Perhaps he needed to work on his manners before he ventured out again.

Hours later, the television was on in the corner as Dylan tried to focus on his sketchbook. The stick figures he was drawing were jumping out the sixth-story window to their fortunate deaths. What a joyful life indeed!

The knock on the apartment door startled him. Maybe if he ignored it, they would go away. However, two minutes later, the sound at the door wafted through the apartment again until the thought of ignoring it was only going to lead to further annoyance.

Whoever was on the other side was determined to reach Sam or Blake. He ran a hand through his hair and opened the door, to find himself greeted by the Amazonian princess from earlier.

"Hey, handsome." She dropped a hand to her hip and smiled. "I thought maybe you'd want to get that pizza."

His head said run, but his stomach moaned otherwise.

"You must have heard my stomach growling from across the hall." Dylan smiled. "You mind if I grab a coat?"

"Grab anything you want."

He ran down the hall and pulled his jacket off the chair as he hollered toward the woman waiting at the door. "I was hoping to find someone who could show me a good pizza joint in New York. I never turn down food, and we only had one place back in Titusville with good pizza."

"Um, yeah, right. I sure do love food."

Dylan didn't want to give Amber the wrong impression that he was interested in her for anything other than food, but sitting in the apartment sulking about his life and drawing stick-figure suicides wasn't exactly doing much for his sanity. "Well, then lead the way, Amber."

Chapter Four

Lucy

"Lilibeth, you can't just walk away from me!"

"Give me a reason to stay, Joel." Lilibeth waited as Joel stared into her eyes, her hands resting against the firm expanse of his chest. All she needed was one word, any word, and she would ruin everything for this man.

"I...I can't." His eyes closed, and Lilibeth felt her heart break into a tiny million pieces, like stardust onto the floor. A single tear stained her cheek. She scrubbed her hand against it, unwilling to let him see her cry.

"Goodbye, Joel." Without looking back, she ran. She ran through the front yard and away from the man who had broken her heart. She ran until she stumbled onto the rocky path that led to Rockmount Ranch.

"Little Bird, are you hurt?" She looked up to find the one person who wouldn't break her. The one person left in this world she could trust.

She looked up, tears staining her face. "Karl, I..."

In one swift motion, he lifted her off her feet and carried her into the house.

"No!" Lucy mashed her bookmark into the current page and slammed the book shut, shoving it to the other side of the table. Lilibeth wasn't supposed to choose Karl. "Ugh!" Karl was safe and boring and wanted Lilibeth to stay exactly the way she had always been. Joel was handsome and daring, and maybe a little grumpy, but he saw Lilibeth for everything she could be.

Lucy rested her chin on her fisted palm and stared out over the city. Something about today had thrown her off. It couldn't just be the book. Sure, it was upsetting her, but it was more than that. She thought back to her encounter on the roof earlier and the man with the brooding dark brown eyes.

Dylan Lancaster.

She bit her lip while fidgeting with the chipped polish on her nails. Dylan wasn't at all like she had pictured him to be. He wasn't as tall as she had imagined, and he didn't have that rugged quality she would have pictured for someone who had been in a bar fight with a famous baseball player.

Not that she found him disappointing. Quite the opposite, in fact. Dylan was more attractive than she expected. Charming, in fact. Maybe it was the way he was trying to hide that he was drawing when she knew, in fact, that was what he was doing. Or that the first time he said her name, her stomach dropped and she nearly bit through her tongue.

And that was before even acknowledging his smile, which was possibly the best she'd ever seen. Though admittedly he didn't smile often. He seemed to spend most of his time scowling or frowning. But when he finally flashed her that first important smile...it felt worth it, earned. It was enough to make her weak in the knees.

"It was nice meeting you, Lucy."

Not it was okay meeting you, or it was all right to meet you, it was *nice!* She sighed and smiled to herself. Maybe Dylan would come up to her sanctuary on the roof more often. They could spend time together; they could talk and become friends. Maybe even get to know each other over the next couple of months.

Perhaps he would be the one to see her.

She groaned. "This isn't a romance novel, Luce."

She wasn't the girl that guys picked. No one was going to carry her off into the sunset. *Growing up Lucy* had been difficult for her. No one ever wanted to date her when there was an actual supermodel in the house. Boys always picked Amber over her.

Her first crush in high school was Byron Frank. He was a year older than her, and Lucy used to dream about him throughout class. She wrote her name next to his in all her notebooks...Lucy and Byron, Lucy Frank. She even thought he liked her back. That lasted all of three days until he walked her home from school one day and met her family. He took one look at Amber, and it was all over for Lucy Frank.

Amber dated him for four months until she broke his heart. He never wanted to talk to either of them after that. That's where Rule #13 came from. *Never introduce Amber to any boy you like.*

Lucy grabbed her book and headed back to her apartment. She wasn't interested in reading anymore today. There was still a lot to do for the potluck this weekend, and she really wanted to impress Dylan by showing him she could put on the best potluck the building had ever seen.

Lucy practically skipped down the hall to her apartment. She would have to ask Blake about grabbing the string-lights out of the basement this week, and maybe figure out what Dylan's favorite colors were so she could hang colored lanterns. She was so lost in her thoughts that she barely registered the commotion on the other side of the door when she swung it open.

Amber scrambled across the couch like a cat that had been caught with a ball of twine. "Luce, I've been looking for you all day."

"Well, you found me," she said, staring at her sister, while recognizing for the first time the man sitting next to her, his arm wrapped around Amber's back.

Dylan Lancaster.

"Dylan, this is..."

"Butterfly Girl." Dylan chuckled, and Lucy tried to ignore the charm of his dashing smile.

"Cartoon man." She snorted. Amber stared between them, with a look of confusion that Lucy had no intention of clarifying for her.

Amber sat up and frowned. "Do you two know each other?"

"We met earlier," Dylan said. "Do you live together?"

"Lucy's my baby sister." Amber smirked, and Lucy felt her blood boil. She made it sound like she were a child. Yes, she was younger, but she was going to be twenty-six in three months, and Amber was only three years older than her. That hardly qualified her as a baby.

"Oh, that's cool. Sam's my little sister." Dylan and Amber continued bonding over their younger siblings, and Lucy felt like crawling under the couch so they could just get on with whatever they were doing prior to her interrupting them.

"Interesting story," Lucy grumbled. "So, what are you doing in *my* apartment?"

"Lucy!" Amber's face turned red with embarrassment. "Dylan and I went out tonight."

"Oh..." Lucy felt her annoyance bubble up, crossing her arms against her chest. Why did Amber jump on every red-blooded man that breathed in her direction?

"Amber introduced me to New York pizza." Dylan grinned, and Lucy felt as if she might pass out.

She turned her ire on her sister. "Oh, did she?" Fun fact, Amber was a vegetarian, and she absolutely *hated* pizza. She never consumed anything that might be deemed even remotely unhealthy for her figure. Lucy had known that something was odd when her sister had texted her earlier asking her about her favorite pizza place downtown, 'for a friend,' she had said.

"Yeah, sadly, she didn't get to eat any herself." Dylan's sad stare at Amber had Lucy glaring at her sister.

"That is sad. What happened?" she asked, her fake concern spilling out in boisterous excitement.

Amber stuttered, holding her stomach. "Oh, uh, st ... stomach cramps, really terrible. Came out of nowhere."

"Sounds like you should go straight to bed. You have an early shoot in the morning." Lucy smiled and glanced at Dylan, who suddenly appeared unsure of what to do next.

"You don't..." Amber protested, touching her hand to Dylan's arm.

"I probably should let you get some rest. Lucy is right." Dylan stood up from the couch.

"Well, it was nice seeing you again, Dylan. I'm sure we will see you at the potluck." Lucy walked over to the door and opened it, escorting a reluctant Dylan out into the hallway. He turned to say something to Amber, but Lucy slammed the door closed.

She spun on her heels and stared at her sister. "Pizza? Really?"

"That was so rude, Luce."

"You don't eat pizza. Why would you lie to him? You can't just meet new people and lie to them." Lucy tossed her book onto the kitchen counter and picked up the dirty glasses of wine that were sitting on the table. "If you can't be yourself, there is no point in being with someone. You just met him, and already you were trying to be someone else."

"Geez, Luce, I was just trying to get laid; I wasn't trying to fall in love with him." Amber stood up and unzipped her dress. "I had an excellent shot, too. I hope you didn't screw that up for me," Lucy groaned and scrubbed at the glass with the sponge.

"You can't just sleep with everyone in the building, Am."

"You know, it wouldn't hurt if you tried to sleep with even one person in the building." Her sister let her dress fall to the floor, leaving her in just her bra and underwear. Lucy frowned and continued cleaning the same glass she had already cleaned twice. She was ignoring the prickle in the corner of her eye.

"Not everyone can be you," she mumbled.

Her sister sighed, leaning against the counter. "Stop comparing yourself to me. You're a beautiful girl." She looked down, staring at her yellow Converse and mismatched socks. There was no comparison between her and her sister. Lucy was a rock, and Amber was a diamond. "Stop doing whatever you are doing in that head of yours, Luce."

She looked up, avoiding her sister's gaze. "I'm not doing anything."

"Rule number eighty-five: be authentically you, because that is who you are meant to be." Her sister reached out and touched her chin, lifting it so that their eyes met.

"Lilibeth is going to choose Karl," Lucy said with a frown, diverting their conversation.

Her sister laughed and wrapped her arms around her. "Oh, Luce," she sighed, running a hand through her hair. "Come on, go pop some popcorn, and you can update me in bed."

She bit her lip and smiled widely. "Really?"

"Yeah, I'm starving. I haven't eaten all day. I'll brush your hair while you talk." Lucy finished the dishes and put the popcorn in the microwave.

"Fine, but you have to tell me all about your pizza date afterward." Amber shrugged and walked into the bedroom. Perhaps Lucy could gather some intel about Dylan tonight, for the potluck, of course.

The next few days were a whirlwind of activity. She spent hours planning the potluck, buying all the supplies, coordinating over text messages with Blake about the menu, and ensuring she invited all the guests.

There was a book event at work coming up, which meant that everyone had to organize each section (of course she always picked the romance section) and then Jared would complain that she spent too much time looking at the covers rather than putting them in the right places, but she couldn't help it if she got distracted. An excellent cover was one of the most important parts of selling a book. If the cover caught Lucy's eye, she was sure to buy it.

And then there was "Little Bird," which she was making a lot of progress reading. The book was sitting on the corner of the table while she watered her plants in the greenhouse. Not that she was angry at the characters in the book; she loved Lilibeth. And Lilibeth had a right to be with whichever man made her the happiest, but Lucy couldn't help but feel like she was settling for Karl.

She lifted her head when a scraping sound jostled her out of her musings. "Hello?" She set her water jug on the concrete floor and peered through the dirty window. The wind whistled through the greenhouse, and Lucy tugged her jacket around her tighter. She stepped out onto the roof and looked around.

"'I don't understand what you want me to say to you, Lilibeth.' Joel's voice was deep and unforgiving as he stood at the edge of the driveway. 'I can't be the man you need me to be.'" Lucy walked toward the voice, turning the corner to find Dylan Lancaster sitting at her table with her book in his hands. "'You're breaking my heart, Joel.' Lilibeth's eyes were glassy, her tear-soaked handkerchief in her hand."

"Hey, put that down," Lucy said, raising her voice as she reached for the book. Dylan held the book out of her reach, his eyes wide.

"I was just getting to the good part."

She exhaled and blew a piece of hair out of her face. "Are you always this annoying, or do you practice?" She looked down at the table between them and saw the open sketchbook. Her eyes trailed back to his. Before he could react, she reached for it and yanked it off the table, stepping away and flipping through the pages.

"Give that back." She turned her back to him, her eyes filtering through the drawings that were coming to life with each flip of her hand. He reached over her shoulder and tugged the book out of her grasp. "That's private."

She folded her arms across her chest. "So was my book."

He glanced up and rolled his eyes, holding her book in the air. "You can buy this on Amazon. That's not exactly private."

She yanked the book away from him. "You act like a child."

"Touché, Butterfly Girl." Dylan dropped into the chair under the umbrella. "Why do you read that trash, anyway?"

"It's not trash. It's a romance novel. And I enjoy reading them. You should try reading something with words in it now and then."

He scrunched his eyebrows and frowned, crossing his arms against his chest. "I read books."

She hesitated for a moment before sliding into the seat across from him. He was staring rigidly across the city. *Crap.* Now she'd gone and ruined her chance of being friends with him.

Rule #28: If at first you don't succeed, try a different approach.

Biting her lip, she muttered. "I like your cartoon figures."

His eyes snapped up to meet hers, and then he quickly glanced away. "They aren't...that's nothing."

"Okay." She kicked her feet beneath her, looking for anything else to focus on besides the attractive man in front of her. "So...Titusville, right?"

"Yup."

Oh my God, why was he so difficult to talk to? Were all men like this? She closed her eyes and sighed. "Blake told me it was a small town. I don't really know much about small towns. I grew up in San Francisco."

"Titusville is definitely not San Francisco."

She picked at the corner of her book, hoping it would give her inspiration for what to say next. "So what did you do in Titusville?"

"Worked on cars, mostly." He shrugged and glanced at his hands. He had strong hands. They were the type of hands that Lucy had dreamed about. Large, firm hands that had done manual labor. His hands were the kind that when he touched you with them, you could feel their roughness on your skin.

She shook her head when she realized she was hyper-fixating on his hands. "Did you enjoy working on cars?"

"No, Lucy, I did not."

"Oh." She swallowed hard, looking up to see him studying her.

"Honestly, I hated my entire existence in Titusville. It's kind of why I'm sitting on this rooftop right now." He leaned forward and lowered his voice. "You see, I drank myself into a stupor each night until I could barely remember my own name. I'm pretty sure everyone I know thinks I was about to off myself, so they all got together for one of those bullshit interventions to save my life."

She twitched involuntarily. "W...Were you?"

He pinched his eyes together until she could just see the slits of his darkened pupils. "No, Lucy. I was not going to off myself." She exhaled and sat back in her seat. "But between you and me, I can't really say if they wouldn't be better off if I got hit by a bus right now, either."

Her eyes widened. "That's horrible."

He shrugged. "I just don't get the point." His voice rose at the end, his head dipping back as he shouted it toward the sky. "I mean, is this really all there is?"

"To what?"

He laughed. "Life? Is this it? Some boring existence where I crank out a few oil changes, disappoint my dad, and literally amount to nothing in life except the ability to drink my weight in liquor?"

It was her turn to laugh because, wow, this guy was something else. "You know, when Blake said his best friend was coming to visit, I assumed he'd be pretty cool after all the stuff he's told me about you. But wow! He never mentioned you were such a...positive-thinking person."

"Oh, I'm a delight."

"What you are is stubborn, and very talented." She touched her hand to his sketchbook. "I know some people who would love to get into illustrating, and they would kill to have the raw talent you have."

"I told you, this is nothing; it's just brain anxiety." Ripping the book from the table, he stood up and walked toward the door. He paused as he reached it. "It's nothing personal, Butterfly Girl. I'll, uh...I'll see you around." The door slammed shut, and her body jumped involuntarily at the sound of the metal pounding in her ears.

She didn't understand how Dylan didn't see his own talent or why he was passing it off as something negative rather than a creative outlet that was generating a positive opportunity for his future.

Maybe if Dylan could learn to appreciate art the way she saw it. If he could see things differently than he was used to, he would see that what he was doing wasn't just anxiety, but talent.

She smiled to herself and dug into the bag sitting under the table. She scribbled a note and left it under a jar and headed back to her apartment. Hopefully, the next time Dylan came up to the roof, he would find her note and then he would see that there really was more to life than the miserable existence he had exiled himself to.

Chapter Five

Dylan

"So..." Dylan looked up from the couch and groaned. His sister was staring at him from the kitchen with that look on her face. The one that said, *we need to talk.* "Blake told me you went out with Amber the other night."

"We went out for pizza; that was all."

Blake walked out of the bedroom and paused, mouthing an apology in his direction. Dylan figured he should have known which side his best friend was on, now that his relationship with his sister included bedroom privileges.

"Do you like her?"

"Sam, it was pizza that hardly qualifies for marriage." Dylan sighed, and Blake dropped onto the couch next to him.

"No one said anything about marriage. Blake and I do more than eat pizza, and we aren't married." Sam finished whatever the hell she was doing in the kitchen and walked past the couch, slapping him on the back of the head. "I just don't think Amber is your type."

"Yeah, sorry, Dyl, no hot chicks," Blake said with a smirk.

"That's not what I meant, Blake, and you know it." She scolded his best friend, and he watched the smile leave his face as he nodded in agreement. It was hard not to laugh at how whipped Blake was.

"No, she's right, man. Amber isn't exactly the type we had in mind for you." Damn, his sister really had neutered Blake. "But, uh, maybe we let Dylan figure out his own dating options, sweetheart?" His sister sighed and left them to escape to the bedroom. "She worries about you, that's all."

Dylan wasn't sure he needed, or even wanted, this kind of mothering from his little sister. "And she complained I was overprotective."

Blake was staring toward the bedroom with a sick and disgusting smile on his face. "Yeah, she's the best."

"Dude, find your balls."

"I got balls." He stared at him with a frown.

"Yeah, prove it." Dylan lifted his fist, and Blake held his hands defensively in front of his crotch.

"Careful, man, I want to have kids." How the hell had it all come to this? It felt like just a few years ago they were joking around in their backyard about going to prom and who was going to score the most touchdowns at the game that Friday. And now they were sitting in a grown-up apartment with actual art on the walls, and Blake was talking about having kids with Sam.

"We're boring-ass adults." Dylan sagged against the couch. "How the hell did we let that happen?"

"We had to grow up sometime. We're going to be thirty next year. Don't you want to settle down and get married? White picket fence, get a dog and all that shit."

Dylan shook his head. "I ain't ever getting married. And neither were you. I remember you telling me that senior year."

"I was drunk for most of our senior year." Blake looked toward the bedroom. "Things change. We changed." He leaned against him. "Love does things to you, man."

He laughed at how ridiculous his best friend sounded right now. "Obviously, it makes you stupid, dumbass."

He worried his teeth over his bottom lip, and Dylan could tell he was about to say something monumental. Dylan had known his best friend his entire life, and right now he had that look in his eye he always got right before he told him a secret he'd never shared with anyone else. It was the look he had when he told him in fourth grade he thought their teacher, Mrs. Sanderson, was hot. Or when he found Blake down by the creek after his dad's car accident, tear-streaked cheeks, muttering that he didn't know how he was supposed to go on with his life anymore. And it was the same look when they sat in that jail cell last year when he told him he was in love with Sam. So, Dylan braced himself as Blake gathered his courage to speak this time.

"I'm gonna ask Sam to marry me," Blake whispered, and Dylan's eyes grew about as wide as they could get. Before he could yell, Blake's hand went over his mouth. "Shh. I'm gonna ask her at Christmas, and I want you to help me find her a ring. You're my best friend, Dylan. I can't do this without you."

Fuck! Just what he needed on his New York finding-himself adventure. Love and Marriage and all that shiny bullshit. But this was Blake, and he wanted to spend the rest of his life with his sister, because he loved her, and that was honestly pretty damn special.

"Alright."

"Yeah?" Blake grinned like an idiot, and Dylan honestly just wanted to punch him in the face to make it stop.

"I said yes. Stop smiling like that. You look like a dumbass."

"Did you kiss Amber?"

Dylan groaned. "Oh my God, I hate you now that you're with my sister. I can't tell who's more annoying, you or her."

Blake shrugged. "Can't be her. She's damn near perfect, so it has to be me. So did you?"

"Yeah, it was alright, I don't know. I didn't even want to. That's why I don't really drink anymore. I make horrible decisions. Her sister came in and interrupted us, which was probably a good thing. But it was awkward as hell. What's her deal?"

"Lucy?" Blake's face flashed a look that Dylan didn't quite understand, something akin to annoyance that Dylan even asked about her. "What do you want to know about Lucy?"

"I don't know. It's not a big deal; I was just curious. I've talked to her a few times."

"You've talked to Lucy? Why? Where? What for?" Blake stood up from the couch and crossed his arms defensively against his chest. Dylan got whiplash from the complete U-turn his best friend just made.

"What does it matter? We've talked. Hell, I just said I was curious about her."

"Well, get uncurious. Lucy's a nice girl. She doesn't have a lot of experience with guys like..."

Dylan's mouth opened, and a noise escaped that wasn't exactly friendly. "Like what? Assholes like me? Is that what you wanted to say?"

Blake shrugged it off yet had the audacity to appear apologetic when clearly he wasn't. "Come on, man, I didn't say that."

Dylan wanted to laugh in his face. "Then what did you want to say?" He stood up, staring at his friend, who towered over him. "Let me make it easier for you, Blake. Guys like me, right?"

"I didn't mean that, Dylan. Lucy's just special. She's innocent. She's not like the girls you date. I'm not saying that as something against you. You're just not in the right place for a girl like her."

"Hey, what's going on?" Blake and Dylan turned toward his sister, who was standing in the hall staring at them.

"Nothing! Clearly I'm in the wrong place right now." Dylan stepped back and grabbed his sketchbook, heading to the front door and slamming it shut behind him.

Noah Kahn's "False Confidence" played in his ears as he exited the stairs onto the roof. If anyone had demons chasing him, it was definitely him. Maybe Blake was right—maybe he wasn't in a good place to be talking to nice girls.

The sketchbook slammed against the table as he sat down. He popped out his earbuds and closed his eyes, listening to the traffic below him. It sure didn't seem like New York was going to be some magical answer for him. It couldn't fix all his problems. Especially when he didn't even know what the hell his problems were.

He was too dumb, too tired, too ignorant to find his way in the world. Pick a problem, pick a lane. Damn, he sounded like a brat.

The wind blew across the roof, and Dylan felt the chill of the breeze and heard the soft sound of paper rustling. He glanced at the center of the table and saw a piece of paper tucked under a jar. He slid it out and unfolded it.

Cartoon Man,

Thought you might like to venture out and see things from a new perspective.

21 Dey Street.

Give them my name at the front desk.

Maybe you need to come down from the roof to find the answers to the questions you're asking.

Unless you're too chicken?!

Butterfly Girl

Wow, this girl was something else. Now she wanted to send him on a scavenger hunt out into the city. He crumpled the note and shoved it into his pocket. There was no way he was going to run all over New York City just because some random girl thought he was being a coward.

The door to the roof opened, and he was surprised to see his sister walk out. "What are you doing up here?"

She held a box in her hands. "Lights for the party."

"You guys are serious about your potlucks." He slid his sketchbook under his leg.

"Oh, it's no joke. Blake and Lucy run a tight ship. Lights, music, food, the whole nine yards. This place is the envy of the block." He sat back and watched her decorate until she struggled to reach the corner where the lights needed to be strung, and stood up to help her.

"So, uh, what's with Blake and Lucy?" His hand instinctively slid across his neck. "I asked about her earlier, and Blake nearly chewed my head off."

Sam laughed. "Blake's pretty protective of her. I think he misses Kelley. So, Lucy's like having another little sister around. You know how he is about women. He's Blake."

"Practically called me an asshole just cause I talked to her," he grumbled under his breath. "Am I missing something?"

"Blake and Lucy do some things together now and then. A few months back, there was an incident while they were out. Things got ugly with a man who showed up and gave Lucy some trouble." Sam sighed. "I've never seen Blake so upset. Lucy didn't get hurt, but she got roughed up. Blake got there in time, thank God, but ever since that day, those two have been pretty close. So Blake watches out for her."

Dylan shook his head. "I guess I get it. Sounds bad, but I'm not one of those guys. I would never hurt a girl like that."

"He knows that." Sam stared at him from the ladder she was on. "But, uh, I thought you liked Amber."

"Forget it." He handed her another string of lights. "You guys are crazy. I went for pizza with Amber, and all I did was talk to Lucy. Can't a guy talk to a woman without you two making a big deal out of it?"

"I'm sorry. It's just that Lucy—well, she's never even had a boyfriend. And you're...Dylan."

"Wow, thanks for that, Sam. That was such a thrilling vote of confidence." He held the box over his head as Sam rooted through it for what she needed.

"You're not exactly serious about women, Dyl. I mean, look at your track record. Donna Draper. Do you want to talk about that now?" Sam glared at him. Why wouldn't anyone let him make a single mistake and forget about it? He needed to text Jax and thank him for letting him walk into this lion's den with no warning.

"I'd really rather not talk about her," he sighed. "That would give her more importance than she's due. And honestly, can we not have these down-to-earth talks every damn minute of my day?"

"Then, I should probably warn you now. Dad's downstairs."

"Well, that's just fantastic. I'm sure he won't ask me anything about how much I've fucked up over the last year or what I plan to do next." He set the box down on the ground and walked over to the edge of the roof, staring down at the street below. Was it too late to reconsider a stick figure suicide? Nah, too violent. He hated blood.

He felt his sister slide up beside him. "Everyone just wants you to be alright."

"Then maybe everyone should back off," he snapped.

"You should talk to someone. It really helps to have someone to confide in. Even if it's just Blake or Jax or—"

"Sam, I'm fine." Dylan had someone he'd been talking to. Every Friday night. Sam didn't know he had talked to Mom, and maybe it wasn't what she meant. But it was someone.

They stood there staring out at the city for what felt like hours, even though he knew it was only minutes. "The potluck is going to be fun. All the neighbors will be there. There's this old couple—Holly and Mike. They're wild. You'll love them."

He doubted that, but he'd upset his sister enough tonight. "I'm sure I will." He looked back at the half-strung lights. "Come on. I'll help you finish stringing those. You're too short to do it on your own."

"Hey! You're not that much taller than me." She shoved his shoulder, and he wrapped an arm around her back, pulling her into a hug.

"I missed you," he whispered into her hair.

"I missed you too, Dilly Bear."

The potluck was everything torture was supposed to be. Intentional suffering in the form of hours of psychological warfare, enduring humiliation while being forced to reveal personal details about yourself to strangers. He hated everything about the joyful event being held in his honor. Yet here he sat, a beer in his hand, forcing a smile to pretend there was nowhere else he wanted to be.

"And then when he was in the tenth grade..."

Dylan's eyes fell closed slowly as his dad droned on for what felt like the fourth hour, wrapped in some story about Blake and Dylan's high school adventures. "Dad, I highly doubt they care about that game."

Everyone paused and looked at him. "I don't know. I'm quite enjoying hearing about the football hero of Titusville." Amber tilted toward him on the couch, her hand resting on his thigh.

"Trust me, that guy is dead and gone. If I tried to run for a touchdown now, I'd probably keel over and die of a heart attack." When he looked up, his eyes met Lucy's. She smiled at him from the other side of the rooftop and then looked away.

"Those boys were inseparable," his dad continued as if Dylan hadn't said a word. "Blake and Dylan against the world."

"Or the Pittsburgh Pirates!" someone shouted from the other side of the roof.

"Here, here." Blake laughed, raising his beer bottle.

Dylan stood up abruptly and smiled. "I never tire of that story, but I need to get another beer."

He walked over to the coolers and away from the revelry of the local hero makes history bullshit his dad was going on about. "Doesn't seem like you're having fun."

He popped the top of his bottle and looked up as Lucy approached him. "I bet your butterflies hate all this noise up here."

"They are roosting," she said. "Like sleep, but not."

"You think they'd mind if I roosted with them?" he said, trying to unclench his jaw. "Can I get you a beer?"

She shook her head. "I don't drink."

"Shit, really? Ever?" He took a swig of his beer. "How do you have fun, then?"

"Doesn't sound like drinking has given you much fun in the last year." She stared at him for a moment, and he wanted to argue with her, but what could he say? "Your dad seems pretty proud of you." She stared back at the riveting discussion happening in the center of the roof as his dad continued talking about all the wonderful things he did back in high school.

"He's proud of Peak Dylan."

She frowned and raised her eyebrow at him. "Peak Dylan?"

"Yeah, I totally peaked in high school. He doesn't have a damn good thing to say about me since. That's why all his stories about me are old." As soon as the words left his mouth, he realized maybe he shouldn't drink anymore tonight. That was the most honest thing he had said in ages.

"That seems unfair to think about yourself that way." She rocked back and forth to the music, some upbeat pop song by a blonde chick all the girls were talking about back in Titusville. "Did you get my note?"

He snorted. "You called me a fucking chicken."

"Are you?" She grinned at him, her eyes sparkling with something that made him want to know more about her.

"Are you sending me someplace where a bunch of angry dudes are gonna jump me and beat the shit out of me?" he asked with a smirk, leaning closer to her.

"You shouldn't swear so much, Dylan Lancaster." His mouth dropped open in surprise. Did she just lecture him about cussing? "And no, it's perfectly safe."

"Aren't you going to give me a clue about where you are sending me in the middle of a city I'm unfamiliar with?"

She pinched her lips together and tapped her finger against them. "Nope, you're just going to have to trust me," she said before walking away. And for the rest of the evening, Dylan couldn't stop staring at the pretty smile sitting on her pink lips every time she looked his way.

"I'll be back at Christmas." His dad peered down the street, looking for his cab. While he hadn't enjoyed last night's party or listening to his dad wax poetically about his son's better days, a part of him hated seeing him leave.

"Where are you off to now?"

"Virginia," he said with a grin that made his dad look ten years younger. "Always wanted to go to Shenandoah National Park. Linda says that...well, anyway." He stared off down the road as if the conversation wasn't for him. "What's the plan, kid?"

"Oh, you know, a little bit of this, a whole lot of that." He smirked.

His dad shook his head with a grunt. "Yeah, that's what I was afraid of. You know, when I took off in that RV, I didn't know if I had made the right decision leaving you kids behind. Once I got out on the open road, I made a promise to myself to try one new thing a day that I was afraid of."

"Dad—"

"Give me a minute, kid." Dylan's shoulders sagged as he rested his hands on his hips and stared down at the pavement. "All my life, I've done the safe thing. I stayed where I was supposed to be. I took care of my responsibilities. But after a while, my well ran dry. I had to figure out what was going to feed my soul." He looked up and met his dad's eyes. "You're the most like me, kid. You need to feed your soul."

"That's pretty deep, Dad, especially for you."

"What can I say? I'm a new man."

Dylan shook his head with a chuckle. "So driving around in a big-ass RV feeds your soul?"

"Nah, that thing is a beast to drive. Half the time I hate it. It's not the RV. It's being free." He watched his face light up, like something deep inside of him was bursting through with happiness he had never seen before.

"Don't you get lonely out there?"

The smile slipped from his lips just momentarily, but enough that Dylan noticed it. "I miss seeing you all. I meet a lot of people on the road, but uh..." There was something there, a smile that turned up on the corner of his lips.

"Son of a bitch, have you met someone?"

The flinch, just a small one, but enough that he caught it. "I, uh...it's nothing I want to talk about yet."

"Dad!" Dylan grinned and touched his father's shoulder. "That's—wow."

"Stop making a big deal of it and don't tell the others. I don't want to say anything yet."

"Let me guess, she's eighty and lives in a shack by the lake," Dylan teased, lightly tapping him on the shoulder.

A yellow cab pulled up beside them. "Just don't say anything, you promise?"

"I'm a steel trap." Dylan zipped his lips.

His dad chuckled and wrapped him in a hug. "You kids can't keep secrets to save your lives." He pulled back, gripping him by the shoulders. "Promise me you will not hide out while you're here. Go feed your soul, kid."

"Feeding, check. You know I love to eat." He stepped back on the curb and saluted his father as he climbed into the cab.

"I'll see you at Christmas."

As the cab pulled away, Dylan dug into his pants pocket and looked down at the crumpled piece of paper in his hand. "Feed your soul."

All right, Lucy Patel, game on.

Chapter Six

Lucy

Lucy stood in front of the self-help bookshelf and deposited the newest deliveries onto the shelves, reorganizing a few of the older books onto the bottom levels. "So?" She looked up as the dark-haired woman approached her. "I've gotten no updates on Lilibeth's plight this week. Was the book that bad?"

Lucy shrugged. "I'm not done with it yet."

"What?" Josephine sat down on the square plush in the middle of the floor. "You've had that book for a week. It's never taken you this long to finish any of the books in the series."

"I've been busy." She shoved another book onto the shelf.

"That's never stopped you before. When 'Robin' came out, you finished it in a day while also helping Amber with her Vogue party." Lucy moved to the other bookshelf and pulled a stack of books onto the floor, rearranging the titles in the correct order.

"My neighbors have family in town, and we threw a potluck over the weekend. I've been trying to help him get out into the city." She closed her eyes the moment the words left her mouth. It was an error on her part to even mention a guy. Jo was like a shark sniffing blood in the water.

"Him?" Damn Josephine and her nosiness.

"My neighbor's brother." Lucy shrugged.

As Lucy expected, Josephine attacked. "How old is he? Married? Single? Is he cute?"

Lucy turned around and held up her hand, pointing to her fingers. "Twenty-nine, no, yes, very."

"Oh, not just cute, but very cute. And how have you been helping him exactly, Luce?"

"Don't get your hopes up, Jo. He's already gone out with Amber. I'm pretty sure I walked in on them making out on the couch." She frowned. "Besides, hot guys don't look at this and think, wow, I want to date that." She stepped back and ran her hands down her body, twirling in a circle.

"Oh, now he's hot!"

"Who's hot?" Jared walked in and leaned against the bookshelf.

"No one!" Lucy shouted.

"Lucy's new hot neighbor," Jo said at the same time.

"He's not my neighbor. He's my neighbor's brother," Lucy said with a frown.

Jared raised his brow. "I'm a sucker for the neighbor's hot brother trope."

"He went on a date with Amber." Jo blinked and then licked her tongue across her lips. Lucy was aware of how much Jared and Jo disapproved of her sister. Jared made a contemptuous groan, and Lucy returned to sorting her books.

"Look, it doesn't matter, anyway. Guys like Dylan are never interested in women like me."

"Dylan," Jared said in a haze. "I like the name. Sounds very *90210*. Does he surf?"

Lucy's brow crinkled. "I don't think so. He's from Pennsylvania."

"You should bring him by the shop." Jo stood up and wiped her hands on her black tights. "That way we can inspect him and see if he's good enough for our Lucy."

"Absolutely not. That would be like bringing him into a den of vipers. And I told you, he's not interested in me."

"Then bring him in so we can figure out what the hell is wrong with him," Jared said with a growl, walking away.

Lucy ran up the stairs to the roof as soon as she got home. She told herself it was because she wanted to check on her butterflies and read her book, but she knew that wasn't the reason at all. The moment she exited onto the roof, the real reason her heart had been pounding was sitting at his spot at the table, scribbling in his sketchbook.

She paused in the doorway, willing her pulse to slow before stepping out into the sunshine. Dylan remained hunched over, focusing on the page in front of him. Although his baseball cap covered his face, she could tell by his tightly pressed lips and jaw that he was concentrating intently.

She reached into her bag and pulled her book from inside. Perhaps she would leave him alone and just read for a bit. It made her feel comfortable sitting on the roof, just knowing he was there on the other side, existing in the same space as her.

She rested against the wall, opened her book and read.

"Do you love him?" Lilibeth stared at the man sitting across from her, trying to hide his eyes from her view as he asked her the question she knew he would eventually pose.

"Does it matter?" She responded with fire in her voice. "He is the only one who loves me."

"Lilibeth." It was a whisper, barely a sound leaving his mouth.

He looked up and met her eyes. "I have only loved one man in my life." She ran a hand across his cheek. "But he does not love me."

Lucy gasped and held her hand over her mouth. She heard a chuckle across the rooftop and looked up to see Dylan staring at her.

"I've never seen anyone get so into a book before." Dylan leaned back in his chair, and Lucy pushed away from the wall and walked toward him.

She slid into the seat across from him and set her book down. "Are you making fun of me?"

"No." He shrugged. "I guess I've just never really felt that attached to something that wasn't real. It's fascinating watching you."

"Just because it isn't real doesn't mean you can't get drawn into it." She frowned. "It's like your drawings. Haven't you ever drawn something and wished you could actually live in it?"

He stared at the book in front of him. "I don't know, I guess."

"That's what a book is like for me. Sometimes I wish I lived in the stories." She flipped her book over. "This one is a series, so I've been reading it for a couple of years. I can almost close my eyes and see Rockmount Ranch."

"Rockmount Ranch?" he snorted.

"Don't make fun. It's an actual place for me. At night, I used to close my eyes before I went to bed and imagine being there." Her eyes slid shut, and a smile ghosted across her lips as she pictured the lavender fields and the horses roaming the prairie.

"What are you running from in your own life, Lucy Patel?" She opened her eyes to find Dylan's locked on hers.

When she swallowed, she turned away from him, ignoring the pit in her stomach. "I don't have to be running from anything to fall in love with a story." She could fib and not be a bad person, right?

When her eyes met his, it was his turn to look away. "Yeah, well, I guess that's where we're different because when I imagine myself in my drawings, I'm absolutely running away from my life." They sat in silence, neither one sure of what to say next. She hoped Dylan might tell her more, perhaps let her know what he was running away from. Maybe he was looking for something in his drawings, like she was in her books. She thought about telling him that, but then...how silly would that sound?

I'm Lucy, a twenty-five-year-old virgin who imagines herself in romance novels because she can't find a boyfriend or even a guy who will look at her as anything more than the plucky fun girl that hangs out with her hot model sister. Pathetic, sad, stupid.

"Did you, um, did you go to the place I sent you?" she asked instead.

He sighed. "Yeah."

She sat up and leaned forward. "So, what did you think?"

He closed his sketchbook and frowned. "Traffic sucked."

That was not the reaction she had expected. "Well, yeah, it's New York City, so you should have expected that, but what did you think when you got there?"

He scratched his nose and looked away. "Yeah, it was okay."

Okay?!

She frowned and stared at her book, flipping the pages through her fingers. Fine, if this was the way he wanted to play the game, she would play. "Well, good for you for getting off the roof." His head snapped in her direction. "Thank you for trusting me." She smiled, stood up and walked toward her greenhouse.

"Hey, where are you going?"

"To water my plants." She felt him behind her, and the corners of her lips turned upward. He could pretend all he wanted to that he was disinterested in everything, yet here he was, following her into a greenhouse.

"Won't the butterflies get out?"

"I don't keep them hostage, Dylan," she said. She picked up the water jug and filled it with water. Dylan was walking around on the other side. "Most of them will be gone next week."

"Gone, are you evicting them?" he asked.

"No, silly. It's too cold here. The monarchs will migrate to California for the winter. A few of the other species will stay here in the safety of their greenhouse and hibernate. But they'll be back in the spring." Lucy pointed to a corner of the greenhouse where a larva clung to a small tree in a planter.

"It's safe for it to stay there all winter?" he asked, and Lucy shivered when she realized how close he was to her. She glanced at him, surprised to see a look of amazement in his eyes as he stared at the small creature in front of him.

"I try to take good care of them. I keep it warm in here, making sure the door is closed all winter." A couple of monarchs flew over their heads, and Dylan stood up to observe them. "They're the most beautiful thing I've ever seen. Sometimes I come up here just to watch them. It's hard to believe they start out so ugly and insignificant and turn into that..." she sighed. "A perfect metamorphosis."

Dylan grunted. "At least they can just fly off wherever they want to go."

She watched the amazement on his face, so enraptured by the butterflies over his head. Yet, even in his amused interest, he looked sad. "So can you."

"I'm not a butterfly, Lucy. But everyone around me might as well be." He shoved past her and out the door of the greenhouse.

She chased after him. "What is that supposed to mean?"

"It doesn't matter," he said, scowling at her with an ugly frown on his face. Dylan Lancaster had a way of going from hot to cold in the breath of a heartbeat.

"It matters because you said it."

He spun on his heels and glared at her, his fists clenched tightly at his side. "Would you stop doing that?" Lucy cowered slightly at the anger on his face.

"Doing what?" Her voice was timid as she gulped with each word.

"Treating me as if I'm someone important." He shook his head. "I'm not a nice guy, Lucy. The shit I say doesn't matter. So stop acting like it does."

As she watched the door slam shut, Lucy wondered what had happened in his life that made Dylan think he was such a bad guy. She was sure it couldn't be that awful. And she absolutely refused to give up on him.

Something about Dylan intrigued her. There was a connection she felt to him. Both she and Dylan felt like they were missing something in their lives and, like Dylan, she too hid away in a fantasy. Maybe she could help him.

Rule #42: Always help those who can't help themselves.

With a determined smile on her face, she pulled the pad of paper out of her bag and started writing.

Entering the apartment, the first thing she noticed was that Amber was dancing around in her underwear to Pink's "Walk of Shame," which usually meant she had a date. The second thing she noticed was that she hadn't eaten the dinner she had set out for her.

"Amber, the food doesn't eat itself." She tossed her bag onto the chair.

Amber laughed and continued dancing. "Who needs food when tequila exists?"

She sighed and grabbed the bottle of tequila off the counter. "You need food if you're going to drink."

"Hey, don't put that away, *Mom*." Amber lunged for the bottle.

Lucy ignored her sister and climbed onto the stool to tuck the bottle on top of the fridge. "After you eat."

"Fine." She leaned against the counter and stuck her fork into the lettuce. "I asked Sam's brother to go to my event tomorrow."

Lucy froze. "What?" Amber had a Vogue event tomorrow evening. It was one of those fancy dress-up events where all her boring and anorexic friends would stand around and talk about how pretty they were and then eat a tomato and drink five gallons of vodka while looking like they just stepped off the pages of whatever magazine they had just posed for. It was superficial and bougie, and Amber always came home drunk as a skunk, and Lucy always had to hold her hair while she vomited into the toilet until three in the morning.

"Yeah, I figured he'd enjoy it."

"Really? Because I don't."

Amber narrowed her eyes and made a choking sound. "Like you know anything about him, Luce."

"And you do?" Lucy shot back. Amber shoved a forkful of salad into her mouth. She chewed and then parted her lips. "Hold on a minute. Are you jealous, Luce?"

Lucy's mouth dropped open, and she felt like her cheeks were burning. "What? No!"

"You are! You like him!" Her sister's accusation hit her like a ton of bricks. "You have a crush on Dylan."

"Oh my God, Am. Shut up, I do not." She stormed off toward her bedroom and slammed her door shut, throwing herself down onto her bed face first, screaming into the mattress. Her sister was being annoying, talking about Dylan like she was some stupid girl with a crush on a boy. She was twenty-five years old. Dylan was a man, and she was a woman. Besides, it wasn't like that. Dylan was...

Crap. She didn't know what it was like. Dylan differed from anyone she had met before. He was interesting, nice to look at, for sure, and clearly he was having issues that were bothering him, and she wanted to help.

"Luce..." She ignored the knock at the door. "Lucy."

"Go away."

"I'm sorry for teasing you. If you like Dylan, I won't go out with him."

UGH! She stood up and walked over to the door, leaning against it. "I don't like him, Am. But I am friends with him. And I just don't think your event is a good idea for him, that's all."

"You realize he's an adult, Luce, capable of making his own decisions, and he agreed to go, so maybe you don't know him as well as you think you do."

"Yeah, whatever," she grumbled.

"I'll cancel."

Lucy stood frozen, staring at the door. Part of her wanted to let her sister cancel the date with Dylan. Everything she had learned about him since she met him was telling her that Amber's events were not something he needed in his life right now. But Amber was right; he had agreed to go, so maybe she didn't know him at all.

Lucy swung the door open. "Don't do that. Go, have fun."

"Are you sure?" Her sister frowned, reaching out to pull a strand of her hair between her fingers. "I don't want a guy to get between us."

"Please, he likes you, obviously. Why wouldn't he?" She rolled her eyes, trying to ignore the ache she felt all the way to her toes.

Amber's shoulders sagged. "I've never seen you interested in a guy before."

"I'm not, really, I'm not," she lied. "We're friends, that's all."

"Alright then. I'll go eat my salad." She smiled. "Want to watch America's Next Top Model?"

Lucy nibbled on her bottom lip. "Nah, I'm just gonna read my book and go to bed."

Amber hesitated at the door. "Alright, goodnight, Luce."

"Night." She closed the door and fell back onto her bed, staring up at the ceiling. Turning her head, she glanced at the bag on the floor where her romance book was nestled inside. She wasn't in the mood for love stories. Not when she had a handsome man like Dylan Lancaster around. And not when she was being forced to once again re-live her high school nightmare, where that handsome man ended up with her sister.

She curled herself into a ball under the covers and closed her eyes, wishing for the first time in her life that she were a butterfly, ready to fly home to California.

Chapter Seven

Dylan

Dylan ventured to the roof early on Monday morning, partly because he wanted to avoid Blake prior to getting out of the shower before he went to school, but mostly because he hoped he might catch a certain dark-haired girl loitering before work.

He had become intrigued by the cute and quirky Butterfly Girl he had met on the rooftop. Maybe it was because she wasn't afraid to challenge him, but honestly he just felt safe talking to her. She wasn't a member of his family, and she wasn't aware of the things he had done in the last year. Lucy also didn't appear quick to judge either, so he felt like he could be slightly more honest with her.

It didn't hurt that she wasn't conventionally typical of women he usually dated, like Donna or even her sister, Amber. Which might have been what made her even more attractive. But it was her smile that stood out to him the most. When Lucy smiled, it was like the entire world lit up with color.

So, it was becoming more common for him to seek her out, but when he swung open the steel door, he found only silence and the rising sun.

The way he had left things with Lucy had interfered with his sleep. Not that insomnia was uncommon for him. Dylan hadn't had a full night's sleep since his senior year in high school, and the growing prospect of his future becoming a reality. But there was something about his conversation with Lucy that had unsettled him. Or perhaps it was just Lucy herself that did that.

He hadn't been exactly truthful with her when she asked him about his visit to Mercer Labs. While he was reluctant to follow an address blindly through a city he had never been in before, something about the fact that it was Lucy asking him to go made him curious. And Dylan had never been one to back down from a challenge.

She hadn't been wrong about the perspective either. Mercer Labs was the place you went when you wanted to experience something entirely different. Lucy didn't just send him to an art gallery; Mercer Labs was a mindfuck. Imagine being sent in to inspect a place after turning the building upside down and shaking it thoroughly—that's the kind of gallery it was. It was amazing, and sort of trippy, like being on drugs, and if Dylan was being honest with Lucy yesterday, he would have told her it was the most interesting place he'd ever been to in his life.

Living in Titusville didn't give him a lot of opportunities to see things outside the ordinary. Most of the time, everyone just went in the same direction. Dylan had been coloring outside the lines his entire life. But everyone he ever knew kept trying to put him back inside the box. He didn't know it was okay to see things or experience them on a different level. He felt as if he needed permission to be unique.

Visiting Mercer Labs changed all that. Dylan had spent hours in one room in particular, lying on the floor with a blindfold on, listening to the sounds as they played all around him. The museum attacked his senses and left him feeling raw and vulnerable in a way that he still couldn't explain.

The museum made him feel like maybe it was okay to be unusual. Perhaps the crazy things in Dylan's head weren't that crazy after all. He just needed to look at them from a new perspective.

After he left Lucy on the roof yesterday, he had felt bad about the way he unloaded on her. He had gone to her apartment to apologize, but ran into Amber instead. Somehow that ended with him getting roped into an invitation he didn't know how to turn down for a party tonight.

That left him in a sour mood. He liked Amber. She was hot, and hanging out with a bunch of gorgeous supermodels would have sounded like a great way to spend his time. But that was last year's Dylan, and he didn't want to be that guy anymore.

Plus, he couldn't get Lucy off his mind or the fact that he might have upset her yesterday. He'd never really had a friend who was a girl before, and he'd already insulted the first one by being rude to her.

He sighed as he glanced around the rooftop one last time, hoping that maybe she was in her greenhouse, when something caught his eye. Attached to the greenhouse door was a note. With a fast-beating heart, he walked quicker than was even appropriate and pulled the note free.

Cartoon Man,

You might not think you are important, but everyone is important to someone.

2227 Bowery. Go between 10:00 AM and 11:00 AM.

Give my name at the front desk and they'll know what to do with you.

Trust me, your own troubles seem smaller when you open your eyes to the world.

Butterfly Girl

Dylan looked down at his phone. He didn't have to go to this party with Amber until 7:00 PM, so he had plenty of time today.

With excitement he couldn't contain, he headed back to the apartment to shower.

Walking in New York City differed from walking in Titusville. The city was loud and busy, and people came at you from every direction. It was easy to get lost in the city without trying. Back home, if you took a wrong turn, you just went down the next street and got back on track. In New York, Dylan followed the map on his phone and didn't deviate for fear that he might end up down an alley or in the river.

The buildings were also very different from the ones back home. Everything in New York had character. Some buildings had distinct red brick, while others were entirely glass. His favorites bore the graffiti of artists and street gangs marking their territory. Something you would never see in Titusville.

If he and Blake had tagged a building back home, Sheriff Draper would have put them in his lockup for the night and called their parents. The town would have painted over it by dawn, and everyone would have spent the next month whispering about how the Lancaster kid was a delinquent who wouldn't amount to anything.

Not that he didn't have a reputation growing up. But *delinquent* wasn't usually associated with his name.

Those poor Lancaster kids who spent all day working at the shop with their dad. The Lancaster boy who's always starting fights. Crazy conspiracy theorist Dylan. That sad little kid who grew up without a mother.

Yeah, he was used to all sorts of whispers back home.

He turned the corner onto Bowery and looked up at the tall brick building with a bright red door. The sign next to it read: The Mission. He pushed the door open and stepped inside. Several people were walking around the hallway, mostly ignoring him. The ceiling extended high above his head, and the building felt old and slightly chilly.

"Can I help you? The line starts outside, but we don't begin serving until 1:00 PM. Breakfast service just ended." Dylan turned to see a man approaching him.

He smiled politely, holding out his hand. "I'm, uh, Dylan Lancaster. Lucy Patel sent me over. She said to check in with the front desk and they'd know what to do with me?" His voice must have seemed hesitant enough, because the man stared at him for what felt like ages.

"Well, Lucy sure likes to keep us all on our toes, doesn't she?" He narrowed his eyes, reaching out to shake his hand. What the hell had she gotten him into? "Why don't you come with me?"

"Uh, sure." Dylan followed him into a darkened part of the building, through a labyrinth of hallways and even colder rooms. Wherever Lucy had sent him, it seemed like she intended for him never to escape.

"So how do you know our Lucy?"

As soon as Dylan entered the small kitchen, he found himself surrounded by people. Everyone was standing in front of various stations, working quietly on different tasks. There was a man chopping potatoes, one dicing an enormous pile of onions, a woman washing dishes in front of a large basin, and a gentleman who appeared to be counting chicken breasts. The man next to him cleared his throat, and Dylan turned his attention back to the conversation. "Um, I met her last week, actually. She lives in the same apartment building as my sister, Sam, and my best friend, Blake."

"Forrester?" The man's voice raised an octave. "Great guy. He's gonna be an excellent chef one day." Dylan wasn't sure how this man knew his childhood best friend. He nodded silently. "Blake usually comes with Lucy. Those two are thick as thieves. Everyone loves Blake's chicken marsala. I think we double the number of people that come through on those weekends."

"Come through?" he asked.

"We serve breakfast, lunch, and dinner here. Seven days a week. That's about one thousand meals a day, but when Blake comes by, sometimes we double that if they know he's coming. And if Lucy and Blake come together, well, those two can spend all day talking to people."

Dylan was clearly confused. What kind of celebrity status had his best friend achieved without him knowing about it? "I'm sorry. Lucy didn't really explain where she had sent me."

The man chuckled and lifted an apron from a hook on the wall. "We're a mission, Dylan. At this location, we provide hot meals, clothing, and shelter to those in need." He passed the apron to Dylan. "We're prepping for the lunch service right now, and we could really use some help peeling carrots. If you still want to stay."

A part of him wanted to run, just head for the door and go back to the apartment. He hadn't signed up for manual labor today. But then there was that other part of him. The curious part that thought maybe slicing some carrots to put food on a few plates wasn't the worst thing he could do with his time.

He shrugged and took the apron. "I think I'll stick around."

"What was your name again?" It was the third time the woman had asked his name. Usually, it didn't bother him when people forgot his name. In fact, there was a woman at the shelter this afternoon who had forgotten his name six times. He was sure she had a form of Alzheimer's or dementia, but the woman reminded him of his grandmother, and every time he walked past her she would ask him his name.

"Young man, do you think you could bring me something to drink? I'm quite parched."

"Of course, Lilly, I'll be right back." The water wasn't exactly cold, but everyone seemed so grateful to receive a glass. The old woman smiled and took the glass, pushing her woven beanie further onto her matted hair before taking a sip.

"Thank you, young man...Oh dear, I've forgotten your name again."

"It's Dylan."

"Oh, I knew a Dylan once—such a sweet young man. He was friends with my son before he died." Dylan frowned, leaning over to take the woman's empty plate.

"Can I get you anything else, Lilly?" He noticed she wore three sweaters and a pair of mismatched boots.

She shook her head and stared up into his eyes. "You remind me of him." Dylan smiled. "My dear, Leonard." The woman sighed and looked around. "Can I bother you for a napkin?" Her eyes dimmed. "Sorry, I've forgotten your name again."

"No worries, Lilly. It's Dylan, I'll be right back with that."

However, the woman standing in front of him asking him his name for the third time tonight was not suffering from any type of memory disorder. She was probably in her mid-to-late twenties, with long blonde hair, had definitely never eaten anything with a beating heart, and was on her fourth glass of wine. She had forgotten his name for the third time because it simply didn't matter to her. In the grand scheme of "where does Dylan's name fit in her universe," he imagined it was somewhere between under her shoe or buried beneath asphalt.

The party that Amber had taken him to was not even within the realm of his comfort zone. Dylan sat on a couch that wasn't designed for comfort, sipping his fourth old-fashioned. "Dylan!" he shouted to the girl over the music, which had a vibe that even felt too bougie for him.

"You told me that, didn't you?" she asked, giggling into her vodka tonic.

"A couple of times." His voice was dry and to the point.

"So how do you know Amber?" She twirled her straw around her glass, bouncing her leg against her thigh.

"We just met. My sister is her neighbor." Suddenly, Amber dropped into his lap, giggling and screeching with another girl that slipped next to him on the couch.

"Isn't he just adorable?" Her fingers slid into his hair, her nails teasing his scalp. "I want to eat him all up."

"You don't even eat meat, Amber," one girl teased from outside his periphery. He couldn't see beyond Amber's tits in his face.

She squeezed her chest against him, her lips pressed into his hair. "I'll make an exception for him." Shit, she was drunk, and he was going to have to make sure she got home safely.

He closed his eyes as soon as his brain caught up with him. He was getting old if the first thought that entered his head when a drunk supermodel had her tits in his face was that he needed to get her home, not to have sex with her, but so that she got home without incident.

He whispered in her ear, "Maybe we should get you home."

She ground her hips against his lap. "Oh, someone is eager." He placed a hand on her hips to keep her from grinding on his now curious dick. He *was* still a man, and his own head was swimming in alcohol.

"How do you call your car service?" he asked. She fumbled with her phone, pressing the screen until it finally came on. His eyes widened when he saw Lucy's name pop up, and she pressed the phone to her ear.

"Luce, girl. I need my car service, sweetie." Amber frowned. "No, of course I'm not too drunk. Only a little. Okay, maybe a lot." She touched his face, her fingernails scratching against his cheek. "Dylan, baby, are we too drunk, honey?" Her lips brushed against his jaw, and he froze. Lucy's voice flittered through the phone next to his ear.

"Fine, I'll call the car now. Please get home safe, Am." The line went dead, and Amber dropped the phone into his lap. Her lips crushed against his, and he heard cheering over the loud music. Everything else blurred around them as her tongue slid into his mouth. He couldn't concentrate on the feel of her lips or the way her hands were gripping the hair at the back of his neck.

His thoughts were drifting in and out of consciousness. It didn't register when she stood up, taking his hand and leading him out of the building toward the car. The moment they entered the darkness of the small space, she climbed into his lap, her breath hot against his neck. "God, you're hot."

"You're sort of crushing me," he mumbled.

She laughed and pulled away, staring down at him. "That's not what I meant."

"Oh, right!" He nodded. "Yeah, you're hot too." Her hands slid under his shirt, and he glanced up at the driver, who was glaring at him in the rearview mirror. She slipped her fingers down his pants, and he gripped her wrist, stilling her movement. "I, uh, I think the driver might want us to cool it."

"I'll tip him extra." She bit his ear, and the pain surprised him, causing him to yelp, but it seemed to only spur Amber on. She dipped beneath his waistband and roughly tugged at his now more than interested penis.

"Woah," he yelped. She bit her lip and grinned. "Let's uh..." He sat up, pushing her hands away from his crotch.

"Come on, don't play hard to get now," she whined.

"I just—we've had a lot to drink tonight." Her smile drifted from her face, and she slid off his lap, flopping into the seat beside him. The driver smirked at him in the mirror. Dylan let out a loud exhale. "Look, Amber, I like you. It's just—I've got a lot going on right now, and I don't think this is going to help any of that."

"Trust me, sex helps everything." Amber leaned against the window, staring out at the lights passing by.

Dylan slouched in his seat and stared up at the dirty ceiling of the car. "Not in my experience. Trust me, Amber, I'm saving you a lot of trouble. I'm not someone you want to fall into bed with right now."

"So what, you're just going to be celibate for the rest of your life?"

Dylan laughed. "Shit, I hope not."

After dropping Amber off at her door, Dylan stared at the apartment across the hall and decided to skip the lecture about being drunk from his sister and his best friend. Instead, he climbed the stairs to the roof and stepped out into the night air.

The steel door slammed shut behind him, leaving him in darkness. He ran his hands over his face and stared up at the sky.

"I came up here so you and Amber could be alone when you got back."

"Son of a..." He jumped at the intrusion. "You scared the crap out of me, Lucy." He walked closer to the table, and the moonlight illuminated Lucy's face as she sat in the table's corner, hunched in the small chair.

"Sorry, I didn't think anyone would be up here at this hour." As his eyes adjusted, he realized she was wearing her pajamas. The pink T-shirt read, "Tonight is going to be Lit-erary."

He slid in across from her and smirked. "Nice PJs."

"Shut up." She crossed her arms defensively, tucking her chin to her chest to hide her smile behind her dark hair. "Where's Amber?"

"Probably passed out in bed by now." He shrugged, staring out across the city. When he turned back, Lucy was studying him. "Vogue parties go pretty hard." He held a hand to his forehead, wiping the sweat from his brow. He'd had more than enough to drink tonight.

Lucy made a noise that didn't sound very approving. "I'm sure you felt right at home." Wow. That was the first time she had judged him. She shook her head and frowned. "Sorry, that wasn't fair of me."

"A little below the belt, actually, but you're wrong." Her eyes met his. "That wasn't my type of party."

"Yeah, I've heard you *hate* drinking," she said sarcastically. *Well, thank you, Blake and Sam, for whatever you've said about me to complete strangers.*

He shook his head and growled. "You know, I'm getting pretty tired of everyone thinking they know what's going on in my life." In the moonlight, he could see her eyes grow big. He held up his hand. "It's not just you. Blake, Sam, my brother Jackson back home, my dad, hell even Donna thought she knew what was going on in my head. Everyone makes these assumptions." His heart was racing. "They think they are in my head, that they know why I'm drinking all the time, or they know why I'm doing this shi—" he watched her face and stopped himself. "Crap."

"You're right. That wasn't fair of me to just assume why you do anything." He could tell she had more to say, so he stayed silent and waited. "So why are you drinking so much?"

Not the question he expected. "What?"

"Has anyone ever asked you what's going on?"

He sighed and sank down into the chair. "Jackson did. He was pretty frustrated with me, watching me fall down drunk every day."

"That seems pretty *cry for helpish*, if you ask me."

"I think I just wanted the voices in my head to shut up." The admission surprised him.

"Do the voices talk to you a lot?" She sat up in her seat and leaned forward, concern filling her eyes.

He chuckled. "I'm not crazy, if that's what you're thinking. It's mostly me just telling myself I'm not good enough, or that I'm never going to get out of Titusville, or that I'll never be as good looking as Jax or as settled as Sam."

She frowned. "You can't compare yourself to your siblings."

"Even you wanted me to be Jax when I got here." He smirked.

Her mouth opened and closed a few times as she stuttered, "I...I did not." In the moonlight, he could tell by the way she hid her face that she was blushing.

He pinched his lips together and smiled. "Hate to break the bad news to ya, Butterfly Girl, but he's got a girlfriend."

"Anyway..." She looked away. "You didn't tell me what you thought of the place I sent you."

He sat there for a moment, formulating a response that would be better than what he had provided her last time. "I think that maybe my problems aren't as bad as they could be," he admitted.

"So I was right then?"

He laughed so loudly that his shoulders bounced. "Let's not get carried away, Lucy Patel. I peeled some carrots for a few hours, served way too many glasses of water, but good news, I have a date with a nice lady named Lilly next week."

Lucy sat up. "I hate to break it to you, but Lilly gets a date with all the men that come in there."

"Damn, and I thought I was special."

Lucy studied him before she replied. "I happen to think you're pretty special." They stared at each other, the wind blowing silently across the rooftop, and for a moment, Dylan wanted to believe her.

Chapter Eight

Lucy

Lucy stood at the cash register, her eyes focused on the book in front of her. "This is an excellent book."

The girl on the other side of the counter smiled. "Have you read it?"

"Twice." The register beeped. "Honestly, the first time I read it, I got distracted by the male character. I had to read it a second time just to feel the love story in my bones."

"Is distracted bad?" The girl frowned, touching the book with her hand.

Lucy laughed, handing her the receipt. "No, not at all. He's just very dreamy."

"Most fictional men are. It's the reason I'm still single." The girl shrugged and walked out with her purchase.

Lucy rested her chin on her knuckles, staring at the counter. She didn't have a clue why *she* was still single. Or maybe she did. It wasn't like she went out often or even met new people. She had only been on one "date" in her life, and that hadn't exactly gone well.

Rudy Sandpiper, a guy she had met at the bookstore last summer. Josephine had encouraged her to talk to him after he had shown up four days in a row and sat in her section to read for three hours. He was pleasant, made friendly conversation, and even seemed to flirt with her. After agreeing to meet up after work and grab a coffee, Lucy was excited to get that first date over with.

Lucy spent hours getting ready for the date. She wore the pink and blue dress she had always wanted to try on but had been too nervous to wear out of the house. She had even slipped a yellow and orange butterfly barrette in her hair for good luck before leaving that night.

Rudy told her she looked pretty, paid for her coffee, and then brought her to a poetry reading where he introduced her to his girlfriend. She felt like a complete fool. Apparently, she had misread all the signs. After that, she refused to put herself out there again.

"What's with the face?" She looked up as Jared approached her.

She scrunched her nose and poked her cheeks with her fingers. "It's the only one I've got, so I'm stuck with it."

"You looked lost in thought."

She inhaled through her nose and let out a large breath through her mouth. "I did something stupid."

"Oh no, please tell me you haven't adopted another store cat, because Randy is still pissed about the last one—"

Lucy chuckled, thinking about Sasha, the black and white cat she found roaming behind the bookstore that she let into the office for a few days. She only planned to feed it and send it on its way, but then it ended up giving birth to six kittens a day later and well...The store manager found the litter when his kids were visiting and he couldn't just toss out a helpless mama cat with a litter full of babies in front of three children. Sasha really loved her home on the Upper East Side at Randy's apartment.

"It's not a cat," she interrupted. "You know that guy I told you about? The friend of my neighbor."

"Very cute, made out with your sister?" Jared asked with a devious smirk.

"Yeah, that one." She blew at her hair and leaned forward on the counter. "I kind of, sort of, toldhimtocomeherebutIwishIhadn'tdoneit," she mumbled, squeezing her eyes shut and putting her hands over her face.

"Okay, well, you're gonna have to run that one by me a lot slower and with actual words this time."

She took a deep breath and opened her eyes. "I told him to come by the bookshop today. But now I'm wishing I didn't."

"Wait, cute neighbor guy is coming here? Today?" Jared rushed over to the register and pulled out the mirror he kept stored underneath. "Dammit, I didn't even dress nicely today. Lucy, you can't just invite hot guys without warning me first."

"I don't even know if he'll show up today. It's this thing we do where I leave him a note with an address, and he decides if he's going to go or not."

Jared's eyes lit up, and Lucy knew she had said too much. "Like a scavenger hunt? What does he win when he shows up? Is this sexual?" His eyes narrowed. "Lucy Patel," he sang, his voice sending customer stares in their direction. Lucy covered his mouth with her hand.

"Of course it's not, Jared." She scowled. "It's more of an enlightening journey across the city."

He wiggled his eyebrows. "Sex can be very enlightening, Lucy. Trust me, one day you're gonna understand that."

"Hey, there's this guy up at the coffee shop. He says Lucy sent him." Josephine appeared next to the bookshelf, and Lucy gasped and ducked behind the counter, mumbling to herself.

"What is happening?" Lucy heard Josephine's voice above her and looked up to see her peering over the counter and staring down at her. "Why are you hiding?"

"Is that him?" Jared asked. "I want to get a closer look." Lucy grabbed him by his pant leg and tugged, keeping him from leaving.

Josephine seemed to catch up. "Good-looking guy, average height, brown hair—wait, is this *the* guy?"

"Very cute, made out with Amber," Jared repeated with a nod, yanking his leg away from her. "I'm gonna go check him out."

"That's Dylan?" Josephine whispered. Lucy nodded anxiously and bit her lip, bracing her feet on the wall in front of her.

"He's hot, Lucy!" Jared had returned, and Lucy felt her face flush. "He just ordered a coffee. I think you'd better say hi."

"He doesn't know I work here. My instructions were to go to the bar and tell them Lucy sent him." Her heart was racing. Was she having a heart attack?

"Alright, then what were you going to do after that?" Jared asked.

"I didn't actually get that far this morning. Yesterday's Lucy was braver than today's," she sighed and fisted her skirt in her hands. Last night, she was sure she was ready to share where she worked with Dylan. She wanted him to see what she loved most about New York. Last night, opening up to him felt like a good idea. But today, knowing he was a few feet away inside *her* bookstore, she felt anxious about him being this close to somewhere she felt most at ease in.

"Are you going to stay down there the rest of your shift or..." Josephine's voice trailed off. "Oh, um, hello, how can I help you?"

"I was just curious about this place. It's an interesting idea, putting a bar in a bookstore." Dylan's voice carried to her hiding place on the other side of the counter, and Lucy felt her heart speed up. She reached for Jared's leg and tugged.

"Oh, um, well, I've worked here for five years and the owner really wanted a place where people could relax, read a book, have a coffee during the day and at night, meet up with friends at the bar." Lucy patted Jared's leg appreciatively.

"That sounds pretty neat..." Dylan's voice trailed off, and Lucy was content to know that he seemed to like the place. "Thanks again." Of course, that was the moment Lucy sneezed. Her hand went to her mouth, and she closed her eyes, sitting perfectly still. "Did your counter just sneeze?"

"There it is!" Lucy shouted, standing up and holding a book over her head. "Found it." She handed the book to Jared, her eyes wide.

"Wow, yes, I have been looking for that all day," he said, staring at her with a look of horror.

"Lucy?"

She turned to face Dylan, her mouth opening in surprise. "Dylan? Wow, you're here. You made it."

"Um, yeah." He looked at the counter she had just appeared from. "Were you down there the whole time?"

"Yup, I mean no. I was uh, crawling..." She hummed. "Looking for the book." She pointed at the book in Jared's hands. "We lose them all the time back there. Very dirty."

Dylan stared at her, then glanced at Jared and Josephine. "Alright, then. Do you, uh, do you work here?"

"I do!" she shouted, and Jared cleared his throat beside her. "Um, I do," she said less forcefully. *Calm the hell down, Lucy.*

"Okay, if no one is going to do it, I will. I'm Josephine, and this is Jared. We're friends of Lucy's." Dylan switched his coffee to his left hand and reached out to shake Josephine's hand.

"It's nice to meet you. I'm Dylan. I'm uh, uh..." he met Lucy's eyes. "I'm a friend of Lucy." Lucy stood up a little taller. *A friend of Lucy.* She liked the sound of that.

"We've heard a lot about you," Jared said. Lucy immediately stomped on his toe and glared at him.

"I hope it wasn't about a bar fight." Dylan blushed as Lucy shook her head to stop him from worrying that she would spread any of his business to her friends.

"Oh, tell me more; bar fights are my kink." Josephine slid her glasses down her nose.

"Ignore Jo. She's kidding...mostly." Lucy stepped out from behind the counter. She noticed then that Jared was definitely checking Dylan out.

"So, how long are you in town for?" Jared asked, his tongue slipping out to glide along his bottom lip. Lucy sent him a glowering look to discourage him from flirting.

Dylan seemed not to notice her friend's flirting. "A few months could be more, not really sure, honestly."

"Well, I'm going to show Dylan around. Why don't you two get back to work?" Lucy grabbed Dylan by the arm and tugged him in the opposite direction of her friends.

"I'm pretty sure I'm *your* boss," Jared shouted as she walked away.

"Ignore them," Lucy said once they got to the other side of the bookshelf. "I'm so sorry. I didn't know if you were going to come today."

"You left me a note, so I came," he said, as if it was the most normal thing he had said all day.

"Well, yeah, but..."

"It's kind of our thing, Lucy."

"Right." She blinked, staring back at him. "So, uh, this is where I work."

"You *really* have a thing for books, huh?" He laughed.

She directed him to sit in the pair of chairs in the middle of the store. "That's like asking if you like to draw, Dylan. I enjoy books; they comfort me. Working here makes me happy."

"But what is it about books that you like so much?" She realized he wasn't making fun of her. He seemed genuinely curious, and realizing that Dylan was interested in knowing something about her made her feel as if a million butterflies had taken flight in her stomach. It took her a moment to think about his question. She knew she could give him a million reasons she loved books. She had sat and written them all down once. But sitting across from Dylan Lancaster in the middle of her safe space at the bookstore, something inside of her blurted out the real reason she loved books.

"I can hide inside someone else's fantasy." His brown eyes remained on hers, and even if she wanted to, she couldn't look away. "Not that I hate my life, I don't. When you said I was running from my life the other day, it wasn't exactly right, but sometimes it's just easier to live in someone else's."

Slowly, he nodded. "Do you ever feel like maybe you might miss out on something important because you were living someone else's story and not your own?"

Lucy chuckled. "My story isn't as interesting as the books I read." She leaned over and lowered her voice. "The only date I've ever been on, he introduced me to his girlfriend at the end of the night." Dylan's brow furrowed with a look of confusion, but Lucy shrugged her shoulders. "Honestly, the story isn't that exciting. But asking why I like books is the same thing as asking why you like to d raw."

"True. I guess. When I draw, it's like having somewhere I can disappear to." He leaned back in the oversized chair and looked around the store.

"Have you ever shown anyone the stuff you create?"

His eyes grew large, and he shook his head. "Not on purpose, no. My brother ran across my drawings a few months back, but before that, no one else even knew I did this."

"You're fantastic, though. Why not share your talent?"

He looked around as if he were trying to find an escape. "It's just for me, it's silly little drawings—"

"But what if led to something more?" she asked.

"It won't," he said, his voice raising louder than the quiet bookstore music.

"How will you know unless you take that risk? Hasn't anyone ever told you, no risk, no reward?" She pushed, and she felt him immediately withdraw. "I'm sorry if I'm upsetting you." He picked at his shoes, something she had recognized him doing before when she pushed him further than he was willing to go.

"When does the bar open up here?" he asked. Lucy could sense his unease. She wondered if his drinking was a way for him to hide from his own feelings of uncertainty.

She shook her head and frowned. "Why do you always move directly to alcohol?"

"Do you think you're qualified to ask me that if you don't even know what it's like to drink?" he snapped.

Lucy rolled her eyes. She didn't need to drink alcohol to know how it affected people. She also knew that when people drank alcohol for reasons other than just having a good time, they usually had a hard time admitting it. "Does it make you happy when you drink?" she asked, curious if he knew the answer himself.

Dylan scoffed and stared off into the distance, not meeting her eyes. "No, but when I'm drinking, I don't feel anything." He paused before his eyes met hers. "Why *don't* you drink?"

She inhaled and looked toward the bar as the patrons began gathering. "Because I watch people come in here and drink and laugh and have a great time together. And that seems like a lot of fun. But then I go home, and I have to watch Amber fall down drunk and cry herself to sleep. And I think that maybe it's not worth the facade of a few hours of fake fun, to have to go home and swim in the reality of whatever you're running away from," she sighed and stood up. "You're never going to find your happiness at the bottom of whatever bottle you're searching in, Dylan."

He looked up at her. "You're never going to find yours at the end of a book, either, Lucy."

He had a point. Lucy had created her own safe space through reading. When she got lost in a book, she didn't have to face the thoughts of loneliness that plagued her. It was easy to hide in her romance novels, away from the frustration of her own romantic disappointments. If she was going to insist that Dylan be brave, perhaps she needed to take her own advice. "Then maybe you and I had better start looking in other places, don't you think?" she said.

Dylan stood up and placed his hand on her shoulder, and she willed every muscle in her body not to react. When he leaned over and whispered in her ear, she felt her entire body shiver. "No risk, no reward."

Chapter Nine

Dylan

"So, what kind of ring screams *tomboy who doesn't even wear dresses*?" Dylan tapped the glass case beneath him. The sparkling diamonds below cost more money than he made at the auto shop in the last three years.

Blake passed behind him and whispered. "I'm gonna start by not getting her anything in that case, Dylan. How rich do you think I am?"

Dylan looked up as the woman behind the counter made a sound and frowned. "Then what are we doing here?" He spun around and followed Blake to the other side of the store.

"Because they have something better that I've had my eye on for months." Blake smiled at the man watching them from the front of the store and ran his hand over another case in the corner by the window. "Sam and I walk to the park every Saturday, and we pass by this place. This has been in the window, and I've seen her looking at it, even though she'll swear she hasn't."

Dylan peered into the case and smiled back at his friend. "I guess you really do know my sister."

"It's the one, right?" The sparkle in his best friend's eye left no doubt in Dylan's mind that Blake already knew the answer. Dylan had known Blake loved Sam, but it was at this moment that the truth of it really hit him. Sam was "it" for his best friend. Not in that *I love her, so I'm folding her clothes and cooking dinner for her,* type of way. But in that, *I think I'm willing to walk through fire and step in front of a moving bus for her,* kind of way.

Dylan had never felt that way about anyone except for his own flesh and blood. And probably Blake. He supposed he'd put his toe in a flame if Blake had somehow ended up in danger and needed rescuing. But beyond that, he'd never cared about anyone else that deeply.

Watching Blake spend his hard-earned cash and genuinely smile while doing it messed with his head a lot. This was the natural progression of life.

When a child is born, the parental figures raise the baby. If the child is lucky, it has a carefree existence growing up. If not, it simply survives to make it to the next stage of life. Either way, it exists as a moody, experimental, financial drain on the people who raised it until they get to wash their hands of it and force the child to survive on its own. Then it sinks or swims. Some soar and become successful members of society.

That would be his sister, Sam. She doesn't know it yet, but she's about to move onto the next phase of life. Marriage, kids, white picket fence. And then there is his brother Jax, living with the love of his life, owning his own business, making the dream work.

Then you have the other side of the coin, the ones who failed to swim, like Dylan, classification: failure to launch.

None of this meant he wasn't happy for his sister or his best friend. It just meant that Dylan's eyes were open enough to see that he was halfway to the bottom of the ocean.

"Phase One complete. Time for Phase Two." Blake stood in front of him. "Earth to Dylan."

Dylan looked up. "Sorry, what?"

"You still with me?" Blake asked. "Thought we could stop for lunch and call Jax."

"Jax?" Dylan worried he must have zoned out for a lot longer than he realized. He couldn't understand why they were calling his brother.

"Yeah, Allison is helping me out with some house stuff. I haven't mentioned the wedding thing. They think I'm just keeping my options open for the future. I wanted to talk to you first about the whole 'popping the question' business. Besides, I don't know what Jax will think about it, and I guess I was too chicken to find out yet." Blake opened the door for him, and Dylan stepped out onto the busy street. "Come on, we can get some dim sum around the corner and make the call." Dylan followed silently, his head racing with anxious thoughts. "You're quiet, Dyl."

"Yeah, sorry, just a lot on my mind."

"You're still cool with all this, right?" Blake slowed his pace, allowing Dylan to match his stride. "I guess I just sort of told you what was happening instead of asking how you felt about it."

"I'm not her dad. You don't have to ask me to marry her, Blake." He paused. "You did ask my dad, right?"

Blake laughed. "Yeah, I talked to him when he was here. I don't screw around with Ken. He still scares the shit out of me." Dylan chuckled because he was pretty sure that his dad loved Blake almost as much as he loved him and Jackson.

"I don't think you have anything to worry about."

"I actually wanted to ask you something, though." Blake shoved his hands in his pockets, and Dylan watched as the cold air came out in puffs of smoke from his mouth. "I was hoping you'd be my best man."

Dylan stopped walking, pausing on the busy street as a man bumped into him from behind. "Loser." Blake stopped a few steps ahead and turned around and, for a moment, Dylan just stared at his best friend.

"You're getting fucking married," Dylan said with a smile.

"Well, she has to say yes first." Blake shrugged. "But yeah, that's the plan."

"I can't believe I'm gonna be the best man at my sister's wedding." When he met Blake's eyes, he was smiling back at him. "We're gonna be brothers for real, just like we always wanted when we were kids."

"You've always been the best brother I could ever ask for."

"Shit, I'm not gonna cry on the streets of New York today, Blake." He stepped toward his friend and shoved him forward. "Let's go rub some dirt on our shins and get in a street fight or something. This is way too up in our feelings for me today."

"How about we just go eat some dim sum and call Jax?" Blake laughed.

Dylan kicked the small pebble at his feet and ripped the page out of his sketchbook, tossing it onto the ground under the table. "Utter crap," he swore, staring up at the sky.

"That kind of attitude does not create a very positive environment for the hibernating butterflies." He closed his eyes at the sound of Lucy's voice, the corner of his lip turning upward. Her voice was the one good thing he had heard in his head for the last hour.

Since parting ways with Blake after lunch, he had spent the rest of his afternoon sitting on the roof, spiraling about his life, or lack thereof, and ruining pages in his sketchbook with mediocre bullshit. "Lucy Patel, please bring some sunshine into the darkness that is swallowing everything in my path."

Suddenly she appeared in front of him in a bright yellow shirt and denim overalls with little blue ribbons on each strap. She held her hair back with a bright yellow butterfly hairband. He wasn't sure if it was simply because his mood was already as far to the bottom as it could get, so there was no way he could feel sadder, but seeing her somehow made him feel ten times happier. "Why are you in darkness, Dylan Lancaster?"

"Because everyone is swimming and I am at the bottom of the ocean, about to be swallowed by a whale."

"Oh." She sat down next to him, not across from him like she usually did. He didn't know why that fact interested him. "So why don't you swim?"

He scrunched his face. "Why don't I swim?" Swim to where? Where was he trying to go? "I suppose I'm not sure if I want to swim or what the point of swimming is."

"Obviously not to get swallowed by the whale, stupid." She bumped her shoulder against him and laughed. It was a simple answer, and he immediately thought about that Disney movie with the fish that kept forgetting everything. *"Just keep swimming!"* she said. Maybe that was life. You didn't have to know where you were going, as long as you didn't stop. "Do you know my favorite thing about butterflies?"

"They fly?"

"Sort of, but mostly because they start off these ugly caterpillars that no one looks at. And then they turn into these beautiful, colorful butterflies that can go anywhere. In the winter, they just fly away to warmer weather and then they come back to the exact place they called home in the spring."

"I'm pretty sure that's what old people do, too. We call them snowbirds. I think my dad's one technically." Lucy pushed him and snorted, her cheeks turning a bright pink color. Dylan was starting to really enjoy making Lucy Patel laugh.

"If I could be anything in the world, I would be a butterfly." She stared, her chin tilted toward the sky, her eyes closed. The way the sun was dancing off the glittery butterfly on her hairband made her face shine.

"You're bright enough today to be a butterfly," he said in a soft tone, reaching out to touch her hair band with his finger. She flinched and opened her eyes. Their eyes met, and for a moment, his heart skipped. Almost as if he forgot to take a breath.

"I, uh, um, so what was wrong with your drawing?" She moved away from him and leaned down to pick up the paper on the ground beneath them. She unfolded the page and giggled. "He's cute."

"He's crap."

"Why?" She frowned, flattening the page and laying it on the table in front of him. The fat rabbit with the ball cap stared back at him. "I like him."

"That's Mr. Jangles, and he hates me."

"Why does he hate you?" She traced the drawing with her finger, smiling to herself.

Dylan lifted the page with his hand. "It's just not right. I don't know. I'm trying to draw from memory. I'm writing a story..." he looked up and found her staring at him. "It's stupid; forget it."

"It's not stupid if it's something you're passionate about." She was looking at him again with those eyes. The ones that said, *"You're special, Dylan."*

"It's a dumb idea," he groaned.

"No risk, no reward." Her eyebrow raised as if she had just thought of something. "Do you trust me?"

He laughed. "Marginally."

She stood up and smiled, but not the sweet, innocent Lucy Patel smile he had grown accustomed to. This was mischievous and not at all the type of smile he thought was wise to trust. She held out her hand. "Come on, Dylan Lancaster, we're gonna do something really stupid."

Stupid was practically his middle name. "Now you're speaking my language, Lucy Patel."

She was definitely NOT speaking his language! In fact, he was almost positive that she wasn't even in the same country as him anymore. They were currently standing twelve-hundred feet above the ground overlooking New York City on a glass platform.

It wasn't like height was a deal-breaker for him. Being on the apartment building roof didn't cause him to break into a sweat.

He felt safe up there. No, the problem was railings, ladders, and the fear of falling to your death.

The highest Dylan had ever scaled into the sky was when he was thirteen years old. He and Blake had climbed the county water tower. It was supposed to be a fun bonding experience. Climb the water tower, spray paint their names for everyone to see, and then climb down. Everything was fine until the moment they got to the top and Dylan looked down. His vision blurred. He realized there was nothing holding him onto the tower except a flimsy rail that had a bunch of screws loose. It took Blake running home to get Jax to talk him off the tower for the next three hours to get him down.

Dylan had never really attempted anything like that again.

"Patel? Lancaster?"

"That's us!" Lucy said with a bounce in her step, moving toward the man calling their names. Dylan stepped tentatively toward him. "Right this way. You'll meet your climb guide, and he'll get you prepared."

"Climb guide? Lucy, I'm not so sure about this." Dylan stared out across the city and bit the inside of his mouth. His knees were shaking, and he wasn't even sure he could walk to where this man was directing them.

Lucy grabbed him by the hand and yanked. "Come on, you said you'd do it."

"That was before you told me what *it* was." They climbed down a flight of stairs on the side of the building, and Dylan felt the wind brush through his hair.

"Let's get you two into a climb suit." A young kid—sure, he was probably in his early twenties—but to Dylan he felt way too unqualified to be shoving him into a jumpsuit at the edge of a skyscraper. "It's time to climb out of your comfort zone."

"How many times a day do you say that?" Dylan asked the kid.

"Enough that I dream about it," the guy said with a smile. "Come on, you're gonna love it."

"Define love." Dylan peered around the guy at the city behind him. There was no way he was going out there.

"How do I look?" He turned around to find Lucy standing behind him in a blue jumpsuit and a helmet that was way too big for her head. His breath caught in his throat. She looked ridiculous and...adorable.

He stepped toward her and grabbed her by the shoulders. "You look crazy!" he shouted over the wind. She peered up at him, pushing her helmet out of her eyes.

"Nope, not crazy, just brave." She grinned.

A helmet got shoved onto his head, and with shaky fingers, he reached up to adjust the straps. Shit, he was really doing this. "Alright, you two, I'm going to clip your harnesses in, and you'll be attached to the rail. That means you aren't going to go tumbling off the edge."

Dylan swallowed hard. "Was that going to be a possibility otherwise?"

"Don't worry, you're perfectly safe. The rail is your new best friend." Dylan looked up at where his clip was attached and mentally introduced himself to the piece of metal that was now holding his life in its metallic grip. "You're both going to go out there with your leader, and then you're going to climb."

"You mean we have to go higher?" Dylan's voice cracked.

"You'll follow the stairs to the top. You can look over the edge as you climb, if you want. Don't worry, you're attached to the rail."

"No, thanks," Dylan groaned.

The man snickered but continued with his instructions. "When you get to the top, your leader will show you where to stand for the lean out."

"The...the what?" His voice was no longer cracking. It was in full-out panic. Complete shut down.

Lucy's hand slid into his. "We've got this, Dylan." He looked down at their hands and tightened his grip. If Lucy had done this and survived, then maybe he could do it too.

His brain disagreed with this deduction, but before he could change his mind, his mouth was moving. "Alright, let's get this over with."

The man showed them the way to the starting spot, and he introduced them to their guide, some idiot named Chance. Who the hell gets a job like this with a name like Chance? He led them to a flight of stairs that was right at the edge of the building *(ironic)* and Dylan was pretty sure his life was about to end. He followed Chance *(again, ironic)* up the stairs. His knees shook, his feet felt numb, but with each step, he was closer to getting this whole damn thing over with.

When they got to the top, Chance turned around and looked at them. "Alright, now walk over to the end and you're going to do a forty-five degree lean out over the edge."

Dylan blinked. Apparently, his hearing had gone bad up here. Surely that guy didn't tell him to lean out over the edge of the fucking building? "You want me to do what?"

"Yeah, go out to the edge and lean over. It's super wicked. The straps will hold you."

"Uh, okay." Dylan turned around to let Lucy go first. She was the one with experience, and there was no way he was going to try this thing before seeing how it was done. When he turned toward her, he saw she was breathing heavier than normal. "Hey, you go first." Her eyes widened.

"What?"

"You show me how it's done, and then I swear I'll go."

She shook her head and stepped backward. "I don't think I can do this."

He moved closer to her and put his hands on her shoulders. "What do you mean? I thought you'd done this before?" His voice carried through the wind.

"I've never done this!" she yelled back.

"What?" His voice cracked as he leaned over, bringing himself eye-level with her. "I thought you said you did this already, and that's why you brought me here?" His heart was dangerously close to pumping out of his chest.

"No, I said we were going to do something stupid." She stared out at the platform behind him. "But this is *really* stupid, Dylan."

"Holy shit!" He looked out at the city as the blood rushed through his ears like a freight train.

"Who's going first?" Chance asked with an excited smile.

Lucy shook her head and took another step back. Dylan looked at the platform and turned to Lucy. She looked white as a sheet. Dylan could easily walk away from this, and right now, he knew Lucy would follow him down. But that wasn't what they had come here for. He turned back to her with determination in his voice. "We're doing this."

"What? No!"

"Just be a butterfly, Lucy." He leaned over and kissed her cheek. Then he looked at Chance and nodded. "Alright, dude, let's do this." If today was his day to die, he might as well get it over with.

With each shaky step, his heart pounded in his chest. He looked back at Lucy and smiled when he reached the platform. With a grimace, he turned to Chance, who gave him the thumbs up. The quiet prayer slid from his lips as he told his mother he loved her.

Closing his eyes, he leaned forward, feeling his entire body falling toward the horizon and then pull back abruptly. For a moment, he wondered if he had actually died. Then he opened his eyes and stared down at the city below him. All the noise, every thought in his head, every doubt in his mind ceased to exist. Suddenly, it was just Dylan Lancaster and the world.

Everything below him seemed so insignificant. All the shit he had been worrying about this afternoon no longer mattered. He could have anxiety tomorrow. Today, he was fearless. He opened his arms and screamed, feeling the weight of months of insecurity and doubt leave his lungs. When the harness tugged and pulled him back to the safety of the platform, he was close to tears. He stepped back and leaned against the wall for support.

He watched as Lucy timidly approached the platform, and smiled the moment she leaned forward, completing her drop over the edge. He couldn't imagine what the moment meant for her, but he hoped it had brought her some of the feeling that it did for him.

He knew that tomorrow the same screaming questions would remain, but maybe today they didn't have to be as loud.

When Lucy was pulled back to the platform and detached from the rail, she raced toward him. The smile on her face told him she had experienced the same emotions that he had on that edge. Before he could stop himself, he picked her up, and she wrapped her arms around him.

"That was the most amazing thing I've ever done," she squealed in his ear.

Her hair was soft as his fingers slid against the back of her neck, and he noticed for the first time that she smelled like lemons. He had an urge to bury his nose in the crook of her neck and inhale, but he set her back down onto her feet instead and smiled. "I can't believe we did that."

"I'm literally shaking." She held out her shuddering hands, and he enveloped them with his own. Lucy flinched and looked up.

"We should get some food in you. Got any good pizza joints nearby?"

Her face lit up. "Pizza is my favorite food. If I were going to get stranded on a desert island with only one food for the rest of my life, it would be pizza."

"Me too. Maybe we'd be okay if we got stranded together." He laughed. "How about this, lets get the hell off this building, and you tell me what else you couldn't live without?" He held out his arm, and Lucy wrapped her small hand around his bicep, giggling as she followed him back inside to the safety of the building.

Chapter Ten

Lucy

Lucy stared down at her fluffy bunny slippers sticking up from the bottom of her blankets. "Good morning, Bumper." She shook her right foot and tapped it against her left. "Hello, Thumper." She stared up at her ceiling and groaned. It had been a week since she and Dylan had gone to the Edge and spent a thrilling and daring day together. She felt like Dylan had embraced the risk she had provided him and was really proud of how he handled it.

But ever since that day, she had been feeling weird about being around Dylan. She didn't understand why. Something about the way he looked at her made her stomach feel funny. Like she had eaten sushi from a gas station.

The way he touched her made her insides go all gooey and her face get warm. She felt embarrassed that she was reacting this way about someone who had called her his friend. So, of course, she did the only thing she could think of. She completely ignored him all week.

Rule #98: When you can't figure out a solution to a problem, go for a walk.

So Lucy walked a lot. She walked to the park. Then she walked to work. After work, she walked to the grocery store. When she saw Dylan head up to the roof, she walked down to the basement and did her laundry. Lucy walked until her feet hurt. Despite that, she didn't find an answer to her problem. She really liked Dylan Lancaster. And not in an *"I want to be great friends with you and talk all day"* kind of way. But in the *"let's kiss and make out"* kind of way.

Sure, she'd never kissed or made out with anyone before, but she'd read about it loads of times in her books. And she really wanted to kiss Dylan. When he kissed her cheek on top of the building, she felt her entire body light on fire. If that was even half of what she would feel when he kissed her lips, then she was ready for all of it.

She swung her feet over the side of the bed and planted her them on the floor. Shuffling across the room, she tugged her bedroom door open and rubbed her eyes as she made her way to the kitchen.

"'Bout time you got your ass out of bed."

Amber stood in the doorway, dressed in a short skirt. Her puffy white coat almost covered her entire outfit. "Where are you going?"

"I gotta get to a shoot. Couldn't wait for you anymore, sleepyhead."

Lucy yawned. "What time is it?"

"Almost nine. Blake came by and asked if you wanted to volunteer today. I told him you always want to, so I'm sure he's going to be by soon to pick you up." Amber slipped on her heels and flipped her hair. "What's gotten into you this week?"

"I'm just tired, that's all."

Amber opened the door and found Blake standing there, just as he was getting ready to knock. "She just got up."

Blake stepped into the room and looked down at her feet. "What the heck are those, Luce?"

Lucy stared down at her feet. "Bumper and Thumper."

He snickered. "Well, get hoppin'. You coming or not?" he asked.

"Yeah, can you give me ten minutes?" Lucy sighed and turned around, heading to her room.

Maybe spending the day with Blake was just the distraction she needed to get over her confusing feelings for Dylan. If, in fact, she wanted to get over them, and she wasn't actually sure that was what she truly intended. But time spent with Blake always made her feel better, so she figured at least the distraction would provide her a good day out of the apartment.

When she finished getting ready, Blake was bouncing at the door, eager to head out. "Marsala day?" she asked as they entered the elevator.

"I got something else I want to try today. Learned it last week in class." He punched the button on the elevator, and the doors slid closed. "Might want to try it at our next potluck."

"Oh, are you thinking we should do another one soon?"

Blake shrugged. "You know how everyone who doesn't go home for the holidays hates to have Thanksgiving meals on their own? I was thinking we could all do a potluck up on the roof together, like our own Friendsgiving."

"I love that idea." Lucy despised the idea of another Thanksgiving with her and Amber sitting around the table eating a sad meal of deli turkey and mashed potatoes from a bag. "Amber isn't exactly the most fun to cook for."

"Well, you're part of our family now." He smiled. Lucy felt the tears well behind her eyes. She didn't realize how lonely she felt not having her parents with her for the holidays. "I'm missing my mom and sister, too," he whispered.

She looked away, scrubbing at her eyes. "Yeah, apparently Dad has a study that he can't abandon right now."

"Ah."

Lucy had gotten the phone call from her parents letting her know they weren't going to fly out to New York for Thanksgiving or Christmas because the grant money had come through on their dad's cancer research and he needed to get to work on it right away. She was proud of her father and all his scientific research, but sometimes she just wished she could see him more. All the work he was doing for the world meant less time devoted to her and Amber.

"Sacrifices must be made for the good of mankind, Luce."

"I'm guessing your mom and sister aren't coming?" she asked.

"Yeah, but they'll be here for Christmas. I'm excited for you to meet them. I think you'll really like Kelley." Blake always spoke so highly of his mother and sister.

She put her hands in her pockets and stared at her feet as she kept pace with Blake's long strides. "So, uh, I'm guessing Dylan is sticking around for the holidays."

"I think that's his intention. I think Sam's older brother is coming in for Christmas, too. Gonna be a busy place." Blake whistled. "Looks like you're gonna get to meet motorcycle man after all," he teased.

"He's got a girlfriend," she said, rolling her eyes.

Blake paused at the steps of the mission. "We'll find you a good man one of these days, Luce."

She nodded and let out a loud sigh. "I'd settle for a half decent one who actually wants me."

"Don't rush it. When the right guy comes along, you'll know it." He patted her on the arm.

She bit her lip and looked around for a moment before staring at him. "How did you know Sam was the right one?"

He leaned against the stair railing. "Well, honestly, there was this feeling in my stomach when Sam looked at me. It's funny because I'd known Sam since we were kids, and I didn't really look at her as anything except Dylan's little sister. But when she came home last year, there was just something about the way she looked at me." He smiled as if remembering something and then chuckled. "I always wonder what would have been different if I'd noticed that she liked me back when we were in high school."

"So she liked you first?"

"Yup, but I was too big of an idiot to notice it." He shrugged.

"Maybe it just wasn't meant to be yet."

He chuckled. "That's what Sam says." He shook his head. "I knew Dylan would be pissed if I went near Sam when she came home last year, so it took us some time to take a chance on this thing. But we had to ignore what everyone else thought and just take the leap, you know."

"But how did you know to leap?"

"Honestly, one day I was sitting across from her at the bar and all I could think about was, damn, I want to kiss her."

Lucy giggled. "So you just kissed her?"

"Hell no, I danced with her, and I swore there was something developing between us in that moment. The way she touched me, the look in her eye...and then Dylan interrupted us, and I pretended like nothing happened." He shook his head with a laugh. "But I kissed her the next day, and I haven't stopped kissing her since."

Lucy sighed, getting lost in her own thoughts. Taking a chance on love had worked out for Sam and Blake, and they had been friends for a long time. "Do you ever regret kissing her, you know, changing the friendship, everything that happened after?"

He stared down the street. "You know, after I kissed Sam, a lot of stuff went down. Dylan and I punched each other in the face. We didn't speak for weeks. Got ourselves arrested for fighting Casey Anderson, and things felt off for a while. But there isn't a single thing I would do differently." He paused. "Except maybe getting Sam to answer her damn phone instead of talking to my ex-girlfriend, but she's stubborn and I can't change that." Lucy stared at him while he revealed a lot of things she didn't know about his relationship. "All I can tell you is that love is worth all the heartache and risk it takes to get there."

She smiled and touched her cheek, brushing her fingers against the spot that Dylan's lips had touched.

"Why are you asking me all these questions about love? Do you have a guy you're interested in, Luce?"

"What?" She felt her face flush. "No, um, no, I was, uh, just curious."

"Alright, just be careful out there. Love can be a bitch, too. Her name is Donna Draper," he said. "Just ask Dylan. We both fell for her stupidity." Blake turned and opened the red door, walking into the Mission. Lucy followed him inside, mentally writing the name Donna Draper in her mind.

Working that diner life #blessed

The caption was under a photo of a busty blonde standing at a register with a smile on her face. The photo was from a few days ago. Scrolling through her Instagram feed, she found Donna worked at Linda's Diner. Lucy recalled it was the name of Blake's mother's diner back in Titusville. It surprised her that Blake's ex worked at his mother's place of business, especially after the way he talked about her.

As she continued to doomscroll further on her feed, she found photos of Dylan and Donna together.

#DoWhoYouLove IYKYK

The photo had been taken at a picnic table at a campground. Dylan sat on the table with the blonde perched on his lap, her face buried in his neck. Dylan wasn't smiling, but staring off into the distance. There were empty beer bottles scattered around next to him on the table.

The photos didn't feature him heavily, but she found a few more showing them at a bar or at other places in their hometown, but always with Donna draped across his lap, either kissing him or practically humping him. None of the photos appeared to tell the story of a happy couple. As she scrolled further, she found photos of Blake and Donna, apparently from when they were dating. She was surprised this woman had never heard of deleting photos once a relationship had ended.

Donna was beautiful. She was tall and skinny, with the biggest boobs that Lucy had ever seen. Lucy glanced down at her own breasts. They were nothing compared to the busty woman on her phone. She squeezed her breasts together and groaned. Even shoved together, they didn't create the spectacle the blonde siren in the photo made. She fell back against her pillow. Why would a guy like Dylan ever be interested in her when he had been with a girl like *that*?

She rolled over, smothering her face in her pillow, and screamed.

Chapter Eleven

Dylan

Dylan stepped out of the shower and cursed when his foot landed on the exfoliating loofah that Sam had left for him in the bathroom. He lifted his foot to avoid crushing it, slipping instead, which sent him stumbling into the counter, causing him to stub his toe.

He pressed his hand to the foggy mirror, and his face stared back at him. He squinted, examining the dark lines under his eyes that had appeared over the course of the last few days. Sleep wasn't exactly something he had been doing lately.

He'd spent more than one or two restless nights, tossing and turning on the sofabed, thinking about that day on the Edge. A few extra nights dreaming about the smell of lemons. And exactly zero nights talking to Lucy, because she was ghosting him.

Dylan wasn't sure if he was making it up in his head or not, but he hadn't seen Lucy since the day he had risked everything and dangled over the edge of a skyscraper for her. And he couldn't deny it. He did it for her. She was the only person in the world who could make him do crazy shit like that. Dylan realized as each day passed that Lucy was becoming an integral part of his day, hell even bigger, his life. When she wasn't there, it felt like a loss.

And the last few days had been a total loss without her. Earlier in the week, he swore he saw her by the elevator, but then the door at the end of the hall slammed shut. He searched the roof, her apartment, but she was nowhere to be found. He'd even stopped by the bookstore and was told she wasn't working that day.

He thought back to everything that had happened, and he couldn't put his finger on one thing that had gone wrong. After their death-defying stand on the roof that day, they went to dinner and enjoyed the best pizza he had ever eaten. It turned out that Lucy dug pizza more than he did. She knew every single pizza joint in the East Village, including the one that Amber had taken him to on the first night he had arrived in the city.

They talked for hours, and Dylan kind of enjoyed the fact that he could just be himself with a woman and not have to worry about what she wanted from him. Being with Lucy felt different from when he was going out with Donna back in Titusville. Donna had expectations. She wanted something from him, usually sex.

But Lucy just wanted to be around him. She was excited to hear what he had to say. In fact, Lucy hung on his every word as if it were the ending to the best novel she had ever read. And Lucy *really* loved books, so that was a pretty big deal. So, the fact that she was ignoring him felt significant.

He stepped out of the bathroom and walked toward the noise in the kitchen, hoping that meant someone was cooking something that would allow him to eat his anxiety.

When he turned the corner, his sister was standing in the kitchen, wearing one of Blake's old high school football jerseys and a pair of baggy shorts, with her hair pulled into a bun on top of her head. She was dancing in circles, sprinkling something into a pan on the stove while she sang wildly off-key to an old Tiffany tune.

"With the way you are singing, I *wish* you were alone right now."

She screamed and turned toward him. "Jesus, Dyl, you scared the shit out of me." She reached for her phone and shut off the music. "I was just making spaghetti for dinner. Blake took Lucy to volunteer at the Mission for lunch service, and I guess they got held up, so I figured I'd get dinner started." She looked into the pot. "And well, this is the extent of what I know how to cook."

"It's a good thing you're dating a chef," he said. She dipped her finger into the sauce and tasted it. "That's gross, you know that, right?"

"Says the guy who used to drink straight out of the milk carton."

He leaned over the counter and plucked a piece of cooked spaghetti from the colander, sucking it into his mouth. "I've matured since then."

"Clearly." She chuckled.

"I'm just impressed to see you cooking, that's all." He chewed on the half-cooked spaghetti noodle, then spat out the rest. "I remember when you only ate Fruit Loops and soda for breakfast."

"Don't knock my breakfast choices, Dyl."

"You eat like a child, Sam." She slapped his arm and continued stirring the sauce. "But you seem happier now...with Blake."

"Did it kill you to admit that?" She laughed.

Dylan leaned against the counter, rifling through the cookbook sitting open. "Nah, I think I was upset at first, because of the whole shock factor."

"Shock factor?" his sister snorted. "Were you shocked because it was me or because I liked *him*?"

Dylan groaned, "Look, you're my baby sister."

"Two years younger—that hardly makes me a baby, Dyl."

"You'll always be the baby, Sam." He kicked her foot with his own. "Blake and I did shit together, stupid shit. We used to have shower fights with our dicks when we were kids!" Sam squealed, leaning over the counter as she tried to catch her breath. "Don't tell him I told you that." He scowled. "But we double-dated. I knew what girls he liked, what girls he..."

"I get it, Dylan. I know you wanted to protect me, but Blake and I have talked about all of that. We were very honest with each other about our previous partners."

"Gross."

"Be an adult," she scolded. "When you love someone, you put all that on the table," she sighed. "Can you answer something for me?"

He held his breath and stared at her. When he exhaled, she laughed. "You wanna know about Donna, right?"

"Why the hell would you run to Donna after everything that went down last year?"

Dylan paused and looked at his sister. "Why did you move to Pittsburgh?"

"That does not answer my question." Dylan narrowed his eyes, and Sam sighed. "Fine, I needed to get out of Titusville. There wasn't anything there for me. I was feeling claustrophobic."

"Exactly." Dylan nodded.

"What does that have to do with you sleeping with Donna?"

"After you and Blake left last year, Dad took off, too. Jax was so excited about running the shop. You should see the big asshole showing up for work, humming and smiling. Even when he was struggling with the shop stuff, he was happy as a clam." Dylan shook his head at the absurdity of it all. "And I was just there, surviving. Everyone was gone. I hated working in the shop. The only person I had any connection with was Donna. Don't get me wrong, I hated her for everything she caused with you and Blake. But I felt so claustrophobic that I was tearing my skin off just to get out."

"So, you slept with Donna?"

"I was just so angry because Blake got out, you got out, Dad got out. Jax was acting like a damn idiot all day long, pretending to hate this redhead he was drooling over, and I just wanted to stop feeling like me for a minute."

"And Donna made you feel like..."

"Oh, Donna made me feel like shit. All she wanted to do was talk about Blake," he said with a loud groan. "But if I drank enough, that didn't matter."

"Dylan, that can't be what you want from a relationship?"

Dylan rolled his eyes. "I'm not like you, and I'm not Blake."

"What's that supposed to mean?"

Dylan pushed away from the counter and walked into the living room. "You always wanted love. I remember you walking around with your headphones on, singing stupid love songs all the time."

"There is nothing wrong with wanting to be loved, Dylan." Sam sat down next to him, putting her hand on his knee.

"And Blake was always the charmer between the two of us. Girls *wanted* a relationship with him. No one wanted to date me; they just wanted...well, anyway, I just don't think I'm going to find a woman who is interested in me, or wants to get to know the real Dylan Lancaster." His sister rubbed his knee in that calming way that only she could, keeping him from spiraling into one of his anxiety fits.

"Do you want to know what I think?" she asked.

"Are you going to tell me either way?" he teased.

She tussled her hand through his hair. "I think maybe if you are looking for a deeper connection with a woman, you need to stop burrowing in with the Donna Drapers of the world."

"Yeah, I'm done with that." He shook his head and leaned toward his sister, resting his head on her shoulder.

"And maybe the Amber Patels..."

He chuckled. "She and I weren't exactly reading the same book."

"Exactly. I think maybe that's your problem, Dylan. You need to find a woman who's reading the same book as you." Dylan smiled to himself as the girl with the butterfly barrette entered his mind. "What is that smile for?"

"Nothing."

"That was not a nothing smile. You were thinking about some-one." Sam poked him in his abdomen, tickling his side.

"How would I have met anyone else? I've been here with you guys this whole time." Dylan sat up on the couch and leaned away.

Sam's eyes focused on him. "Fine, keep your secrets."

The front door opened, and Blake walked through with a bag of groceries in his arms. "Who wants dessert?"

"Once you taste dinner, that may be the only thing we eat," Dylan said with a chuckle. Sam elbowed him in the side, and he jumped up from the couch and ran toward the kitchen as Sam chased after him.

Blake watched from the hallway. "Is this what you two do while I'm gone?"

"Nah, we mostly drink out of milk cartons and play dodgeball with Fruit Loops." Dylan winked at his sister, who snorted and tossed a piece of uncooked spaghetti at him.

"How was volunteering today?" she asked.

Blake sat the groceries on the counter and put them away in the cabinets. "It was great. Lucy is amazing." Dylan scratched the back of his neck and ran a hand through his hair at the mention of her name. "She had everyone laughing today."

"She usually does," Sam said, leaning up on her toes to peck a kiss against Blake's lips. Dylan envied the ease of their relation-ship. They were already practically married, and Blake hadn't even popped the question yet.

"Yeah, but today, she was telling this story about how she went to that skyscraper place, The Edge." Dylan stood up straighter and leaned against the counter.

"When did she do that?" Sam asked.

"Last week, apparently. She said she went with someone but wouldn't say who." Blake shrugged, and Sam made a soft cooing sound.

"Is our little Lucy finally getting a boyfriend?" Sam giggled.

Blake shook his head. "Don't get ahead of yourself. She said she went with a friend." Blake seemed completely against the idea of Lucy dating. Dylan sagged against the granite countertop. "Anyway, the way she told the story, the two of them dared the lean out, and it was apparently terrifying, and this dude somehow got her through it. And she said, in the end, they both faced their fears."

"That's amazing. I'm proud of her for doing that, especially knowing that she's always wanted to do it, but Amber refused to take her."

"That's because Amber only does what is on Amber's schedule." Blake chuckled, but then turned and shoved a box of Fruit Loops into the cupboard a little more forcefully than necessary.

Sam reached up and scrubbed her hand through Blake's hair. "Her sister means well. I just don't think she realizes that she's a bit selfish when it comes to Lucy."

"That's because she never thinks of her at all. Lucy practically acts like her mother, and she does nothing for her at all. Did you know their parents aren't coming for the holidays?" Blake frowned.

"Her dad's grant came in, so they can't travel. So that means they are on their own this year."

"Oh no, Lucy must be heartbroken. She was really looking forward to seeing them." Sam stirred the sauce and grabbed the noodles.

"She's not saying it, but I could see it on her face. She was practically in tears talking about it this afternoon, even though she tried to hide it from me."

Dylan pushed away from the counter and grabbed his sketchbook, walking toward the door. "Where are you going? Dinner is almost ready?" Sam called out.

"I just remembered I need to do something. Eat without me." Before they could respond, he closed the front door and escaped to the end of the hallway.

Chapter Twelve

Lucy

Lucy sat alone in her apartment window with the lights off. While she wouldn't admit it to anyone, she had been listening to the same song on repeat since Blake had dropped her off thirty minutes ago. The last beats of Colbie Caillat's "Fallin' For You" played in her ear, and she clicked the repeat button to start the song again. She laid her head back against the windowsill and sang softly until her stomach growled.

Lucy hadn't eaten all day. It wasn't like her not to eat, but she didn't *feel* like eating. All she could think about was the fact that she missed Dylan and she hated not talking to him.

It had been a week, and now it would be embarrassing to explain where she had been. What exactly was she supposed to say? *"Sorry, you're making me feel sick to my stomach, so I can't be around you right now."*

When she realized she was about to listen to her song for the tenth time, she knew she needed to get out of her apartment. At least Dylan would be eating dinner with Blake and Sam now, so she could escape to the roof for a while and get some air.

She pulled on her coat and beanie and climbed the stairs to the roof, but the moment she opened the door, she froze. Dylan Lancaster was sitting at the table, drawing in his book.

Maybe he wouldn't see her if she just closed the door!

"There you are!"

Crap!

"Oh, hey Dylan. Here I am." She stepped out onto the roof and nervously walked toward him.

He slammed his book shut and slid it under his leg. "Haven't seen you all week. I thought maybe you were avoiding me."

She frowned and dropped into the seat across from him. "Just busy. I can't drop everything all the time." She picked at the paint on the table, unsure of what else to say. She had never felt this way around Dylan before, but between her nerves and her disappointment in her family right now, she wasn't in the mood to explain herself.

"Everything alright?" She felt his foot nudge hers under the table and looked up at him. The right corner of his lip turned upward, and she felt her entire stomach drop to her knees.

Maybe now she was finally understanding all her romance novels. There was that line about the main character holding a breath they didn't know they were holding. Which Lucy always thought was stupid, because how did they not know they were holding their breath? Only right now, Lucy felt like she might pass out if Dylan didn't stop looking at her, and she realized she wasn't breathing.

She exhaled and choked. "I, uh, I'm fine."

"No, you're not." Dylan was still staring at her with those dark brown eyes that were making her feel like liquid. "But I didn't think you were the one to lie in this relationship." And then he smirked, and she felt like her body had set on fire. She should totally move on from his use of the word relationship, right?

"It's nothing; it's stupid." She scraped her fingers against the paint on the table.

Dylan sat up, his large hand hovering over hers, stilling her movement. "It's not stupid if it's upset you. Come on, Butterfly Girl, talk to me."

Her skin tingled as she watched his thumb caress her hand. "My parents aren't coming for Thanksgiving or Christmas," she whispered. "And it's not their fault. My dad—he's a scientist, and his grant came through, so he has to work, but I haven't seen them in over a year, and I just thought they would be here this time." She ducked her chin against her chest, burying it in her jacket to hide her face as she felt a tear trickle down her cheek. "I feel like a jerk being upset about it because I know he's helping people."

"Don't be sorry for wanting to see your parents. I'd give anything to see my mom." He squeezed her hand, and she looked up. Sam hadn't spoken much about her mother. All Lucy knew was that she had died when they were all very young. "She died when I was eight." He shrugged. "Cancer sucks."

Lucy recoiled and sat back in her chair. "Oh God, I *am* a jerk."

"Hey, no, seriously, you aren't."

"My dad isn't coming because he's trying to *cure* cancer, which is the reason your mother can't be here with you, and I'm sitting here crying because my parents won't come visit so they can eat deli turkey with me."

Dylan chuckled. "Okay, first...deli turkey? What kind of Thanksgiving are you having, Lucy Patel? And second, seriously, stop being so hard on yourself." She groaned and slumped in her seat. The silence felt like it was going to choke her the longer it sat between them. Dylan sighed and pushed her foot under the table. "How's Lilibeth doing?"

She let her head fall against the chair. "Lilibeth is getting on my nerves."

"So she hasn't chosen Joel or Karl yet?" he asked.

She shook her head. "In her heart, she knows she belongs with Joel, but she's afraid." She sighed and stared at her hands, folded neatly on the table. "She's afraid that he can't love her. So she's staying with Karl. He says he loves her, but really he just wants her for what she can give him. He wants Lilibeth to stay exactly as she is, even if that isn't who she wants to be."

Dylan was chewing on the inside of his lip, his jaw clenched tight. "Does Joel love her?"

Her eyes met his, and she felt her heart race. "Joel loves Lilibeth more than anything. He loves her even though she doesn't know who she wants to be, or that she isn't even sure if Rockmount Ranch is still her home." She blew out a large, angry breath. "But Joel won't tell her."

Dylan laughed so loudly his shoulders shook. "Sounds like the people in your book suck at communication."

"Have you ever read a romance novel before?"

Dylan shook his head. "Can't say that I have." They sat quietly, staring out into the city. Narrowing his eyes, he leaned forward. "I noticed you haven't sent me anywhere else since you tried to kill m e."

Her mouth dropped open. "I wasn't trying to kill you."

"How about we try something different?" He slid out of his seat and stood up. "Tell me one place in the city you've always wanted to go, but have never been."

"Why?" She chewed the edges of her finger and frowned.

"Because we're going to go there."

She blinked. "What? When?"

He held out his hand and smiled. She noticed the way the corners of his eyes crinkled when he did. "Right now."

"We can't just go there right now. What if Amber needs me or...?"

"Nuh uh, Amber is an adult and can take care of herself. This is about you, and it sounds like you know where you want to go." He took her hand, and she immediately felt the warmth of his palm against hers as he pulled her up from her seat.

"Dylan..." He tugged her toward the door. "Are you sure you want to do this?" She ran a couple of steps to catch up with him.

"There's nothing else I want to do." Lucy wasn't sure if she had swallowed a few of her butterflies because her stomach was positively fluttering. She followed him down the stairs, through the lobby, and out onto the street. But it wasn't until they were on the sidewalk that she realized he was still holding her hand.

She had been living in New York City for years and had never been to Rockefeller Center during the winter. She and Amber had planned to visit a few times, but there was always an event that caused them to cancel. "That's where they put up the tree after Thanksgiving." She pointed to the area above the bronze statue of Prometheus.

"And you've never been here to see the tree, either?"

"Nope, Amber always gets busy around this time of year."

"We'll have to come back and see it later." Lucy was pre-occupied with the word 'later' when he tugged on her hand and pulled her toward the rink.

"Where are you going?"

"Ice skating, of course." He smiled and tugged her with him.

She grabbed his arm and pulled him back. "We don't have to do that. I just wanted to come see it."

"Lucy, don't be ridiculous. We can't come all this way and not skate." She pulled her hand out of his and stood firmly in her spot as people pushed past them. "What are you doing?"

Dylan shook his head and stepped in front of her, running his hands along the seam of her jacket. She frowned and stared at her feet. "I don't know how to skate."

Dylan's fingers felt warm against her chin as his hand guided her softly until her eyes met his. "I won't let you fall, I promise."

She glanced over at the rink. There were people skating every-where—children with their parents, couples holding hands, but mostly people laughing and having fun. It looked fun, and she had always wanted to try it.

Rule #66: Always take chances.

With a deep breath, she nodded. "Alright."

Her palm rested against his as he guided her to the entrance. Her heart was pounding while she waited for him to bring her a pair of skates. The entire time she was lacing them, she kept imagining falling on her face in front of Dylan. "That's not tight enough, Luce. Let me help."

She watched as he knelt in front of her, the top of his dark wavy hair just inches from her face. She closed her eyes and inhaled. He smelled of vanilla soap and a hint of cherry that she had recognized in the markers he would spend his day drawing with. When she opened her eyes, he was looking at her, and her heart skipped a beat to the tune of his name. "All better?" He patted her skates and smiled, and Lucy realized just how close he was to her. All she needed to do was lean down and kiss him. She nodded silently instead.

He stood up and held out both hands, lifting her off the bench. "Oh boy, I have a feeling you are not going to be able to keep your promise." Her knees were shaking as she stepped onto the blades beneath her feet.

When his face brushed her cheek, his jaw against her ear, she wanted to giggle as his breath tickled her skin. "If you fall, I fall." Suddenly, she shivered. Looking into his eyes, she knew she had already fallen.

He led them carefully to the entrance of the rink, and the moment her blades hit the ice; she slid out of his grasp. A pair of strong arms wrapped around her waist, hoisting her upright. "I'm not letting you fall down that quickly, Lucy." He held out his hand, and she reached for it, grasping it with all her strength. "Don't let go, alright."

"My legs are too terrified to move right now. You'll be lucky if I don't just ride you at some point tonight." Dylan stopped skating abruptly, and Lucy lost her footing, reaching out for the side of the rink to keep herself from falling onto the ice. She turned toward him and frowned. "Are you alright?" she said, his eyes level with he rs.

"Uh, yup, yeah, totally fine." He reached for her hand and smiled. "Just um, you caught me off guard, sorry."

"I don't know why you're not scared," she squealed as people whizzed past her.

Dylan skated slowly beside her, gripping her hand as if she were some sort of precious cargo. "I've been skating on frozen lakes since I was a kid."

"We didn't have a lot of frozen lakes in San Francisco." She wobbled on her feet as a kid grabbed her coat, trying not to fall on his own. The child's parent picked him up and skated past them. "My parents didn't have a lot of time to do things with us. Amber and I basically raised ourselves. Fun in the Patel home was reading a book, or watching television. That's how Amber got interested in modeling. She loved watching America's Next Top Model."

Dylan navigated them around a group of kids that had fallen in the middle of the ice. "I can't say my dad did much with us either after Mom died. The three of us kids were really tight growing up. Dad was too busy trying to keep everything from falling apart."

She squeezed his hand and smiled at him. "I think it's pretty amazing how close you and Sam are."

"She sucks." He scoffed. "Can't stand her."

"Do you miss Titusville?" Lucy tripped, but Dylan kept his grip on her, making sure she didn't fall.

Dylan slowed his pace and skated toward the edge of the rink. "Not really. There isn't anything back there for me."

"I'm sure you miss your brother or maybe even a girlfriend or something..." She stared off in the distance, not wanting to look at him.

She could feel his grip on her tighten. "Jax is so busy with Allison. I'm sure he's happy to have me out of his hair." She peeked to her side and noticed the tick in his jaw. "I, uh, I didn't have a girlfriend back home."

"Oh, I thought—"

"What did they tell you?" Dylan's tone was rough and accusatory. "Let me guess, Donna."

"She's pretty." Lucy inhaled and held her breath.

Dylan shook his head. "Lucy, she's not worth your time. Trust me, she wasn't worth mine."

"She must have been worth something if you were with her that long." Her voice felt foreign, and she knew she should stop talking before she ruined the night.

"You know how Karl wants Lilibeth to stay the same, and Lilibeth knows that he's not the person for her, yet she keeps fucking around with him, anyway?" Lucy flinched, but nodded anyway. "Donna was my Karl. Pointless, useless, a waste of my time, yet I did it anyway. There is no story there, Lucy. I was just a coward who was too afraid to leave Rockmount Ranch."

"You're not a coward, Dylan," she said. "You were brave enough to come to New York City." Dylan's head snapped in her direction just as his foot snagged on the ground. Before he could adjust, his body lurched forward, tumbling toward the ice. He spun onto his back just as Lucy began tumbling after him. She landed with a thud on his chest as they slid down a patch of ice.

"Lucy, are you okay?" Dylan's concerned voice filtered to her ears as she lifted her head. His brown eyes stared up from beneath her.

She blinked and then smiled. "I told you I would end up riding you tonight."

Dylan closed his eyes and groaned. "Lucy, you really have to stop saying that." She blinked again. *What had she said?* Then she filtered the words through her brain and opened her eyes.

"Oh..." she blushed. Dylan's eyes were piercing hers, and he most definitely wasn't smiling.

Chapter Thirteen

Dylan

"Oh..." Lucy's cheeks had reddened to an adorable shade he had never seen on her. It was mesmerizing and distracted him from his task of getting up off the ice. He lifted his head, and Lucy tried to move, brushing her hand against his thigh. That definitely wasn't helping matters. She braced her other hand on his chest and pushed, slipping on her knees and falling onto her back. She giggled, and Dylan looked over, watching her laugh.

A man skated over to them. "Are you two alright?"

"Yeah, yeah, we're fine. Thank you." Dylan rolled to his side and got up on his hip. "Come on, you menace, let's get you off this ice."

"I'm a menace?" Lucy's mouth sat slightly agape, and he couldn't help but stare at her lips. He suddenly needed to know if they tasted like lemons.

He chuckled and got to his feet, holding out his hands. "Come on, before you make me self-destruct." Dylan lifted her off the ice and carefully led them to the exit of the rink. Lucy continued to stare at him as if he were talking in an unfamiliar language. He wondered if anyone had ever really flirted with her before.

She plunked down on the bench and bent over to undo her laces. He knelt in front of her. "Let me do that." She smiled and lifted her foot, and he slowly undid each lace, every so often looking up to catch her staring at him. "What?"

"Nothing. No one has ever untied my shoes before," she said.

He slid his palm along her calf as he tugged the skate from her foot, smiling to himself when she stiffened under his touch. He glanced up and noticed her breath hitch. She blinked once, then again, and her tongue slid out across her bottom lip. He had an urge to press his lips against hers and suck her tongue into his mouth. He didn't know what was happening to him, but despite the cold he was feeling very warm all over.

He yanked the other skate free, letting his hands slide further along her leg than necessary. She squeaked, and he froze. Why did taking off a pair of ice skates feel so seductive? It wasn't like he'd never had sex before, and seducing a woman was something he was very good at. Yet touching Lucy felt almost sinful.

Her eyes were wide as she stared down at him, blinking slowly between dark lashes. His eyes drifted to her lips.

He dropped the skate to the ground as he knelt between her legs, his hands gripping her waist. She stared back at him with big brown eyes, as if she were unsure of what to do. She appeared frozen. Her breath was heavy against his cheek as he lifted his eyes to hers. "Can I kiss you?" he whispered the moment their eyes met.

She swallowed and nodded ever so slowly, and Dylan leaned forward and pressed his mouth against her lips, and the world as he knew it ceased to exist.

It wasn't as if sound dulled, or time stopped. It was that everything that Dylan had ever known until now was a lie. Because the world changed in that instant.

In fact, in twenty-nine years of life, Dylan Lancaster had not felt this kind of longing, need, *no*, desire, that he was feeling until he had kissed Lucy Patel.

The hand gripping her waist slid up her back, slipping into her hair. His tongue pressed against hers, causing a quiet moan to exit his throat, and he felt her stiffen momentarily. His hand pressed against her cheek, and then her fingers rested against his hand, pulling away from him, panting. "I, uh..." Her eyes glanced at his chest, not meeting his, and in that moment he recognized panic.

He rested his forehead against hers. "Sorry, I uh..." He felt like a jerk as the reality of the situation caught up with him. Lucy hadn't been in a relationship before, had been struggling to flirt with him all night, and most likely had just had her first kiss, and Dylan reacted like a dog in heat.

"Please don't apologize," she said in a timid voice. "Can we just go home now?"

"Yeah, of course."

Three days. It had been three days since the kiss, and Dylan was quite certain he was losing his mind.

His sketchbook was no longer focused on the cute little animals he had been drawing. Now, every single page was butterflies and Lucy. He couldn't stop thinking about her or that kiss. She had taken over every inch of space in his mind. There was nothing he wanted more than Lucy Patel. But Lucy Patel was not like any other girl he had dated before. Lucy was innocent and perfect, and Lucy was most definitely a virgin.

Dylan Lancaster was an asshole. He drank too much. He was the guy who got into stupid fights. And he was definitely the type of guy who had sex with his best friend's girlfriend. He didn't deserve someone like Lucy. No matter how much he wanted her.

Even though all of that was a fact, he still found himself standing outside her bookstore, staring in the window, trying to sneak a glimpse of her. He hadn't seen her in days, and he wanted to make sure she was all right, since that night, since the kiss.

"She's out back if you want to go in and say hello." Dylan jumped at the sound of a man's voice. He turned to see one of Lucy's co-workers he had met previously standing at the door.

"Sorry, I was just, uh..."

"Stalking her?" The guy laughed and stepped out onto the sidewalk.

"Sorry, I don't remember your name." Dylan frowned.

"Jared." He reached into his pocket and leaned against the building, pulling out a cigarette. "You smoke?"

Dylan shook his head. "Don't need another vice. I just came by to check on her. I haven't seen her for a couple of days." He ran a hand across the back of his neck. "How's she been?"

Jared puffed on his cigarette and breathed out a large chain of smoke. "She's been quieter than usual. Anything you want to tell me?"

Dylan frowned and shook his head. "She's a good friend of yours, then?"

"Lucy's the best, rare for her sex. If they made more like her, I might not have switched sides." His eyes swept over Dylan's body in a way that made him feel like he was being gawked at. "Nah, who am I kidding? God made me this way. You love who you love." He winked at him, and Dylan chuckled nervously.

"I suppose so."

"Lucy sure seems to fancy you, though." Jared snorted, and Dylan looked up so fast he felt his neck crack. "Ah, so it's not just our girl that's interested?"

Dylan frowned and kicked at the curb. "She's really never had a boyfriend?" Dylan asked, hoping for some secret affair that no one knew about.

Jared pushed off the wall and dropped his butt to the ground, stepping on it with his shoe. "Only in her books. So, you better be careful with our girl, you hear?"

"Can you carry the mashed potatoes upstairs, please?" Dylan got off the couch and picked up the large container from the counter.

It was heavier than he had realized. "This looks like it could feed five families."

Blake stopped and frowned. "I hope it feeds more than that. We have a lot of people coming tonight."

"Did you text your brother yet?" Sam emerged from the hallway with her phone in her hand. "Jax wants to make sure you say happy Thanksgiving to Allison."

"I'll do that when I get upstairs." Dylan set down the container and pulled on his jacket. "Isn't it going to be cold upstairs?"

"We got heaters to keep everyone warm," Blake said.

"Alright, I'll meet you guys up there." Dylan picked up his giant container of mashed potatoes and headed for the roof. He opened the door and was surprised by the sizeable crowd already milling about.

"Dylan, I hope that is the mashed potatoes." Holly, the elderly woman who lived a few floors down, greeted him the moment he arrived.

"It certainly is. The Forrester special." The woman took the container and set it down on the table next to the rest of the food. "They are coming with the turkey shortly."

"Bless you and your family for doing this. Mike and I would have been alone this year without it." The woman patted his shoulder, and Dylan smiled, leaving her to walk over to the sitting area. He pulled out his phone to text his brother and Allison before he forgot.

He laughed to himself and tucked his phone back into his pocket. "Hey there, haven't seen you in a while."

"Hey Amber, I've been busy." He looked around for Lucy, hoping to find her now that he knew Amber was here.

"Yeah, I was sad that we hadn't connected again." Dylan nodded absentmindedly. "You've missed some really crazy parties."

"I've been keeping to myself, really." The door to the roof opened, and Sam walked out with Blake and Lucy. He sat up in his seat hoping she would look his way.

"Work anything out yet?" He barely heard Amber. All he could focus on was Lucy. She was beautiful. She was wearing a brown dress with orange and yellow flowers on it. Her hair was pulled back with a yellow hair ribbon that stood out against her dark hair. She was wearing light-pink lipstick. He had never seen her in makeup before, and he had a sudden urge to find out if her lipstick was the kind that came off when you kissed.

Amber was staring at him with a look of annoyance. "I'm sorry. Did you say something?"

"Apparently, nothing of importance," Amber said, rolling her eyes.

He hadn't realized how much he missed Lucy until he saw her, and now everything in his body was screaming to be near her. Dylan stood up. "Sorry, I need to go do...something." He walked toward the door, trying to reach Lucy before she could get away. Their eyes met, and Lucy flinched and disappeared behind Blake. He wasn't going to let her get away from him that easily. Dylan dodged a few guests, trying to reach her before she could escape.

He found Sam instead. "Hey, can you help me with the turkey?"

"I was actually—" He didn't have time for this. The only thing he wanted right now was to talk to Lucy.

"It won't take long; I just need to set it out and make sure the plates are somewhere close to it...Oh, and maybe you could help me with the drinks, too." Dylan groaned. His sister was, in his opinion, the worst cockblock he had ever encountered. At this rate, he'd never have time to talk to Lucy.

Chapter Fourteen

Lucy

Lucy watched Dylan from the other side of the roof while he talked to Amber. Of course, they looked cozy, smiling while sitting at *their* table, and a part of her felt irrationally angry about that. Her sister didn't deserve his attention. She hadn't earned the warmth of his smile. Lucy was the one who spent weeks getting to know him, trying to understand what turned up the corner of Dylan Lancaster's lips.

And she knew a lot about his lips. She had been thinking about them more than ever since their disastrous yet earth-shattering first kiss.

Lucy had panicked when he kissed her. She had been unsure of how to react. She had waited years to experience her first kiss. And it was thrilling, amazing, and absolutely terrifying. It turned out that kissing was not at all like she had read in her romance novels. Sure, there were lips touching, and yes, her body felt warm, but no one mentioned that her brain would turn off or that the moment his hands moved against her cheek she would literally forget her name.

Lucy didn't realize how different her body would feel when his tongue slid against her own. It was strange and thrilling, yet alarming. Her thighs felt tingly, and suddenly, she needed to push him away. She had been too terrified of how her body was behaving to let him continue to touch her.

She felt mortified and completely embarrassed by her own reaction. Dylan would never want to touch her again after the way she behaved. She had gone home and buried herself under her covers. When she called out sick the next day, Jared showed up at her apartment demanding to know what was going on. Since being hired at the bookstore, Lucy had never missed a single day of work.

So, she told Jared everything, right down to the embarrassing details of how she told Dylan she would ride him. Jared found the whole sordid affair hilarious, as only he would. He seemed to think the situation was salvageable and that she needed to slow down and let things progress on their own. But Lucy was sure that her inexperience would never allow things to work between her and Dylan. She knew she needed to fix it, and there was only one way to do that.

She needed experience, and she needed it now. But of course, she couldn't just go out and sleep with random men. So that left one other option. That conversation didn't go well with Jared, either.

"You could help me!" Lucy had asked at the bookstore the day before.

Jared stared at her with apprehension. "Help you with what?"

"Getting experience. You know, getting rid of my V-card." She shrugged as if she had just asked him to help her get her driver's license.

Jared shook his head and snorted. "I'm not having sex with you, Luce. Even if women did it for me, you shouldn't have sex just to get it over with."

"But if I don't have sex with someone, how am I going to know what to do with someone who's already very experienced with that stuff?" She frowned and kicked over a pile of books lying in a stack next to her bookshelf.

Jared's eyes widened. "Lucy Patel, you did not just defile books. You wouldn't even watch Wicked because Jonathan Bailey stood on those books during that one song."

Lucy growled and slumped down into a chair in the middle of the store. "How am I supposed to keep Dylan interested when I know nothing?"

"He already kissed you. It sounds like he's pretty interested, Lucy."

She frowned. "But what if he wants more and I panic again?"

"You know how communication is always shit in romance novels." Jared glared at her, and she nodded. "You aren't in one, so talk to him."

Amber's hand slid to Dylan's thigh, and Lucy saw red. This was high school all over again. She was going to lose Dylan to Amber because she was a twenty-five-year-old virgin who didn't know how to seduce a man.

She stomped toward the food table, tossing turkey and mashed potatoes onto her plate. As she got to the end of the table, she looked down at the drinks. Floating on top of the ice was a pink can. Sparkling Rosé Wine. The can glittered under the lights. She glanced back at Dylan just as Amber's laughter flittered across the ro of.

The laughter mocked her. She stared at the can. What she really needed was to not feel like herself for a while. All her life she had been perfect little Lucy Patel, but where had that gotten her? Amber was the one sitting with Dylan.

She picked up the can and walked back to the corner. She was done being perfect; for once, she wanted to be something else. A rebellious thrill buzzed through her veins as she popped the top of the can. She sputtered as the first sip hit her tongue, a sweet mixture of bubbly wine and rebellion causing her to break out in a giggle. Her lips curled and her eyes squinted at the taste, but the mix of anticipation and defiance had her lifting the can to her mouth once mor e.

Three hours later, Lucy noticed that noise sounded different. Words felt fuzzy. No, that didn't make sense. But she swore she could feel the sounds all around her. Words seemed fluffy, almost as if you could touch them.

Her feet looked farther away too. She was sitting on the floor with her legs stretched out in front of her, trying to touch her toes, and she had been unable to for the last twenty minutes, so they must be farther away, she reasoned.

What she could touch was her hair. She loved her hair. It was the softest hair she had ever felt. And it was so dark. Was her hair always this dark?

"Lucy, did you drink all of those?" She leaned back on her hands and peered up, her blurry eyes finding Blake's upside-down face looking down at her.

"Mr. Blake!" she shouted. "You are very tall."

"Lucy Patel, are you drunk?" He put his hands on his hips and smiled momentarily before bending down next to her. She could smell his aftershave. How had she never noticed that Blake smelled like a man? She'd always thought of Blake as a goofy big brother type. But he was very manly with his shaving smell.

"I only had these pretty pink drinks." She fell over onto her side and rolled to get one of the empty pink cans sitting beside her. When she finally reached it, she sat up and produced it in front of her, holding it out proudly. "It sparkles."

"Lucy, that's alcohol." Blake appeared to be lecturing her, and Lucy didn't appreciate that. She was an adult, and she could drink whatever she wanted.

She pressed her lips together and poked her finger against his chest. "I don't see anyone telling you to put away your beer, Mr. Blake."

"Alright, I think you've had enough." Blake's arms wrapped under hers, and he lifted her with ease until she was standing on her feet. She swayed slightly and leaned into his chest. When did her feet get so wobbly?

She looked up just as he was waving at someone. That's when she noticed Sam approaching them. "What's up?"

"I think I should get Lucy downstairs. She was drinking the Rosé."

Lucy pushed away from Blake and stepped backward, tripping over a chair. "I'm not going anywhere!" she shouted.

"Luce." Blake stepped toward her, but Lucy continued to walk in the other direction.

"What's going on?" Dylan was suddenly at her side. She knew immediately from the distinct smell of vanilla soap that it was him. His hand rested heavily on her back, and she melted against him. "Are you alright, Lucy?"

"Cartoon Man!" Lucy pressed her hand against his chest and sighed. "Blake is trying to remove me from the party."

Dylan's hand wrapped more firmly around her waist. "Did you have a little to drink tonight, Lucy?" He turned to stare at Blake and Sam, something passing between them that Lucy didn't understand.

"I drank the sparkly cans." She pointed to the cans littering the ground. "Now they want me to go downstairs. I'm not a bad girl, am I, Dylan?" He bit his lip, staring at her silently, his eyes locked on hers. The way he was looking at her made her stomach do those summer saults that Dylan was always causing, but right now they were also making her feel woozy.

"I can take her downstairs." Dylan's voice echoed in her ears as he spoke softly to Blake and Sam, and Lucy's eyes closed as she rested her head against his chest. She could hear sounds around her. People must have been talking, but everything was blending together.

"Hey, Lucy, let's get out of here." Dylan's voice vibrated in her ear. She'd go anywhere he asked her to.

She nodded in a daze and let him lead her away from the roof.

"Don't let go, alright?" His voice was dark and heavy as his arm wrapped around her. She leaned against Dylan, her arms tight around his waist as he fidgeted with the lock on her door. She didn't know where he had gotten her keys, but she was glad he hadn't asked her to open the door. Standing on her own was a difficult task right now.

She felt her feet move on their own as they tumbled into the apartment, and she heard the door close behind them.

"Let's get your jacket off, okay." She spun in a circle, suddenly regretting that decision.

She tried to stop and then stumbled. "Dizzy."

His arms wrapped around her. "Don't do that, Lucy."

Lucy looked up into a pair of eyes that stopped her heart from beating. "You make my heart do funny things, Dylan." She giggled.

He exhaled and smiled. "Yeah, that might be the alcohol." He slid the jacket off her arms, and it dropped to the ground with a thud. "You should lie down now before you get dizzier." He looked around their apartment. "Which room is yours?"

"You want to see my bedroom?" She bit her lip and held her breath.

He laughed, grabbing her hand. "Come on, Lucy."

She followed him down the hall until he pushed open the door to Amber's room. "Nope, no way. That's not your room."

She frowned. "Why not?"

"Too dark, not enough sunshine and happiness." He went to the second door and opened it. "See. Told you."

She thought letting Dylan see her room for the first time would embarrass her, but the way he smiled when he walked in only made her feelings more complicated. "It's ridiculous, right?"

"It's you." She didn't know if that was good or bad. Her room was a rainbow of butterflies and poems. She had handwritten pages on her wall with quotes she loved from her favorite books. There was a photo of Colin Bridgerton hanging by her mirror, a character from her favorite Regency television show. She had an entire bookshelf devoted to books about the care of monarch butterflies, which she had been collecting and studying since she was twelve.

He was right; everything in this room screamed Lucy Patel. "It always helped me when I got dizzy to hang a foot over the edge of the bed so I wouldn't throw up."

She stared at him, and he shoved his hands into his pockets. She suddenly wished he were touching her again. "I should, uh, get back upstairs if you don't need anything else."

"Can you—"

His response was immediate. "Anything. I can do anything you need."

Her brow raised playfully. "Can you stay for a bit?" She stumbled toward him, kicking off her shoes. He stared back at her wide-eyed, as if unable to move.

"Um, I'm not sure that's...Lucy, you've had a lot to drink tonight and..." Lucy thought it was adorable when he looked nervous. The alcohol was making her feel braver than normal. Or maybe she just wasn't thinking at all. Either way, she wanted to kiss Dylan Lancaster.

She lifted onto her toes and pressed her lips against his. It was soft and timid, and this time she was the one setting the pace. He stood rigid in front of her, his hands still in his pockets. That would not do. Lucy wrapped her arms around his neck, pressing her body against his as her tongue slid across the crease of his lips. The tips of her fingers slid into the hair at the back of his neck.

She was wrong earlier. His hair was softer than hers, and she wanted to run her fingers through every inch of his silken locks all night long.

His tongue met hers, and she moaned. It sounded weird to her, the way she sounded so needy, so desperate. His hand slid against her back, pulling her closer to him. Lucy felt the fire ignite. *This* was a kiss.

Suddenly, his mouth wasn't just on her lips; she felt him everywhere. On her jaw, her neck. Each place he touched scorched her. She was sure there would be a Dylan tattoo etched onto her skin by morning, memorializing the trail of his tongue. His breath was hot in her ear, accelerating her heartbeat. "You drive me crazy, Lucy."

He was saying these words about her? Lucy Patel drove Dylan Lancaster crazy. Even if this was an alcohol-induced dream, she would remember those words forever.

She stepped back and stared up at him, reaching down to tease the hem of her dress with her fingers before tearing it over her head, closing her eyes. When she opened them, Dylan was staring at her chest. His own was heaving in quick breaths as he panted her name.

Her head was dizzy, but the way he was looking at her made her feel hot all over. Dylan's reaction to her was like a drug, and she needed more.

She pressed against him, running her hands under his shirt and feeling the hard ridges of his chest. She'd never felt a man's bare chest before. His eyes were darker than she'd ever seen. He looked feral, staring back at her. She supposed she should be terrified, but currently she didn't care. She stumbled backward, pulling him with her until she fell onto the bed and he toppled over, bracing himself with his arms. "Luce..." His voice sounded distant, dark,

almost as if he was begging her for something. She enjoyed hearing hi
m beg.

She kissed him again, and he pressed his weight onto her. The
intrusion at her hip felt long and heavy. He rubbed against her,
and when she opened her eyes; he had his own pinched shut. She
moved her legs, opening them further to let him settle between
them, and then she felt it. Oh God, she felt it. His body pressed
into hers, and she felt the length of him grind against her panties,
and for a moment, her entire body pulsed as if lightning had struck
her. "Oh!" she squealed. Dylan's head lifted, and he stared down at h
er.

Suddenly, he rolled over, staring up at the ceiling. "What's
wrong?"

"Everything," he sighed.

"Did I do something wrong?" she whispered.

He frowned and sat up on the bed. "No, I did."

Chapter Fifteen

Dylan

*D*anger, *Will Robinson, danger.*

Dylan needed to get out of a very drunk Lucy's bedroom, and fast. Yet here he was, still staring at Lucy Patel like she was the only thing holding him together.

"I should, uh, get back upstairs if you don't need anything else."

"Can you—"

"Anything. I can do anything you need." *Idiot.*

Lucy stumbled toward him, and he knew this was his immediate cue to turn around and exit the room. "Can you stay for a bit?"

The answer, of course, was no. That was the only word that needed to leave his mouth. "Um, I'm not sure that's...Lucy, you've had a lot to drink tonight and..." That sounded like a lot more words than no.

But then she kissed him, and all reason left his head. He tried to maintain control. Dylan kept his hands in his pockets. He couldn't get in trouble if he didn't touch her. Kissing was one thing; touching was dangerous. And then her hands slid into his hair, and damn, her fingers felt good against his scalp.

It couldn't hurt to let his tongue explore hers. It was still just kissing. And that's where it all went so terribly wrong. Because then she moaned, and if that didn't completely undo him, the need to touch her did. He could just hold her; that couldn't hurt anything—to hold her. So he did, and maybe that was a mistake, but kissing her didn't feel like one.

He got lost in the way her lips tasted, not at all like lemons, but a hint of strawberries from her shiny lip gloss lingered with each swipe of his tongue. When he kissed her neck, he inhaled a scent of coconut and lemons as he nipped at her earlobe. "You drive me crazy, Lucy."

She pulled away, and in a haze, his body followed her. But then she tore her dress over her head, and she was standing there in a white cotton bra and panties, and he swore his vision blurred. "Lucy." Her name fell from his lips like a prayer, but he wasn't sure if he was praying for his survival or a quick death. The warmth of her skin woke him from his stupor as her fingers danced under his shirt. He was tumbling forward onto her bed, and he reached out to stop himself before he crushed her with his full weight. "Luce."

He was waking up now, as his mind raced with her body underneath his. His thoughts didn't have time to catch up to him when her lips assaulted his, pulling him down to meet her. She felt so good underneath him. He felt himself growing hard against her hip, and he couldn't stop himself from thrusting against her. She opened her legs, and he settled between them. And dammit if he didn't fit so perfectly between her legs. He kissed her, pushing her hair back from her face as he ground himself against her, needing the friction. Wanting more than anything to peel her panties down her legs and sink inside her. He kissed her neck and squeezed his eyes shut.

"Oh." The squeal she made sounded so sudden, surprised, as he felt her stiffen underneath him. He lifted his head and looked down at her. Her face was flushed, and horror rushed over him. She was drunk. She had never had sex before. And Dylan was an asshole.

He rolled over, staring up at the ceiling as he lay on the bed in the happiest room he had ever been in his life. "What's the matter?" Lucy's beautiful face looked back at him with such innocence it broke his heart.

"Everything," he sighed.

"Did I do something wrong?" she whispered.

He frowned and sat up on the bed. "No, I did."

Lucy sat up and covered her chest. "I don't understand?"

"You're drunk. We shouldn't be doing this." He shook his head and ran a hand through his hair. "*I* shouldn't be doing this."

"Gee, Dad, thanks for the lecture." Lucy stood up and walked over to pick up her dress, tripping over her feet twice before giving up. "I'm sure all the other times you've had drunk sex were just fine."

"That's not fair, Luce." Dylan stood up from the bed and picked up her dress, handing it to her. "This is different."

Lucy laughed and held the dress over her chest. "Yeah, because I'm not some hot blonde chick with huge tits, right?"

"That's not it. You don't understand—"

"Get out!" she screamed as tears began pooling at the corners of her eyes.

He stepped toward her, and she hurried away from him. "Lucy, would you—"

"I said, get out. Just leave, please."

Dylan reached for the door and opened it, pausing before he left. "I'm really sorry, Lucy."

"There you are." Dylan had been sitting in the darkened living room since leaving Lucy. He looked up to see Sam with an armful of dirty dishes. "You didn't come back up after you took Lucy downstairs. Did you get her to her apartment alright?"

"Uh, yeah, she's fine, all tucked in." He returned his attention to the window and the streets below.

He heard her rustle around in the kitchen and then felt the couch dip as she sat down next to him. "Everything okay?"

"Can we not talk about it and just let me pout a bit?" He leaned his head against his sister's shoulder and enjoyed the way she ran her hands through his hair like she used to when they were kids.

They sat in silence for a few minutes. Dylan closed his eyes and tried to block out all the voices that were trying to invade his thoughts. But it wasn't working. Everything was so loud. "Do you think all the awful shit a person does in their past follows them forever?"

"Dylan, no. What are you talking about?"

He sighed. "Do you think I'm an asshole?"

"Of course not. Who said you were? I'll beat the shit out of them." Sam's grip around his shoulders tightened.

Dylan laughed, because of course his sister would resort to violence. "All that stuff I did last year, fucking with Donna when she was with Blake. Being a total dick to Jax. I don't know if I know how to be something better, Sam." She moved, and he clung to her. "I want to be something different. I want to be more; I want to be a good person, but..."

"Dylan, you aren't an asshole. You just get caught up in your head."

"The shit in my head sucks."

"Did something happen tonight?" She leaned back and looked at him.

He wanted so badly to talk to her, but something stopped him. "No." He looked out the window again. "I think it's just meeting new people, good people. It just causes me to ask a lot of questions about myself. Things I don't like the answers to."

The room got quiet again. "Lucy's...a really sweet person," Sam whispered. "You spend a lot of time with her, don't you?"

Dylan kept his focus on the window. He couldn't look at his sister. "We talk on the roof sometimes."

"Ah." She cleared her throat. "I see." It was that Sam tone. The one that said, "I'm on to you."

He closed his eyes and sighed. "It's nothing, Sam. I can hear you thinking."

"I didn't mean anything by it. I just said, I see." She shifted on the couch. "But..." Dylan groaned. "I think it's nice that you have someone to talk to, like Lucy."

He turned and looked at her. "You're not going to tell me to stay away from her like Blake did, are you?"

She laughed. "Blake is overprotective and ridiculous. Lucy is a twenty-five-year-old woman. She can take care of herself." Dylan rolled his eyes. "Everyone needs friends, and Lucy doesn't have that many of them."

"I'm kind of an asshole, remember?" he grumbled.

"You're my brother, and she's damn lucky to have someone like you around."

Dylan sat up a little taller and smiled. "Thanks, Sam."

She stood up and laughed. "How did she ever get you to lean out over the side of a skyscraper, anyway?"

Dylan's eyes grew wide. "I, uh, um...what?"

"Never mind, you can tell me some other day."

Dylan woke up the next day with a new attitude. Maybe there was a way he could get closer to Lucy, and prove to himself he wasn't an asshole. He'd never dated a girl before. Donna was purely sexual. In fact, every encounter he ever had with her led to sex. They never went out just to have dinner or go to the movies. They never talked about their favorite things or their hopes and dreams.

In high school, he didn't have a girlfriend. He took Patty Windsome to prom just so he could lose his virginity. After that, there were makeouts behind the bleachers, girls he asked to dances so he could have sex in his dad's truck after. But nothing that said, *"Hey I have feelings for you. Let's go steady."* Not that he would ever say something that stupid. But he sort of wanted to with Lucy.

If he was going to get that, though, he needed her to talk to him. And after last night, that was going to be a challenge.

Finding her was easy because she was hunkered down at the table on the roof with a pair of sunglasses and a ball cap on her head. Apparently, this challenge of keeping things chaste would not be easy because hungover Lucy looked sexy as hell.

Approaching the table, she didn't even bother to look in his direction. "Good morning, Sunshine."

"Go away." Her icy attitude was not unexpected, but still stung.

He sat down anyway. "Alright, so you've chosen anger today."

She turned to face him, and he wanted to remove those ridiculous shades so he could see her pretty eyes. "I'm sorry if my attitude is not to your liking, Dylan. We can't all be what you want, apparently."

He hadn't expected that she would take his trying to be a good guy last night as an outright rejection. Looking at it through her eyes, he supposed he should have. Maybe he should have been clearer. "Lucy, please look at me."

"I would hate to ruin your day by making you stare at me," she said, crossing her hands over her chest. Her bottom lip was jutting out, and all he could think about was pressing his mouth against it.

He chuckled. "Trust me, Lucy, the only thing ruining my day is the fact that I haven't seen your eyes today," she groaned and turned her body away from him. "Do you have any idea at all what you do to me?"

"Repulse you, apparently," she mumbled.

Dylan dropped his head into his hands and growled. When he looked up, Lucy was still staring out toward the city. "Lucy, last night...was about the fact that you were drunk."

"I was fine."

He snorted. "Then why do you have such a lovely pair of dark sunglasses on today?" He leaned back and raised his voice. "Should we go to a club and listen to some loud music?"

"Do you mind not screaming?" She held her hands over her ears and groaned.

"Headache, Luce?" he said in a much louder tone than necessary.

She slouched in her chair and pouted. "Fine, I might have had a bit too much to drink."

"Exactly, and I was not going to take advantage of you last night. Especially not with you being a..." He paused and looked away. "I'm just...despite who people think I am. I'm not that guy."

"But it was okay for you to be drunk and sleep with Donna?"

He closed his eyes and sighed. "That was different. I didn't care about Donna." His jaw clenched as he opened his eyes. "You deserve to remember your first time, Lucy. It should be special. It should be with someone you have feelings for."

"Did you?" she asked.

"Did I what?" He pinched his eyes shut and sat up.

"Have feelings for the girl you had your first time with? Was yours special?" She pulled her glasses off her face and sat them in her lap.

He met her eyes, blinking. "No, Lucy, I didn't. Honestly, I just wanted to get it over with. I didn't even like the girl. It sucked pretty much."

"Did it get better after that? You know, after you were with a girl you liked?"

Dylan gripped his hair, groaning slightly. "Honestly, Lucy, I can't answer that. I've never liked a single girl I've had sex with." He leaned across the table. "But I'm not going to lie to you. Sex is great; it feels amazing. But an orgasm doesn't even require a partner, so technically I can do it by myself and get the same satisfaction out of it."

She paled slightly, and Dylan wondered if she had ever done that by herself. He needed to stop thinking about it immediately if he was going to stick to his plan of not seducing her. "So if it sex means nothing to you, why did you care last night?"

"Because it matters to you. Hell, I don't know. Maybe I want it to matter to me."

She stared out at the city for a while, and Dylan wondered if she was ever going to speak to him again. She blew out a very large breath. "I don't know how you drink alcohol. I woke up and my mouth tasted like I had eaten rotten eggs."

Dylan chuckled. "At least you didn't throw up."

"Oh no, I did." She frowned. "I'll never wear my rain boots again."

She put the glasses back on her face, and he couldn't stop the smile from forming on his lips. "Friends again?" he asked.

She shook her head. "Friends."

"You have a lot of anger in there, Butterfly Girl." He pulled out his phone and shuffled through it as he searched for what he was looking for.

"I do not." Her voice was sharp, and that made him laugh even harder. He found what he was looking for and stood up.

"Come on, I think I found a way for you to let out your anger issues."

"What are you talking about? I don't have anger issues." Lucy stared at him. "I'm literally the happiest person you know."

"Everyone has something inside them that's buried. Maybe we need to let yours out." He grabbed her hand and tugged her out of her seat. "Come on, Luce. Trust me."

Chapter Sixteen

Lucy

"A hockey game?" Lucy frowned as she looked up at Madison Square Garden in front of her. "I hate sports." Lucy wasn't sure what Dylan was thinking. She didn't have anger issues, so the entire idea was stupid.

The only reason she had gotten angry was that she had tried to have sex with Dylan and he had rejected her, making the entire ordeal that much more embarrassing.

Okay, maybe that wasn't exactly true. She thought back to how angry she had felt at the party when she saw Amber flirting with Dylan. Perhaps she was a little uptight.

"I think you might enjoy yourself." Dylan slipped his hand in hers and showed their tickets to the attendant. She wasn't sure about wasting a day watching a hockey game, but sitting next to Dylan with his arm around her shoulder didn't feel like a waste.

Dylan leaned over, and his lips brushed against her ear. "That's the goalie. His job is to keep the puck out of the net behind him."

"And I'm guessing everyone else's job is to knock it in there?"

"Pretty much." Dylan shrugged. "Whichever team scores the most points, wins."

She sat back in her seat and frowned. "That doesn't seem that hard."

He chuckled. "The guys on the other team don't exactly make it easy." Lucy stared out at the ice as the men skated onto the rink. They were gigantic men wearing pads and helmets.

"Why do they have on so much stuff? Isn't this like ice skating?"

Dylan leaned over and kissed her cheek. "Oh, Lucy, you have so much to learn. This is nothing like ice skating."

Lucy frowned, leaning back in her seat as she took a bite of her nachos and watched the men skating around the rink in circles. The next few hours were going to be the most boring time of her life.

This was the most exciting thing she had ever seen in her life.

"Get him, Matt!" Lucy stood up, waving her arms as the fight broke out on the rink. The two men ripped their helmets off and started pulling at their jerseys. She sat back down and stared at Dylan, who was smiling at her. "Did you see the way he shoved him into the glass like that?"

Dylan nodded with a light chuckle. "I did."

She shook her head. "He didn't even see it coming." She turned back just in time to watch another player get clipped from behind. It was a dirty move. The other player ripped off his gloves and rushed toward his teammate. The ref seemed to turn a blind eye to it. Lucy jumped out of her seat. "Hey Ref, watch the game." She sat back down and pushed her sweaty hair out of her face, reaching into Dylan's bucket for another piece of popcorn.

"You were right. This is fun." She smiled, plopping the popcorn into her mouth.

Dylan continued staring at her. "I don't think I've ever seen anything this amazing."

"But the Rangers are losing." She frowned, looking up at the Jumbotron.

His hand touched her cheek softly as it slid down to her ear. "I wasn't talking about the game." She felt her cheeks warm and looked away.

Someone nudged them from behind, and Dylan grumbled, looking at the man seated to his left. "You're on the screen, Love-birds." She looked up and saw her face on the giant screen in the middle of the rink.

A few people started chanting. "Kiss, kiss, kiss."

Dylan smirked, flipping his baseball cap backward. "Well, Lucy Patel, are you going to kiss me or not?"

She bit her lip, staring at the large screen over the ice rink with their faces on it. Everyone around them was chanting and cheering them on. Dylan's smile, and that it was directed at her, astonished Lucy. This gorgeous man wanted her to kiss him.

Lucy leaned over, pressing her lips to his. His hand came to rest on the back of her neck as his mouth slid across her lips, firm yet tender. She heard clapping in the distance, but the only thing she could focus on was the fact that Dylan was kissing her like she was special. He had a grip on her jacket like she might disappear if he let go.

Slowly, he pulled away, and she bit her lip, peering through her lashes. He was still grinning like he knew something she didn't. "What?"

"Nothing." He shrugged. "I just think you're adorable, that's all."

She slapped his chest and sat back in her seat. "Stop it."

For the rest of the game, she was distracted by the man sitting beside her. She wasn't sure what to think. She only knew that her heart had stopped beating properly, and that he hadn't watched a single second of the hockey game.

"So tell me, what is one thing you regret about moving to New York?"

Lucy was sitting on a stool at her favorite pizza joint across from Dylan. "Oh, I don't regret anything." She frowned.

Dylan shook his head and threw a piece of pepperoni across the table at her. "Bullshit, Luce; everyone regrets something."

She groaned and took a bite of her pizza, chewing while she gathered her thoughts. She didn't regret things, mostly. "Fine. I miss my friends—well, the few I had. Sometimes I wish I didn't have to make a choice between my sister and dropping out of college to come here."

"What were you studying in college?"

She played with a piece of pepperoni on her plate. "Nothing important. Literature. I was only going to City College. It wasn't a priority."

"Who said that?" Dylan asked, his eyes focused on hers as if she was the most important person in the room.

"Amber." She shrugged. "She didn't want to come here alone. I get it. I was supposed to go back to school when I got here, but then I started working at the bookstore and helping Amber stay organized, and I just didn't find the time."

"You do a lot for Amber."

"Her career is important. Vogue is huge and everything."

Dylan snorted. "Vogue is huge and everything." He sounded ridiculous trying to mock her. "What does any of that have to do with Lucy?"

"She's my sister," Lucy said, squaring her shoulders and crossing her arms firmly against her chest.

"Does it ever make you mad you had to give up your life and friends back home for your sister's career?"

"Of course not. Why would you ask me something like that?" Her voice rose, and she sat up in her chair, leaning toward him. "I love my sister."

"You can love your sister, but still be mad that you lost something because of her."

"I'm not mad, Dylan. It's not her fault that I'm out here all by myself." She slammed her hand on the table and flinched when she realized what she had done.

Dylan stared back at her. "You gave up everything for her, and it doesn't seem like she appreciates it."

"Stop it!" she shouted. "She cares in her own way, even when she doesn't show it. It's not her fault that I'm lonely." She hadn't meant to say that out loud. Dylan had a way of making her feel comfortable enough to admit her deepest thoughts.

She felt a tear slide down her cheek, got up and excused herself from the table, rushing out the front door onto the busy sidewalk.

She leaned against the brick wall and hunched over as tears fell from her eyes. Gasping for breath, she tried to stop herself from feeling the emotions that were overtaking her. She had never told anyone that she was lonely before. She had spent most of her life trying to ensure that everyone around her was happy. Her parents, her sister, people she worked with, her friends, everyone she came in contact with received the Lucy Sunshine effect.

Rule #9: Always leave the room with a smile

Dylan made her admit her deepest secret. Something she only said in the darkness of her own room at night when she was by herself. She was lonely, and she was afraid she was always going to be that way. She had spent so much time taking care of her sister that she had forgotten to take care of herself.

"I'm sorry you're lonely, Lucy. No one should feel that way." She looked up to see Dylan standing a few feet away from her on the sidewalk.

She stood up and leaned against the brick wall. "There's nothing wrong with being alone. There are people who go through their entire lives alone. I've read about it."

Dylan walked over and leaned next to her, shoving his hands into his pockets and staring out at the road in front of them. "Yeah, I'm sure there are." He leaned his head to the side and stared at her. "Maybe you and I can be lonely together?"

"Are you lonely too?"

He closed his eyes. "Sometimes I can be with my entire family and still feel like I am the loneliest person in the room. Does that make any sense?" When his eyes opened, theirs met, and Lucy smiled at him.

"I never feel like I'm alone when I'm with you."

His fingers laced with hers, and she folded their hands together. "I really like you, Lucy Patel."

She giggled and leaned toward him, resting her chin on his shoulder. "I think I like you too, Dylan Lancaster."

Walking back into the apartment building with Dylan's hand in hers was the happiest Lucy had been in years. She'd never had a man walk her to her door, or stare at her like she was the most beautiful girl he had ever seen.

Currently, Dylan was doing both. "Can I see you tomorrow?"

She giggled as he slowed down in front of her door. "Dylan, you see me all the time. When have I ever said no?"

"I don't know." He grinned, lifting his arm to brace against the wall as he leaned toward her. "You seemed pretty angry with me this morning."

She looked at him and licked her lips. "I'm not angry with you now." Flirting with Dylan was becoming one of her favorite things to do.

"No?" He smirked and bent over, pressing his lips near her ear. "Does that mean I can kiss you goodnight?"

She shivered, biting her lip between her teeth. "Mm hm." She couldn't even say words. What was wrong with her?

His mouth touched her jaw, and her eyes slipped shut. She tilted her head to allow him better access. His hand was at her waist, his fingers gripping her hip, and she slid her hand into his hair. He groaned. "God, I love it when you do that." Score one for Lucy, she thought. Touch the hair. Check. She was going to need to add a new X-rated section to her guide.

His mouth scorched a trail along her jaw until she couldn't stand it anymore. She grabbed his face with her hands and pulled his mouth to hers, igniting the flames inside her as their lips touched. It was glorious.

His tongue pierced inside her mouth, wrestling with her own. His fingers danced against the piece of flesh exposed at the small of her back, and she arched into him. She wanted him to touch her. She needed so much more.

"Dylan, what the hell!" The voice at the other end of the hallway startled them, and Lucy clutched Dylan's shirt, panting into his chest.

Blake Forrester was storming toward them from his apartment.

"Blake, hey, it's uh..." he looked down at her and smiled reassuringly. "I was just bringing Lucy home from a Rangers game."

Blake was standing in front of them now, and he wasn't happy. "Is that so?" He looked at Lucy and nodded. "Are you alright, Lucy?"

"She's fine, Blake, Jesus, what the hell are you asking her that for?" Dylan straightened up, still nowhere near the height of his much taller best friend.

"Blake, I'm fine. Dylan was just dropping me off." Lucy smiled and put her hand on Dylan's chest. Blake glared at it as if he expected her hand to catch fire.

"Why don't you tell her goodnight then, Dyl," Blake said in a flat tone. "You and I need to talk."

Dylan exhaled angrily and turned toward her. "I'll talk to you in the morning, Luce." He smiled at her and brushed his hand against her cheek. "Everything's fine, okay."

Lucy nodded and stared at the two friends. "Yeah, alright, goodnight." She opened the door and stepped inside, but she was pretty sure that nothing was all right.

Chapter Seventeen

Dylan

The door slammed shut, and Dylan didn't even wait for Blake to finish setting his stuff on the counter before he set his sights on him. "What the fuck was that? Asking her if she was alright—like I raped her in the damn hallway!"

"You had her trapped against the door. How was I supposed to know what was going on?" Blake slammed the cabinet door closed with a loud bang.

"We were just kissing, Blake. Sorry, I know that might have been confusing for you walking in on us like that. Not everyone can be that innocent. I still had my pants on!" he shouted at him, knowing very well that he was throwing something in his face he shouldn't have.

"Are you ever going to get over that?"

"Hard to get over a blowjob in the forest."

"Oh, fuck off."

"What the hell is going on in here?" Blake and Dylan stood frozen in the middle of the living room as Sam walked out in her pajamas.

Blake glared at Dylan and then turned to Sam. "I found him with his tongue down Lucy's throat in the hallway."

Dylan threw his hands in the air. "We were kissing. That's what people do at the end of a date!"

"A date!" Blake hollered. "You can't date Lucy."

"Oh really? And just who do you think you are? Her father?" Blake and Dylan took a step toward each other.

"Okay, that's enough, you two." Sam reached for Blake and tugged his arm. "This is ridiculous. Dylan is right. You aren't Lucy's father, Blake."

"Are you kidding me? You're taking his side after the way he behaved last year," Blake growled. "Lucy's never even had a boyfriend before, and Dylan's—"

"Say it, asshole!" Dylan yelled.

"Stop it." Sam glared at Blake. "It is none of your business what goes on between Dylan and Lucy, and it's not fair of you to make the assumptions you're making."

"He was fucking around with Donna right before he got here. He shouldn't be messing with a girl like Lucy after what he was doing with a girl like Donna." Blake pointed in his direction, and Dylan snorted.

"That's rich, considering she was your girlfriend for years," Dylan growled.

"Can you two stop yelling at each other for a minute?" Sam sighed.

"Nah, forget it." Dylan walked down the hallway, ignoring his sister's pleas, as he let the door slam shut behind him.

Dylan rolled over and groaned. The pain in his hip radiated all the way down his leg. He was too old to be sleeping on the corner of a greenhouse floor wrapped in a tarp. He sat up and wiped his eyes, holding his hands to his mouth and blowing warm air into his palms.

After his fight with Blake last night, he was so angry he didn't want to go back to the apartment, so he spent the night trying to get comfortable on the roof. New York City in December wasn't exactly warm. He looked at his phone to make sure that Blake had already left for school and headed downstairs.

Before he could get into the apartment, the door to Lucy's opened. "Dylan!"

"Oh, hey Amber."

She rushed toward him in very high heels and a short black miniskirt. "I'm so glad I ran into you, because I need you desperately."

His hand froze on the doorknob. "Oh, uh, um—"

"I need a date. Now." She put her hand on his arm and bit her lip.

Dylan's head raced to come up with an excuse. "I actually can't because I was planning to talk to Lucy about—"

"Lucy's at work," she interrupted. "You'd be doing me a really huge favor. It's this whole affair, and the model who was going with me got sick, and I can't show up alone. That would be humiliating."

He snorted. "I'm not a model, Amber."

"Yeah, but the people I work with do wonders. Clothes, hair, the whole nine yards. You'll be like a whole new Dylan Lancaster for the day." Amber pushed her bottom lip into a pout and crinkled her eyes. "Please, I'm desperate."

Dylan didn't need this right now. He was tired, cold, and in desperate need of a shower. But this was Lucy's sister, and he didn't want to be rude either. Besides, she looked frantic. "How long will it be?" he asked, groaning.

She jumped up and down on her heels. Dylan was surprised at her ability to avoid breaking her ankle. "Just a few hours. I promise I'll have you back in time for dinner."

"Fine, but I'm not drinking. And no funny business, Amber. I'm doing you a favor, as a friend, that's all." Dylan opened the door to the apartment, but before he could go inside, she wrapped her arms around him.

She squealed in his ear, and Dylan was already regretting his decision to be a nice person today. "Thank you so much. I really appreciate it."

"Yeah, just give me ten minutes to shower," he grunted.

"Thank God I wasn't going to say anything, but you smell like you slept outside."

An hour later, Dylan was sweating from sitting in a trailer with six people hovering around him, and he felt like a damn dress-up doll. "No one said I'd be wearing makeup," he grumbled into Amber's ear as she sat next to him in a chair, getting her hair done.

"It's just eyeliner, Dylan. It makes your eyes pop."

He adjusted his face from side to side, examining it in the mirror. "I didn't need my eyes to pop. They looked just fine before."

"It looks better for the camera." Amber bent over and ran her hands through her hair, tossing it back and shaking her head. "Trust me, you're gonna look hot."

Dylan pinched his eyes shut and groaned. "Maybe I should have asked more questions before I agreed to this." He looked down at his outfit. He felt like an idiot. This was definitely not something he would ever wear. "I thought there was a rule about wearing all white after Labor Day or some shit."

"It's an all-white party, Dylan."

"These pants feel weird. I think you can see my underwear through them." He pinched the flimsy material with his fingers against his skin. Yup, everyone was going to see his ass through this stuff.

Amber shook her head. "That's what the jacket is for."

Dylan glanced at the long white jacket sitting on the chair beside him. Why did he agree to this? At least he wasn't being subjected to dress shoes. The white Converse suited him fine. "How long do we have to be out there?"

"The party lasts three hours. You're really bailing me out of a jam, Dylan. Seriously, I couldn't get anyone to cover for Jimmy on such short notice." Amber ran a hand over his knee, and Dylan smiled at her.

"I just want to get this over with and get out of here before anyone sees me with makeup on."

Amber giggled and patted her face. "Well, maybe don't show Blake or Sam the magazine then."

Dylan choked. "Magazine?"

"Dylan, there are going to be a lot of people out there. I'm a Vogue model. They won't know who you are, but you're going to be with me all day today. You're bound to show up in some photos from the event today. Definitely going to end up online on the Insta."

Dylan stood up and struggled to put on his jacket, anxiety already creeping into his thoughts. "I definitely should have asked a lot more questions."

She slapped him on the ass and walked to the trailer door. "Come on, sexy, let me show you how the other half lives."

The music overhead was becoming noise. Dylan followed Amber through flashes of light and mobs of people milling about the room.

He picked up a piece of food from the tray and stuffed it in his mouth. It burned immediately, and his eyes welled with tears. He couldn't chew without feeling like flames were going to shoot out of his ears. Looking around discreetly, he spat out the remains in his hand and strolled over to a large potted plant in the middle of the room, depositing it into the planter.

"Want some?" He jumped as Amber approached him with one of the offending crackers he had just spat out. "Wasabi bites!" she yelled over the music. He shook his head and wrinkled his nose.

A man with a white feather boa approached them. "Where's Jimmy?"

"Vomiting since breakfast!" Amber yelled into his ear. Dylan stood off to the side with his hands in the pockets of the long coat he was wearing. He wanted to find a corner and disappear into it.

"Who's this? I haven't seen him at any events before? He's not one of ours?" Dylan felt their eyes turn to him, and he smiled nervously.

"I'm Dylan."

"IMG? Ford? Elite?" The man was rattling off names of things he didn't understand.

Dylan shook his head. "Excuse me."

"Who are you with? Where are you from?" he yelled.

"Titusville." He raised his voice over the loud, thumping music.

Amber snorted, and the man seemed even more confused. "Is that international?"

Dylan leaned closer to the man. "It's in Ohio."

"Interesting." His eyes swept over him, and Dylan stared back at Amber, who winked at him with a smile. "He's got a very different feel than our other men. Down to earth, small-town charm." Dylan suddenly had the feeling of being scrutinized like a prized fish for sale at the market. The man looked back at Amber and kissed both of her cheeks. "Good job, Am, I love him. Call me on Monday; we'll talk."

Amber giggled as the man moved on. "He's interested. I think you have a future in modeling."

"Hell no. I just want to get the hell out of this scratchy fabric." Dylan tugged at the material around his balls, ignoring the disapproving looks from the surrounding guests.

Amber nodded at the gigantic clock on the wall. "I promise we're almost done."

Dylan dropped the bag of Amber's clothes onto the counter and laid his face against the cold granite. "I don't know how you do that every day."

"I don't do *that* every day. Sometimes it's photo shoots or runways." She laughed when she turned and saw him. "You look ridiculous."

He lifted his head, a piece of paper sticking to the side of his face. "What?"

"You still have your eyeliner on."

He immediately reached for his face. "Fuck, I can't go home like that." He scrubbed at his eyes and Amber tugged them away.

"Stop that. You're making it worse." She pulled something out of her bag, and Dylan recoiled.

"No more makeup."

"It's to take it off, stupid. Otherwise, you're going to have streaks down your face all night." She held up the small white cloth. Dylan sighed and removed his hands from his face. With a light touch, she ran the cloth under his eyes. "Look up." He stared at the ceiling as the cold cloth skimmed his eyelashes. "Thanks for today, Dylan. You really saved my ass."

"Yeah, I guess it wasn't so bad once you get over all the men staring at your ass." Dylan and Amber both laughed, and it was the first time that day they both shared a comfortable moment together.

"Can't really blame them. You've got a great ass." And the moment was gone.

His eyes drifted back to hers, and he noticed she had gotten a lot closer to him than she had been before. "So, uh, I should probably get going." Her hand slipped from his face to his neck and into his hair. "Amber, I need to tell you something."

"Yeah, we can talk later..."

Two things happened at once. First, Amber moved like a puma, pushing him back into the kitchen counter and assaulting his lips with a force so strong that he lost all the air in his lungs. Second, the front door opened, and the sound of Lucy's voice filtered through the apartment. "Amber, I'm ho—"

Dylan and Amber stood at the counter like a pair of deer caught in headlights. Lucy dropped the bags of groceries in her arms as she turned around and ran out of the apartment.

"Fuck!" Dylan pushed Amber away from him and headed toward the door.

"She'll be fine. I don't know why she's being so dramatic. She just has a crush on you, that's all."

Dylan turned and looked at Amber and groaned. "Sometimes I swear you're clueless. I'm gonna go talk to her."

Dylan climbed the stairs to the roof, wondering if the entire universe hated him. His best friend thought he was an asshole, undeserving of love. He was trying to do the right thing with Lucy by taking it slow and properly courting her like some old-fashioned Regency romance show. He did a nice thing by helping Amber out with her stupid event and got all dressed up in scratchy material and even wore eye makeup. And what did the world do? It sent down a literal Fuck you, Dylan!

Once he got to the roof, it was settled. The world not only hated him, it wanted him dead. At the table, knees pulled under her chin, sat Lucy, tears streaming down her face with some sad song he recognized playing on her phone.

"Leave me alone." She turned away from him and curled into a tighter ball.

"Lucy, please listen to me. What you saw wasn't what you thought it was." He sat down beside her and tried to reach for her, but she immediately recoiled.

"So, you weren't kissing my sister, then?"

He groaned. "Okay, well, yes, that is what you saw, but it's not what you think happened."

She turned toward him and narrowed her eyes. "Then please, Dylan, by all means, explain how your lips became infused with my sister's."

"She kissed me."

Lucy scoffed. "Sure." She looked away and stared out over the horizon. "Why were you even with her alone in our apartment?"

Dylan's eyes slipped closed. "I helped her out today with this stupid event. Some Jimmy guy got sick, and she asked me to stand in for him. She seemed desperate."

Lucy rolled her eyes. "Of course she was."

"Lucy, I have done some terrible things in my past. I have been the first person to admit to you I'm not a good guy, and I don't blame you if you don't want to believe me. Hell, I probably wouldn't listen to a thing I said if I were you." He touched her hand, his thumb sliding across her knuckles. "But I'm telling you the truth. I didn't kiss your sister."

"You were my first kiss," she whispered.

He closed his eyes. "Yeah, I'm *really* sorry about that."

Her hand slid across his cheek, and he leaned into her touch. "Don't apologize for that. It was better than anything I've ever read in a book."

He chuckled as he opened his eyes and smiled at her. "That's pretty high praise from you, Lucy Patel."

She scrunched her nose and frowned. "Are you wearing makeup, Dylan?"

He shook his head and dropped his chin to his chest. "Can we please not talk about that?" She giggled. "No seriously, Lucy, like, can we never talk about it ever again?"

"I think you look sexy," she said. He looked up and bit his lip as Lucy stared at him. There wasn't a single reason in the universe that he deserved this woman. Everything was working against him. Amber, Blake, his past. There wasn't a scenario he could think of where Dylan got to keep Lucy for himself.

For the first time in his life, Dylan wanted something for himself. Really wanted it. Really wanted her. The universe had given him something amazing and perfect just to remind him he could never have it.

His heart thudded in his chest, and he was finding it harder to breathe. Dylan swore he could hear the blood moving through his eardrums. His skin was itching, and his fingers tingled. He tried to take a deep breath, but only gasped for air.

He lifted Lucy's hand to his lips and pressed his mouth against her knuckles, trying to ground himself to something that was real. "Are you alright?" He shook his head and rested it against her chest. Lucy buried her hands in his hair. "Hey, what's wrong? Talk to me?" He felt dizzy as he wrapped his arms around her waist and pinched his eyes shut, willing the tears to stay behind his eyeballs. "Dylan?"

He gasped and blew out a breath, watching the first tear slip from his cheek onto Lucy's dress. *Shit.* Lucy's fingers grazed his scalp. "Just breathe."

He lay there in her arms, weeping like a child until he could catch his breath again. He knew he should feel embarrassed, but her touch soothed him. Lucy would never judge him, and he knew he needed her.

When he finally recovered, she didn't ask questions. She let him sweep her hair from her forehead, brush his lips lightly against her temples, take her hand, and walk her back to her apartment.

He spent the rest of the day walking around the city, lost in his feelings. He'd never been in love before. Lucy Patel was the most beautiful thing that had ever come into his life, but he didn't have a clue what he had to offer her. She was his sunshine, his butterfly, and maybe it was in her best interest if he let her fly free.

Chapter Eighteen

Lucy

Dylan's panic attack concerned Lucy, but she didn't want to press him to talk about it. She was sure he would have shared with her the reason behind it if he had wanted to. Instead, she just tried to be there for him.

Dylan had a hard time seeing himself the way she saw him. She knew he had a past he wasn't proud of, but Lucy didn't care about any of that. Everything he had shared with her didn't matter to her. She liked Dylan because he seemed like a nice guy, despite what he claimed otherwise.

She slammed the front door of her apartment closed, and Amber looked up from the television. "There you are."

"Here I am." She shrugged, dropping her coat onto the chair and walking into the kitchen to make herself dinner.

"You alright?" Amber asked, turning off the TV. "You got a little dramatic earlier."

Lucy gripped the can of Spaghetti O's tightly in her hand, shoving it toward the can opener. "Sorry if my dramatics upset you, Am."

"Is there something going on between you and Dylan?"

Lucy dropped the bowl of Spahgetti O's onto the counter. "Crap." Amber jumped off the couch, gathering a handful of paper towels to help clean up the mess. "Thanks." Lucy blotted at the spilled sauce, pushing it into the sink. "Guess I'm eating ramen again."

"You want to order in?" Amber asked. "We could get Thai food."

Lucy sighed. "That sounds good, actually."

"Are you sure you're alright?" Her sister asked as she sat down with the takeout menu in her lap. "You just seem off recently."

As angry as she was at her sister, there was no point in bringing Dylan up with her. Amber didn't understand relationships. To her, men were just something she used for her own pleasure and threw away when she was done with them. She had no use for them after she got what she wanted.

"I guess it's just Mom and Dad not coming for the holidays. I just thought we were going to see them. And with Christmas coming and—" Lucy frowned. "Well, you know, I was looking forward to i t."

"What do you want to do this year? Anything at all. Your choice, of course." Amber rubbed her knee, and Lucy thought about all the years they would go out on Christmas Day back home.

Lucy sank down onto the couch. "Remember when we used to go to Pier 39 right after we opened all our gifts on Christmas morning?"

Amber laughed and leaned her head against her shoulder. "And Mom would let us ride on the carousel, and you always had to go up on the second floor."

"That's because it was the highest part, and I felt taller." She laughed. "Remember how Dad would always wander off to a bench and end up talking on the phone the whole time?"

"And Mom would get mad, and they would spend their whole time fighting about it," Amber sighed. "It was always just you and me, kiddo, wasn't it?"

"Do you ever wish things were different?" Lucy asked.

Amber looked up at her. "Different how?"

Lucy shook her head. "I don't know. Do you like being a model? Do you like your friends? Are you lonely?"

Amber sat up and stared at her. "That was a lot of specific questions, Luce." She scrunched her face and laughed. "But yeah, I love it. I have a ton of friends in the industry, so it's hard to be lonely around here. Why?"

"I'm just asking. No reason." Lucy shrugged.

"Luce..." Amber stared at her with those long eyelashes. Her sister would never understand. Amber's entire life had been one long string of people wanting to be around her, just to sit in her shadow for a mere moment. She was tired of languishing in the shadow of her sister's presence.

Lucy pushed away from the couch. "Just forget about it. I'm gonna order the food."

Lucy sat in a nook tucked away in the back of the bookstore, reading her book, tears streaming down her cheeks.

"Joel! What are you doing here?"

"I came back. I came back for you, Lilibeth." Joel was standing in the open doorway.

"Why? Why would you do that after I told you to leave? I'm going back to Karl." Lilibeth had her hands balled into fists at her side.

Joel stepped toward her. "Because I love you, Lilibeth. I love you even if you've given up on us."

"You can't."

"I can't lose you. I had to take the risk because...we're evergreen, Lili." He took another step toward her and touched her cheek. Lilibeth sucked in a breath. "Tell me you love me, and I'll be the strength for both of us." Joel slipped his hand to her chin and tilted her face to his. "I'll fight for this, for us."

Lilibeth let out a sob. "I've always loved you, Joel. I've never stopped."

Lucy slammed her book shut and sighed. "She loves him, and he loves her." She tossed the book onto the table and stood up, spinning in a circle. "Turn that up," she yelled to Jared at the counter. Jared turned up the radio, and Andy Grammer's "Don't Give Up on Me" played louder over the speakers, and Lucy started bouncing on her feet.

She skipped to Jared and pulled him into the center of the floor. "Come on, we're dancing."

Jared spun her in circles until they were both laughing and her stomach hurt. When the song finished, he pulled her into a hug. "What was that about?"

"Lilibeth is going to pick Joel."

"You were that happy just because of a book?" Jared glared at her. "What gives?"

Lucy shrugged and walked back to the counter. "Can't a girl just be happy?"

"You can always be happy, Lucy, but it wouldn't have anything to do with a certain handsome man from Titusville, would it?" Jared leaned against the counter and grinned.

Her smile betrayed her. "I think I'm falling for him, Jared."

"Wow, Lucy." His eyes widened and focused on her. "That's...this is a big deal."

"It's crazy, right? I mean, I've only known him for a couple of months, but..." she stared across the bookstore. "I can't tell what's in his head. He likes me, trust me, I know that, but he's just so angry at himself."

Jared sighed. "Guys like that are tough. You can't save them from themselves."

Lucy leaned against the counter and rested her chin on her palms. "I just feel like we're good for each other. I'm just not sure if he sees me that way or not." Lucy was ready for him to see her that way. She wanted him to see her as a sexual person, not just happy, sweet Lucy that he kissed sometimes.

After work a few days ago, she had bought an extra-spicy book to read. She wanted to gather the courage to kiss Dylan again, and she needed to stop being so timid about it. Dylan was keeping her at arm's length, and she was ready for less PG-13 and more R-rated attention from him.

"Hey, Lucy." Her hands slipped off her palms as she jumped at the sound of Dylan's voice.

"Dylan, uh, what are you doing here?" She glanced nervously at Jared and then back at Dylan.

He stood with his hands in his pockets, staring at them, and shrugged. "Figured I'd stop by and see if I could walk you home from work." He glanced at his phone. "You're off in ten minutes. I can wait for you."

Jared chuckled. "Get out of here, Luce." He stepped behind her and whispered. "Seems like your hot boyfriend is eager for your attention."

She spun around and hit Jared in the chest and then glanced at Dylan, who was meandering around the store. "Okay, let me just go grab my coat." Dylan's face lit up, and her heart skipped a couple of beats with each step to the break room.

"I'm glad you stopped by." Lucy looked up at Dylan, who was walking slowly beside her.

He squeezed her hand, and she swung it between them. "I missed you." She bit her lip and looked away.

"I missed you too." It was almost a whisper, and she wasn't sure if she wanted him to hear it or not. Things were still so new between them, and she wasn't sure exactly how to behave around him. Was it too clingy to want to be around him every moment she wasn't at work or sleeping? Was it too soon to say she really wanted to find out what it was like to have him next to her while she was sleeping?

They turned the corner, and she tugged on his hand. "Come here. I want to show you something." She dragged him into the Botanical Garden park she would cut through on her way home from work. "This is one of my favorite parts of the city."

Dylan looked around and smiled. "Wow, it's like a little forest right here in the city." His relaxed expression made Lucy want to spend all day just studying his face, memorizing every detail.

"In San Fran, we have these woods I used to go to when I was little. It's something I miss about living there. But sometimes I stop in here and just close my eyes and pretend."

She sat down on a bench under a tree and patted the spot beside her. Dylan sat next to her, wrapping his arm around her. "This is great, Luce. Thank you for sharing it with me."

She watched him out of the corner of her eye. His arm sat innocently on her shoulder, his fingers rubbing small circles into the bare flesh on her arm.

Something came over her that threatened to spill over. A desire she couldn't contain. She bit her lip, deciding to seize the moment. If Dylan wouldn't do it, she was going to have to be the one to take this to the next level.

Lucy leaned into his touch, resting her head on his shoulder. His hand brushed her neck and left tingles on her skin. She moved her hand to his chest and tilted her chin, pressing her lips to his neck. He swallowed, and she could feel his chest rise and fall. She tested the waters further, sliding her tongue against his skin, along the stubbled flesh to his ear. He sucked in a breath and brought a hand to her arm. She pressed her mouth against his jaw and nibbled a path to his lips. His hand slid to her cheek, forcing their mouths together in a kiss that was desperate and full of passion and need.

She reached up and took his hand in hers, dragging it down her body until it rested on her breast. He groaned, trying to pull his hand away, but Lucy held him firmly against her. She opened her eyes and found him staring at her. She nibbled on her bottom lip and smirked. "Lucy." It was a warning, and she wasn't in the mood for any resistance today, not when she had her own desire to nurture.

"Please, Dylan." Her lips pressed against the bottom of his jaw. "I just need you to touch me."

"I...you can't ask me to do that. Not here." She brought their lips together again, her hands brushing into his hair. He moaned, bringing a smile to her face. His hand gripped her breast through her shirt, and her head fell back. She didn't recognize herself. She was outside in the garden, where anyone could wander upon them, and she didn't care. All she wanted was Dylan's hands on her.

His mouth pressed against her jaw, kissing her neck with wild abandon. She had unleashed him, and his mouth was now burning a trail on her skin. His fingers tickled her stomach as they slipped under her shirt. Goosebumps lit the path his hand took across her abdomen until he reached her breast. She couldn't stop the moan when his hand slipped under her bra. "Shh, baby, quiet."

Baby... The single word was causing a reaction in her body she couldn't explain. She bit her lip and mumbled against the top of his head. His entire palm covered her breast, squeezing it in his hand. Her entire body turned to liquid. Her thighs were tingling with each brush of his tongue against her collarbone. She gripped his shirt in one fist and his hair in the other, pulling him against her chest. She heard him chuckle, and his eyes met hers. "Relax, Luce."

"I feel like I'm on fire," she panted, staring back at him with widened eyes.

"Tell me what you need?" he asked.

She shook her head. "I don't know. I just—I..." She couldn't stop gasping, unsure of what to say. What did she need? All she could think of was more...more of him.

Dylan pushed a strand of hair out of her face, bending to kiss her lips. "Be quiet, alright, and I'll take care of you." Lucy's head fell back as she nodded at Dylan's words. She would let Dylan take care of anything as long as he kept touching her.

She squeezed her eyes shut when she felt him pull her shirt down with his chin, his mouth grazing the top of her breast. But it was the feeling of his hand sliding under her dress that caused her heart to race. His fingertips teased the edge of her panties, and Lucy thought she might crawl out of her skin trying to press herself closer, forcing his hand where she needed him. He cupped her through her panties and groaned when he found her soaked through. He wasted no time pushing them aside, and she squirmed the moment his bare hand touched flesh. "Stay still, Lucy."

"I can't," she cried out. Dylan lifted his head, pressing his mouth against her lips.

His hand nudged her legs, pressing them wider apart as she tried to relax, and then his fingers slipped between her legs. She closed her eyes the moment she felt him enter her, crying out. He pressed his mouth against her lips, silencing her. It felt weird and intrusive having something inside of her, and yet she couldn't stop herself from wanting more. With each thrust of his finger, she ground against his hand. This was so different from when she touched herself. This was intoxicating and almost like standing on the edge of a cliff just waiting to be pushed off. His thumb was in that spot, the one that made her see lights, and she felt like she was going to have a heart attack at any moment.

And then it happened. When she didn't think she could handle any more than his finger, he slid in another, and stars and the universe erupted behind her eyes like dust. Dylan's tongue was in her mouth; her fingers were digging into his shoulder; and one of her fists was so tight in his hair she feared she'd pulled some out.

When the kaleidoscope stopped spinning, and Dylan's kisses had become small pecks against her mouth, she opened her eyes. She released her grip on his hair and sat up. "I think I just died."

He laughed. "I hope not. I don't think I could live with myself."

She kissed him, wrapping her arms around the back of his neck. His face broke into a grin when she finally let him go. "That was brilliant," she said.

"I would have to agree with that."

She frowned and looked down at his lap, her eyes going as wide as saucers when she saw how large the bulge in his pants was. Good Lord, and she was concerned about two fingers being inside of her. "You can't say it's that good if it leaves you like that."

He shook his head and covered his hand over the large intrusion. "I'm fine. This was about you."

Lucy watched him as he stood up and adjusted himself. "Are you thinking about awful things now?"

"Usually I try to think about mundane tasks, or my sister and Blake going at it in the woods."

Lucy scrunched her nose. "Eww, why would you think about that?"

"Trust me, I'd rather not, but it works." He spun around and held out his hands. The situation appeared managed.

She looked up at him and asked the one question on her mind. "Would you ever have sex with me?"

He choked and took a moment to catch his breath. "Lucy..."

"It's a serious question, Dylan."

He ran a hand through his hair and sat down next to her on the bench. "You should give your virginity to someone you're in love with." He patted her knee and stood up again. "Shall we?" He held out his hand and waited for her to adjust herself before taking his hand.

For the rest of the walk home, Lucy thought of a million different ways to tell Dylan Lancaster that the only person she was in love with was him.

Chapter Nineteen

Dylan

In the week leading up to Christmas, Dylan had filled his sketchbook with the exciting adventures of Mr. Jangles, Grumpy Gus, and Dilly Bear.

For the first time in his life, something he drew—a vibrant world of eclectic characters that reminded him of home—felt exciting to him. It took him back to a time when he was happy with his siblings back in Titusville. But it was more than that. The world he created on the page was different and bold and...kinda awesome.

It wasn't just that the idea was exciting either; Dylan was getting more confident in his drawing. It was like a sense of purpose overtook him when he sat down to draw. The stories flowed from his mind onto the page like lava, and before he knew it, he'd been sitting for hours and had drawn entire storyboards full of ideas from his past.

But the more books he filled, the less he knew what to do with them. What good was a storybook that sat on the floor and collected dust? How was that supposed to give him a purpose? After a while, he drew other things to distract himself from those answers, like butterflies and flowers. Or Lucy.

He was thinking about Lucy all the time now. Ever since the day in the Botanical Garden, she was on his mind in every task he did during the day, and in every dirty dream he had at night. In the morning, he woke up in a sweat, harder than a rock as he raced to take a cold shower.

He'd tried to avoid being alone with her. He didn't trust himself to be intimate with her for fear of losing control of himself and taking more of her that could never belong to him. But his feelings for her had spiraled so far out of his control that there was nothing he could do to deny them anymore. He was in love with Lucy Patel.

And it wasn't just because of the physical stuff, either. Yes, he wanted her more than he'd wanted any woman in his entire life. But it was more than that. Lucy understood him. She looked at him in a way no other woman had. Dylan wanted to be with Lucy outside of the bedroom, and that scared the hell out of him.

Dylan hadn't spoken to Blake since their argument the week prior, which was making him feel even more alone in his thoughts as he tried to isolate himself from everyone in the apartment.

Lucy was spending more time at the bookstore leading up to the holiday shopping week, and Dylan was falling back into his old patterns of anxiety and self-doubt. At least that was something he was familiar with.

The steel door to the roof scraped on the ground, and Dylan looked up to see if Lucy had come home early, only to be surprised and somewhat annoyed to see Amber emerge from the entrance.

"Hey, I was looking for you." She waved and sauntered over on another pair of shoes that were too tall for normal people relaxing at home.

"You found me."

She squeezed into the closest available seat, and he stared at the empty chairs across from him, wondering why she never seemed to take a hint. "I haven't really seen you around since the whole kiss incident."

This was the last thing he needed today. "I've been busy." The pen on his page slipped the moment her hand slid to his crotch. "Woah." He slammed his pen down and grabbed her hand. "Amber, stop."

"What?" Her mouth sat agape, and Dylan thought he might be the first guy who had ever turned her down.

"Look, you seem great and all, but I'm really not interested."

She blinked and rubbed her temples. "Wait, I thought you said you weren't gay?"

Why did some attractive women assume that if a man turned them down, he must be gay? "I'm not, Amber. I just...I'm interested in someone else, and I don't want to screw that up."

"Oh, I didn't realize you had met anyone else while you were here."

Dylan rubbed his neck, suddenly feeling warm. "Uh, yeah, I—"

"Wait..." Amber tilted her head and gasped. "You don't mean Lucy, do you?" Great, just what he needed—the nosy sister who was always trying to get in his pants asking questions. "I don't know how I didn't see this before. How long has it been going on?"

He didn't want to have this conversation, yet here he was. He sighed and leaned back in his seat. There was no point in denying it anymore. "I think I've had a thing for Lucy since the day I met her." Amber's mouth dropped. "I don't know why you're so surprised. She's the only person I've ever known who calls me on my bullshit. I swear, it's like she's in my head sometimes. Lucy's the most amazing person I've ever had the pleasure of calling my friend." When he finished speaking, he took a deep breath, trying to gauge Amber's reaction.

"Are you sleeping with her?" The accusation was swift and not at all surprising.

"No." Dylan lifted his hands defensively. "Look, I'm not gonna kiss and tell. If Lucy hasn't told you anything, then I'm sure she has her reasons."

She scoffed. "My sister's never even had a boyfriend before."

"I know. We've been very honest with each other."

Amber stood up, pacing in front of the greenhouse. Dylan felt the anxious pit in his stomach churn as his own negative thoughts surfaced loudly in his mind about why he wasn't good enough for Lucy. He wasn't sure he was ready to hear someone else verbalize those feelings out loud. "Before Lucy and I moved to New York, she had a rough time. She didn't have a lot of friends, maybe one or two, but mostly she got bullied for being quiet, for living in her books." Dylan couldn't imagine anyone being rude to Lucy. "Guys never even looked at her. Why would they when I was her sister?"

Dylan felt sick to his stomach. "Jesus, Amber. Don't you think that's a tad vain?" Why would she say that about her own sister?

Amber shook her head. "I'm just being honest. I'm not saying it's right. It's just how it is." Dylan thought about how much Lucy catered to her sister, how she prioritized Amber's needs over hers, and he wondered how Lucy felt growing up with an older sister as beautiful as Amber. "My parents never put her first. She's never been the special one."

He shook his head, his nostrils flaring. "You know that's a really shit thing to say, considering you're her sister."

"Look, I love Lucy. And I haven't always been the best sister to her. Did you know her birthday is on Christmas Day?" Dylan did not know that. "I mean, how shit is that? Growing up, we always had the worst Christmases because our parents weren't exactly attentive. But it was also her birthday, and our parents were busy with other things." Amber laughed. "But she never cared. She always made the most of it. Do you know what she remembers the most? That damn carousel that she and I used to ride on her birthday. That's what she thought was amazing. It was literally somewhere our parents took us so they could get rid of us for a while, but to her, it was something that made her happy."

"Sounds like Lucy," he chuckled, though he found nothing she said amusing; in fact, the situation made him feel sick. Finding out that Lucy's birthday was on Christmas, a fact he was unaware of, made the heartbreak of her family's decision not to visit for the holidays even heavier.

"It really does. She deserves to be chosen for a change." She looked at him with a raise of her brow. Suddenly, he felt like she was placing all the hope for Lucy's happiness on him.

Dylan frowned. "Amber, I agree with you. Lucy deserves to be loved and cherished and shown that she's important, but I'm not sure I'm the right person to do that for her."

Amber sat down next to him. "I'm confused. You just told me you were interested in her."

"I am." He scrubbed his hand through his hair. "I care about Lucy more than anyone I've ever been with before. But I've got my own shit to figure out, and I'm not sure I'd be the best thing for her."

"That sounds like bullshit."

Dylan groaned. "I'm just trying to be a good guy here."

"Look, I get it. I haven't been the best person for Lucy, either. But I love her, and Lucy—well, she's got a big heart, and she loves me despite how terrible I am. She reminds me every day when I wake up that it's another opportunity to be better."

He sighed. "The road to hell is paved with good intentions, Amber."

"Are my eyes deceiving me, or is my brother actually showing his face?"

Dylan expected everyone to be gone when he headed to the apartment to shower that afternoon. So, when he walked out of the bathroom and found his sister waiting for him in the middle of the living room with her arms crossed against her chest, he was mildly surprised and not exactly in the mood for another emotionally charged discussion.

"Do we really need to do this today?"

"You got somewhere you need to be right now?" Sam's eyebrow rose, and Dylan knew he didn't have a good enough excuse to evade his sister.

"Fine. Which topic do you want to discuss today? My failure as a human being, your boyfriend being a dick, or would you also like to give your opinion on my love life?" Dylan scrubbed the towel through his dripping hair.

Sam sighed, her shoulders slouching. "Blake said some things he shouldn't have said."

"Which things were those? The one where he said I'm too big of an asshole to date nice girls, or the one where he insinuated I'm just a whore who practically raped Lucy in a public hallway?"

His sister flinched at his words. "I think you're over-exaggerating."

"Oh, am I?" His voice remained calm, but the back-and-forth conversation was getting exhausting.

"Dylan, I'm on your side here." Sam sat down on the couch and patted the spot beside her. Dylan reluctantly tossed the towel next to him and sat down. "It was wrong of Blake to say what he did, but I also don't think he meant it."

Dylan massaged his temples. "Yeah, Blake, the guy who has shot straight his entire life, didn't mean to insinuate that I didn't deserve to be happy."

"Are you?"

"Am I what?" Dylan squeezed his eyes shut and shook his head. "Undeserving?"

"No, are you happy? Is that what you are trying to tell me? Does Lucy make you happy?" Sam's hand grazed his knee, and Dylan sunk back into the sofa.

In all the years growing up with his sister, she was always the one person he confided in. Sam always had a way of seeing into his mind. Yet, for the last year, she had been absent from his life. It was a void that had become a black hole the longer he sat in it. "Is it so wrong that I want to be happy?"

"Dylan, of course not."

"With Lucy, she makes me dare to dream things could be possible with her. Things I have no business even imagining." Dylan buried his face in his hands.

The comforting hand on his back was helpful, but his thoughts were tumultuous. "Or...maybe it took meeting Lucy for you to open your eyes to the scenarios you're imagining."

"It's like, you know how I get all those anxiety attacks?" Dylan stared at his sister, letting his thoughts wash over him.

"You, anxious? I didn't know that." His sister's sarcasm aside, it was widely known that he was the most anxious of all the Lancaster siblings. Growing up as the middle child, Dylan often felt undervalued. He had fought for his father's attention all his life.

This led to feelings of inadequacy, which manifested itself into his stubborn and rebellious behavior in high school. He knew he had put his father through a lot growing up.

He chuckled and pushed a shoulder into Sam. She pushed back, urging him to continue. "When I'm with her, all the noise in my head stops. I've never met anyone who could do that. I...when I look at her, when she smiles at me, it's like she becomes my entire world."

"Wow, that's pretty serious!" He could tell that Sam was trying to temper her surprise at his admission, but the way her voice cracked told him she was holding back her response.

"It is, and that's entirely the problem. I don't know what I'm going to do." He ran his hand through his wet hair.

"Have you thought about the future? What about Titusville? Are you still going home? How does this change any of that?" Sam was firing off questions in rapid succession that Dylan had no answers to.

"I don't know, I really don't. Honestly though, you and I both know I'm not good enough for her."

"Shut up. Stop saying that," Sam growled. He sighed and closed his eyes. There was an awkward silence until Sam cleared her throat. "I think you should talk to Blake." Dylan opened his eyes and stared at the ceiling.

"For what reason?"

"He's your best friend, and he feels awful. Besides, it might help if you talked to him. You two have been best friends since you were toddlers. Maybe you need a male perspective."

On one hand, he missed Blake, but on the other one, which was a clinched fist, he was still angry at his reaction. "Yeah, well, he's a big boy. He knows where to find me."

Dylan climbed the stairs to the roof. Instead of helping him, his mood had soured since talking to his sister. He knew the only thing that could salvage his day was Lucy. Stepping out onto the roof, he quietly watched her as she sat in the corner reading her book. He leaned against the door frame, his arms crossed against his chest as he observed her silent smile. With each word she absorbed, she scrubbed at the corner of her eyes.

He'd never met anyone who got such joy out of a book. Lucy didn't just read a book; she lived it. He envied the way she could open the front cover and dive in without a life vest. He thought maybe it made him love her even more, watching her cry over the ending of her book.

"I can feel you watching me." She was still reading the page in front of her, a dainty smile teasing her lips.

He pushed away from the door and walked toward her. "You seem happy. Does that mean Joel finally learned to communicate?"

She continued reading, holding her hand up as he sat down across from her. It made him smile the way she commanded him so easily. The moment she closed the book, her eyes met his. "Lilibeth and Joel left Rockmount Ranch together."

Dylan nodded, expecting that to be her answer. "And Karl?"

"Karl stayed at Rockmount. It's where he belongs." Her fingertips tapped on the cover of the book as she glanced at him. "I think this is the first time you and I have been alone in a week," she said with a loud exhale.

"Oh really, I...is it?"

"So, you want to tell me why you've been avoiding me, or are we just going to continue pretending this is normal?"

Chapter Twenty

Lucy

"*So, you want to tell me why you've been avoiding me, or are we just going to continue pretending this is normal?*"

Lucy usually enjoyed the way Dylan's face lit up when he smiled. The corners of his eyes would crinkle, and the dimples on his cheeks would curve in.

Today, however, when he smiled, it was different. His smile was subtle, more reserved in response to her question. He hadn't shaved in a few days, so the stubble that sat on his chin and cheeks had grown fuller. She wondered what it would feel like to run her hands across his face. Would it tickle her lips if she kissed him?

He swallowed, and she watched the Adam's apple bob at his throat. Her mouth felt dry as her tongue stuck to the roof of her mouth. "Lucy...I, uh, I guess I have been doing a bit of avoiding."

"Aha, so you admit it," she said, slapping the table, sinking back into her chair. The victory stung. She knew the answer already, but it hurt to hear him say it out loud. "What I don't understand is why. Was it something I said? Did I..." She sat up, leaning forward. "Did I do something wrong in the garden?"

"Lucy, no," he said forcefully, reaching across the table to take her hand. "No, you were perfect. Please, this has nothing to do with you." Great, this was sounding like the *"it's not you, it's me"* speech from all the books she read. She rolled her eyes and pulled her hand away. "Luce, I don't know how to explain it to you without upsetting you."

"Start with honesty and go from there."

He sighed and closed his eyes. "I'd never lie to you, Lucy. Never." When he opened his eyes, she saw only truth behind the brown eyes she knew so well. "When I came to New York a few months ago, I was not in a good place. I hated everything, and pretty much everyone." She watched the hurt flash in his eyes. "Blake moving here felt like a betrayal, but the longer I sat with it, it was just another reminder of my failures."

"Failures?"

"Blake and I are the same age by only a month. But he was always smarter, better looking, *taller*, and he always knew what he wanted to do with his life. I think a part of me took some sick pleasure that he was stuck in Titusville working at his mom's diner, because that meant he was as miserable as I was. And then the bastard went and fell in love with my sister last year." He snorted. "Asshole had the nerve to find love *and* leave town to follow his dreams."

"And you didn't think you could do the same?" Lucy interrupted.

"That's the point, Lucy, I couldn't. In Titusville, I didn't have dreams. I had nightmares. Once Blake left, it was like I got left behind, and I started living in those nightmares. Jax took over the family business and, of course, he was good at it, because why the hell not? I'm the only Lancaster who's not good enough for anything. Sam works for the fucking New York Yankees. What's better than that?"

"Well, if I understood sports, I might have an answer for that question, but you're kind of putting me at a disadvantage here, Dylan."

"It's irrelevant. The point is, Jax is brilliant, Sam is spectacular, and I'm the idiot at the bottom of the stupid tree."

Lucy snorted. "You're being ridiculous. I doubt either of your siblings would say that about you."

He reached for her again, his eyes slanted as he pinched them together. "Have you ever felt like you could never measure up to Amber?"

Lucy's heart sped up. She couldn't ignore the question, or her own insecurity hiding in the back of her mind. For years, she'd tried to compare herself to her sister and her success, and every time she had come back lacking. "Amber and I are different, but..." She stared down at her hands and closed her eyes. "Sometimes it's hard when everything is about her. She's always been the priority; she's more important, more valuable.."

"First off, none of that is true, but I think you and I are a lot alike, Luce. We're always chasing our siblings, thinking we'll never be as good as them, as smart as them." He squeezed her hand. "Or as pretty as them." She felt like he was shining a bright light in her eyes and exposing her secrets.

"Even if that's true, Dylan, we aren't them. Their success is different from ours, and maybe it's bigger and flashier, and comes in a prettier package, but that doesn't mean that you or I can't find our own thing."

Dylan growled, fisting his hands in his hair. "Doing what? Drawing stupid cartoons? Sitting around talking to my dead mother about all the crap I can't do right?" Lucy gasped as he shouted and looked away. He sat there in silence. "Damn it. You always have a way of getting me to say things I don't intend to say out loud." His voice was so low she barely heard him.

She stood up, walking to the other side of the table. Dylan turned away from her, wiping at his face. Lucy lowered her voice as she placed a hand on his arm. "I know last year you said that things were bad, and I know you think you screwed everything up. But it sounds like your family loves you, and it doesn't sound like anything you did was unforgivable."

"Lancasters always stick together, no matter how stupid you are. It's kind of our thing." He wiped his face with the sleeve of his hoodie, turning toward her. The wet cheeks made him look so vulnerable. Somehow, that made him even more attractive to her.

"Then I think the only person left to forgive you is yourself."

"How do I forgive myself for all the damage I caused?" he asked.

She laced their fingers together and rested her head on his shoulder. "It sounds like the most damage you caused was to Dylan."

Slowly, she tilted her face to his neck and nuzzled into him. Her lips pressed again him, and the hair tickled her nose.

She needed him to understand that she cared about him and that none of the other stuff mattered to her.

"I'm damaged goods, Luce," he whispered a warning into her hair.

"Do you know what I see?" She looked at him. "When I first met you, I saw so much sadness in your eyes. You wear your scars on your sleeve, Dylan." She pressed her hand against his chest. "You carry them in your heart." She crawled into his lap and cupped his cheeks with her hands, wiping the errant tears from his face. "You are sensitive and scared, and I think most of all, you are unapologetically authentic."

His hands slid up her back, resting at the nape of her neck, his forehead pressing against hers. His eyes were closed as he spoke, soft, yet firm. "No one deserves you, Lucy. You are..."

Her lips cut him off, their tongues clashing in his mouth. He groaned the moment her hands slid into his hair. This was becoming her favorite thing to do. The way his hands gripped her shoulders, firm and desperate, pulling her against him, made it clear he had missed her as much as she had missed him this past week.

The scruff on his face scratched her neck as his lips burned against her jaw. Her eyes blew open when she ground down against him and felt the protrusion between her legs. It made her crazy to know she could do that so easily to him.

His hands were on her back now, under her shirt. She was tingling as they settled on her waist, gripping her hips firmly, pulling her against his erection with a soft growl. She nipped at his chin, her teeth grazing him, and felt his hand slide to her bottom. Lucy's legs were shaking, her cotton panties getting wetter each time she pressed down against him. She was sure his sweats were going to be soaked when they were done with...she honestly didn't know what they were doing, or where this was leading.

His hand slid to her breast, his fingertips tracing the underside of her bra. Her eyes swept over him, his pupils blown wide. "Dylan..."

He shook his head. "You have no idea what you do to me, do you?"

She glanced down between their bodies. "I might have some idea," she teased. He squeezed her breast and closed his eyes. Lucy wanted to be brave. She slid her hand down his chest, her fingers dancing over the waistband of his sweatpants. His eyes popped open, and his hand grasped her wrist.

"Luce, don't..."

Her mouth touched his, with a teasing smile playing on her lips. She'd been thinking about this all week, or even longer. From the moment she saw the bulge in his pants in the garden, she'd been curious. "I just want to touch it." A soft groan emitted from his throat.

"I might die if you do. Do you want to be responsible for my death, Lucy Patel?"

She shrugged and frowned against his mouth. "I've never even seen one before. I don't even have the slightest clue what to do with it." She pouted, pushing out her bottom lip. "Please?"

Dylan's shoulders sagged, and he released her wrist, dropping her hand into his lap. "You're gonna be the death of me, I swear." With a wide grin, she looked down and peeled his sweats and boxers away from his body. It sprang free, landing on his belly.

It wasn't at all what she had been imagining. Long and veiny, thicker than she expected it to be. Her tongue slid out of her mouth as she wrapped her hand around it. Dylan let out a strangled moan. It was soft yet firm in her hand. She lifted it from his stomach and slid her hand to the head, slipping her fingers across the tip, which was slightly wet to the touch. "Son of a...Lucy, holy..." Dylan's head fell forward against her shoulder.

"What do I do now?" she asked, concentrating her attention on her fingers tracing along his shaft.

Panting into her shoulder, he wrapped his hand around hers and placed it back around his shaft, sliding their hands up and down his in a slow rhythm. He shook his head rapidly twice against her neck, murmuring words she didn't understand before he raised his head and kissed her. Panting into her mouth with each stroke, she could feel Dylan slowly unravel in her hand. "Like this?" she whispered against his jaw, testing the way she slid her hand with his.

The noise he made sent chills down her spine. His hand squeezed around hers once, then dropped to his side as he relinquished control to her. Hands snaked through her hair, his mouth assaulting hers in an explosion of passion she couldn't describe. It only took a few more tugs of her hands sliding up and down his velvety skin before he pulled her closer, and she felt him tense and explode beneath her. He was panting, his eyes squeezed shut as his lips pressed firmly against her mouth. Her hand was coated in a sticky, glorious mess, and she felt a surge of pride in helping create it

.

Dylan was clutching her in a way that told her she must have done something right. His lips slid up her neck, so tender, almost as if he were murmuring soft prayers into her skin. "Was that alright?"

He lifted his face, flushed and sweaty, and for a moment she wasn't sure he knew what to say. "I, I..." He shook his head and lifted her hand, wiping her fingers on the underside of his hoodie. He stared down at their hands, bringing her palm to his mouth as he kissed it. "You are a marvel."

She laughed and leaned against his shoulder. "Learning new things is fun."

He chuckled, still panting. "You ever need practice, just let me know. But I think you're a natural."

Lucy ran her hands along his cheek. "I like this." She scratched the scruff along his jaw. "It tickles my face."

He smirked and raised a brow. "I know other places I think you might enjoy it." She furrowed her brow, and before she could ask him to explain, he lifted her up, placing her on top of the table.

"Dylan, what are you doing?" The mischievous grin should have been a warning, but she had no time to think before his head was under her skirt and his hands were firmly on her hips, pulling her toward him at the edge of the table. She squealed as his hands tugged at her panties, pulling them down to her knees.

The table was cold, but none of it mattered the moment his mouth pressed against her center. She might have uttered an actual curse word, but that was between her and the Lord, because Dylan Lancaster had his tongue in places that no one had ever dared go before and Lucy was sure that the birds were singing just for her.

He was right, of course. She absolutely loved the way his stubble felt against her. And she couldn't fight the urge to grip his hair and tug him closer. She should have been embarrassed by her own eagerness, but then she felt him smile against her flesh, and all of those feelings disappeared. Their time in the garden had been exciting, but watching Dylan between her legs, feeling his tongue slip into her so intimately, Lucy couldn't describe the way it made her insides turn out.

When she screamed his name the moment the euphoria washed over her, one hand in his hair, the other gripping the table, she tried to keep her eyes open, to watch him. But it was impossible. The weight of it all hit her so suddenly, her head fell against the table and her entire body clenched.

Before she came back to herself, Dylan was pulling her panties up and settling her skirt around her knees. She lay on the table, inhaling deep breaths as she stared up at the sky. Dylan climbed onto the table opposite her, his head lying next to hers. "I might have recorded that in my brain so I can watch it over and over again when I go to bed," he said breathlessly.

She closed her eyes and swallowed. "I'm pretty sure I need a nap."

He lifted his hand, leaning over to press it to her cheek. "Thank you for everything, Lucy." His eyes grew wide. "I don't mean what we just did. I mean, yes, thank you, that was hot as hell, but I mean, for everything before that."

"You're welcome, for all of it, though I can't imagine it was that exciting considering the experience you have."

He sat up quickly, staring at her as he slid off the table and lifted her up, standing between her legs, his eyes locked on hers. "You really have no idea, do you?"

"What?"

"I was doing everything I could to hold it together. The minute you touched me, hell, I almost blew my load." He kissed her forehead. "You are all I think about, night and day. I don't even trust myself to be alone with you half the time."

Her eyes widened as the reality of what he said hit her. "Is that why you've been avoiding me?"

He kissed her cheek, his lips grazing her ear. "I'm trying to be a good guy, Lucy. But every minute I spend with you, my defenses crumble, and all I want to do is bad things to you." The hair on the back of her neck stood on end. He pulled back and grinned, looking all the while like an innocent man who didn't just devour her on a table. "How about we go out for pizza before I forget myself and do something you'll regret?"

She was sure there was nothing he could do to her she would regret. "But..." He cut her off with a kiss, one of those Dylan Lancaster specials that had her melting inside like butter.

"Food first, and then maybe we can stop at the bookstore." He tapped her on the nose. "You've finished your book, and I can't have my girl without a book to read."

He tugged her toward the door, and Lucy tried to keep up, but her body was emotionally still at the table, her heart still pounding with the sound of his voice.

Two words, a simple admission she wanted more than anything to be true.

My girl.

Chapter Twenty-One

Dylan

"Can you put the pillows in the closet until tonight? I just want everything to look clean when Dad gets here."

Dylan took the pillows off the couch and carried them to the closet. "You want me to move my stuff from the bathroom?"

"No, of course not." Sam moved through the kitchen, scrubbing the counters. "You live here."

"I'm just crashing, Sam. I don't live here."

The door opened, and Blake walked in. Dylan froze beside the couch, still holding a blanket in his hands. He hadn't spoken to his friend since their fight, and Dylan had done a good job of avoiding him. "Hey, uh, you think we can talk before everyone gets here?"

Seeing his dad and Jackson again was already stressing Dylan out. Talking to Blake about all the shit that had gone down between them wasn't at the top of his list of things he wanted to do.

"Oh, I can, uh..." Sam looked like the cat that ate the canary.

Blake tipped his head toward the door. "You want to go to the roof?"

His eyes were pleading with his sister for an excuse, but she gave him that look that said, *"Get your ass upstairs and fix this* now,*"* and he knew he needed to go.

He followed his friend apprehensively up to the roof, and immediately Blake walked to the edge and leaned over the side, looking down to the street below. "Do you think we might get a white Christmas?"

"I'm not a weatherman, but it's definitely colder lately." Dylan leaned against the wall, his arms crossed against his chest. He had no intention of making this easy for his friend.

"You remember that one year we got snowed in, and Sam wanted to go sledding on the hill behind my house?"

Dylan chuckled to himself, thinking back on the memory. "Dad said that Jax had to finish at the shop before we could go, but none of us wanted to wait, so we snuck out."

"When you guys got to my house, Sam looked like a stuffed teddy bear. You put her in like six layers of clothes." Blake laughed, staring out at the horizon. Dylan wasn't sure where this story was going. "That whole day I remember you were a buzzkill. Sam would fall off the sled and you'd have a panic attack."

"Dad would have kicked my ass if she got hurt, especially after sneaking out."

"That's the thing, though. Sam was like fourteen. She wasn't a child." Blake turned and leaned against the banister. "You were always taking care of her."

"She's my sister. That was my job, asshole. What's your point?"

Blake exhaled in frustration. "I'm not trying to be an ass, Dylan. I'm just saying you've always been there for Sam. And growing up, you were always there for me. And maybe I should have been there when you needed me."

Dylan pushed away from the wall. "Oh, fuck that, we're not doing this."

"What?"

"The pity party shit. I fucked up all by myself last year. So, don't act like I was some awesome friend to you. You want the truth?" He stared at Blake before admitting what he was least proud of. "I was happy when you were miserable, because it meant you and I got to be miserable together." Dylan waved Blake away when he approached him. "Don't. Seriously, dude. I was a shit friend last year. You remember the black eye, right?"

"I seem to recall you had a matching one."

"I fucked your girlfriend," Dylan shouted.

Blake shrugged. "Yeah, that was a shit move. But you were right. It's in the past. We need to get over it. We all moved on."

"Did we? Cause it keeps coming up." Dylan closed his eyes and rubbed his temples. He didn't want to fight with Blake, and it was getting exhausting being angry all the time. "I screwed up. And I kept doing it after you left. I've been struggling, Blake, but that's not even the part that killed me. What hurt the most was that the only part of me that my best friend saw was the darkest scars I was doing my best to destroy."

"Dylan, I'm sorry. I was upset and angry, and I said things I didn't mean. Lucy is like a sister to me, and I—"

"Sam told me about what happened with Lucy. How you protected her."

"I just don't want to see her get hurt." Blake sighed.

"I don't either."

"She deserves to be with someone who's serious about her." Blake opened his mouth, but he knew there was nothing more Blake could say about Lucy that Dylan didn't already know.

"Did you know I've never been in love before?" Dylan cut him off, his chest rising and falling as he spoke. "Not once in my entire life. I sat up here the other day and thought about every girl I've ever been with. I barely even liked half of them. There wasn't a single reason I was with them besides the obvious."

Blake had gone silent now, and Dylan supposed he expected that. What could he say, really? *Sorry about all the sex?*

"I know you think I went after Lucy for the same reason, and hell, I don't blame you for thinking that, because of my history. But, the day I met her, it was like I cut out the black parts of my heart and laid them on the table when I was with her. You're right. She is special and amazing, and I don't deserve a damn thing she gives me, but I *am* in love with her. My God, I'm in love with her. I have no idea how I let that happen. I've been torturing myself over it for weeks, but I'm telling you, Blake, I would walk through fire for that woman."

The look of shock on his best friend's face was worth the price of admission that night.

"And I am terrified of the day I walk away from her, because I'm afraid I won't be able to come back from it."

Blake finally found his voice. "I don't understand."

Dylan shook his head. "I have to go home eventually, and Lucy deserves better. Better than who I am, better than whatever I can offer her."

He narrowed his eyes in obvious confusion. "Are you sleeping with her?"

"There you go again, thinking the worst of me." He crossed his arms against his chest, and it felt like he was protecting his heart when he spoke again. "I would never sleep with her. She deserves to be with someone she's in love with."

"What if she's in love with you?"

His laughter filled the rooftop. "Not even I'm that lucky. What the hell would I have to give a girl like Lucy? She'd be a complete fool to fall in love with me."

"Now you're just pissing me off," Blake said. "Look, I got angry at first. Yeah, it was shocking to catch you with your tongue down her throat. But the longer I thought about it, the less shocked I was." Dylan couldn't believe what he was hearing. "Lucy is an amazing girl. She deserves a good guy who will care about her."

"Are you deaf now, Grandpa? That's what I just said."

"You're a good guy, Dylan. In fact, you're the best guy I know."

"Oh, fuck off." Dylan pushed away from the wall and started stalking toward the door.

Blake chased after him. "I'm being serious, and if you're in love with her, then tell her."

Dylan groaned, scratching his head. "I can't tell her I'm in love with her."

"Why not?"

"Because..." Dylan stared out into the city. The answer wasn't that simple.

"Love is a great adventure—"

Dylan's eyes grew wide. "Oh my God, Sam has ruined you. You sound like a moron."

"Just think about it, maybe?"

Dylan nodded. "Yeah, sure, I'll think about it." Dylan wished it were as simple as Blake made it sound. But Lucy and Dylan were a math problem that didn't add up. She was a vibrant rainbow that graced the sky after a storm, and Dylan was a tornado, laying waste to everything he touched.

"Are we, uh, are we okay?" Blake ran a hand through his hair. "Cause we are about to have a house full of family for Christmas and I'm about to propose to your sister, so I need my best friend and I'm sort of freaking out here."

Dylan grinned, leaning into his best friend. "Yeah, man, we're fine. Look at us—no punch to the face this time. Looks like we're maturing and shit."

"That's absolutely awful," Blake groaned. "We're getting old."

Dylan wrapped his arms around his best friend's back and hugged him. "I'll hit ya next time if it makes you feel better, Gramps."

"We're even now though, right?" Blake asked.

"Even?"

"You caught me and Sam in the forest. I caught you in a compromising position with Lucy in the hallway. So, we can let that little thing go now?" Blake shrugged and patted him on the back.

Dylan snorted. "Fuck no. I had my tongue down her throat. That is very different from catching my sister with your di—" he started.

"Alright, alright, point taken."

"Where's that asshole brother of mine?" Dylan jumped off the couch and rushed to the door, launching into his brother's arms. It had only been three months, but Dylan really missed Jax. His brother tussled his hair and pushed him toward the ground. "The fuck's up with you?"

Dylan shoved back. "Nothing's up with me. I was just trying to get to Allison." The redhead behind his brother was smiling.

"There's my favorite Lancaster." Her open arms welcomed him with a smile.

"Hey, Allison." Dylan shoved past Jax to get to her. "Come meet Sam." He gave a dirty look to his brother as he led Allison down the hall to the kitchen, where his sister was getting the drinks together.

"Dad and Linda are right behind us with Kelley and Gretchen." Jax followed them into the kitchen.

"Who the hell is Gretchen?" Blake was standing at the end of the hall with a perplexed look on his face.

"What does that mean?" Jax asked. "You didn't know your sister brought her girlfriend?"

"Kelley has a girlfriend?" Sam asked.

"What the fuck?" Blake's voice cracked.

Hell yeah, this was going to be the best Christmas ever.

Sam sat perched on Blake's lap in the oversized chair in the corner. Things had finally died down after the drama exploded once his dad and Linda had arrived with Blake's sister and the uninvited but *"very excited to be here"* girlfriend, Gretchen.

Dylan *should* feel some sympathy for Blake. After all, his best friend had spent all week freaking out about Lucy having her tongue down a man's throat only to have an immediate *shit-the-bed* moment catching his sister feeling up her girlfriend in the bathroom ten minutes after arrival.

Karma sucked ass.

His lack of compassion was petty. Maybe Dylan would get over his encounter with his sister and Blake in the forest next year. New Year's resolutions were still a thing, right?

"So, Kelley, how's California?" Sam asked, and Dylan could almost feel Blake's grumble all the way from his spot on the floor by the window.

Kelley was leaning on the girl beside her, and Dylan didn't miss the way she smiled and laced their fingers together before she spoke. "School is amazing, but the best part is the weather, and Gretchen, of course."

"And how did we meet Gretchen?" Sam continued questioning.

Blake cut in. "And why do *we* not know about Gretchen?" Sam glared at Blake, and Dylan swore he saw her pinch him behind his back. Blake winced. "Ouch." Ah, the bliss of domesticity. Dylan shared a look with Jax, who bit his lip and snickered under his hand.

"Gretchen and I met at the coffee shop on campus. She's studying journalism."

"Is Gretchen not allowed to speak for herself, or do you just keep her locked in the bathroom?" Blake asked his sister pointedly.

"Blake!" Linda's firm voice came from the kitchen.

"Twat..." Kelley directed the insult at her brother under her breath

"I just asked a question, Mom," Blake whined, his shoulders slumping.

Gretchen rubbed Kelley's knee before she spoke. "Kelley warned me her brother was overprotective, but I don't think I was quite prepared for this."

"Welcome to the family, Gretchen," Dylan said, leaning back on his hands. His thoughts drifted across the hall to the dark-haired girl, who was having a quiet dinner with her sister tonight. As much as he enjoyed seeing his family again, he wished Lucy were here with him as well.

The thought hit him like a ton of bricks. He'd kept Lucy separate from everyone. He had wanted their relationship to stay private. It had been something selfish that he had kept to himself. But sitting around his family, enjoying the holidays, the smile on his lips didn't feel real without her.

"You look good, asshole. But did you move to New York so you could become a hippie?" Jax tugged on the unshaved facial hair on Dylan's chin.

Dylan slapped his hand. "I'll shave tonight. I've been busy." Jax shoved him against the sink, and water sprayed onto his shirt. He grabbed the towel and scrubbed it against his clothes. "And I didn't move here, you know."

"It's been three months. I just assumed." His brother shrugged. "Thought maybe you found something that made you want to stay."

Dylan thought about Lucy, and for a moment he considered it. But he didn't even know what that would mean. "Yeah, well, I can't keep sleeping on Sam and Blake's couch. Besides, after tonight..."

Shit...he tried to close his mouth, but it was too late.

"What's happening tonight?"

"Shut up." Dylan punched his brother in the arm, and Jax immediately scrubbed at it with an open hand. "Don't make a scene..." He leaned over and whispered. "Blake's gonna pop the question."

"What?" Jax's voice carried through the kitchen to the living room.

"You guys alright in there?" Sam popped her head in, and Jax and Dylan turned like raccoons who had just been caught eating trash.

"All good!"

"Everything's great!"

Sam stared at them suspiciously until Blake appeared behind her. "They're acting weird." Sam peered up at Blake, and he kissed the top of her head.

"I'll investigate," he whispered, and Sam returned to the other room. "What's up with you two?"

Jax turned and crossed his arms. "Dylan was letting me in on his little secret."

Dylan groaned, gripping the sink. "Oh, damn, I didn't think he'd tell you already. It's crazy, right? I never thought I'd see the day that Dylan fell in love." Dylan spun to face Blake with his eyes wide.

Jax's head turned on a swivel. "Hold up, you're in love?"

"Yeah...I mean..." Blake noticed the reactions and frowned. "Wait, what were you talking about?"

"You asshole, I was talking about your thing with our sister," Dylan said between gritted teeth.

The realization hit Blake suddenly. "Oh…Oh! Shit. Sorry."

Jax leaned back with a shit-eating grin and turned to stare at Dylan. "And just who the hell is my baby brother in love with?"

Blake stepped closer, lowering his voice. "I think maybe we shouldn't interrogate Dylan right—"

Jax put his hand on Blake's shoulder. "Oh no, pretty boy, don't get too excited. Your turn is coming after I sort this out with Dylan." Blake gave him an apologetic wince and cowered in the corner.

Dylan sighed. "It's not a big deal, Jax. Honestly, can we *not* talk about it?"

Blake looked at Jax and shrugged. "It is fairly new. She's pretty awesome, though. You can meet her tomorrow. We can invite her over for Christmas dinner."

"Blake, you're not helping," Dylan growled.

"Come on, Dylan, I know you wanted her to come over. She and Amber are alone for the holidays, anyway." Dylan's head dropped against his chest. Lucy would have to meet his entire family in one sitting. There would be so many questions. But it would also mean he would get to spend the entire day with her for Christmas and her birthday.

"It is her birthday," he sighed in resignation.

"Shit, really? Hell, I've known her longer than you, and I didn't know that." Blake had his hands on his hips, shaking his head. "I'm a terrible friend."

"She didn't tell me. Amber did. I was actually going to do something special for her tomorrow night, just the two of us after dinner."

Jax stood quietly, watching the conversation from his place at the sink. "I don't even know what to say right now. I think I'm in shock."

"He's a changed man," Blake said proudly. Dylan stood in the middle of the floor, blinking at him. "She got him to dangle off the edge of a building. I thought there was no way after the water tower fiasco, but love is a powerful thing, man."

"Did Sam tell you that?" Dylan huffed in annoyance.

Blake chuckled. "Nah, after I caught you two making out, I started thinking back over some of the stuff Luce has been saying about this mystery friend of hers, and I realized only you could say some of the dumb shit this guy said."

"Gee, thanks."

Jax turned to Blake. "And you!" Blake flushed. "What makes you think you get to marry my sister?"

"I...uh...well, I asked your dad." Blake swallowed.

Jax narrowed his eyes. "Oh, did you now? Yet you couldn't pick up a phone and give Ole Jaxxy a call or send a text? What kind of brother are you going to be, shithead?"

Dylan held his hand over his mouth and snorted into it. Blake looked absolutely sick to his stomach. "I...I, uh."

Jax wrapped an arm around his neck and pulled his head into his chest, scrubbing his hand into his hair. "Welcome to the family for real, Forrester." With his other hand, he patted Dylan on the shoulder. "Congrats on using your heart instead of your dick for once."

"What the hell are you doing to my boyfriend?"

Everyone turned to face Sam as she walked into the room. "It's all love, Sam."

"Well, love him more gently. He needs those hands to cook."

Jax released Blake from his hold. "Is that what we're calling it now? *'Cooking'* in the bedroom."

"Fuck off, Jax." Sam kicked him, dodging him as he lunged for her. Dylan leaned against the sink, watching his siblings dance around each other as Blake tried to lift Sam off the ground and carry her to the other side of the room.

These were moments that Dylan would cherish forever.

Watching his family spend time together, calling each other out, horseplay in the kitchen like they used to do when they were kids.

When they all settled in for dinner around the table and his dad said the blessing, Dylan damn near had tears in his eyes thinking about how far they had come. Sure, they argued over who got to cut the ham, and Jax ate more than his fair share of mashed potatoes. Blake and Kelley fought through dinner about her use of the word "twat" at the table, and Gretchen proved she was more than capable of speaking up and putting Blake in his place.

There wasn't a dry eye in the house when Blake dropped to his knee, holding out the tourmaline ring that slid perfectly onto Sam's finger. Another grand adventure, he told her, because that was kind of their thing now.

He watched his dad and Linda sitting together, smiling at their children, sharing a private thought. When his dad caught his eye, he thought maybe they were both thinking the same thing. Maybe his mother and Bobby were up there somewhere, smiling down on all of them.

Chapter Twenty-Two

Lucy

It was a lazy but happy Christmas Eve. Her parents had called just before dinner to send early birthday wishes and open their Christmas presents over FaceTime. Lucy smiled politely at the annual gifting of her Christmas scarf. This year's had books sewn on it, with the words, "I stopped reading to be here." She wrapped it around her neck, striking her best pose as she walked down an imaginary catwalk to her family's applause. She only cried for twenty minutes when they hung up the phone. A personal best for her.

Lucy was still washing dishes when the knock on the door interrupted her quiet thoughts. Amber groaned as she crawled off the couch in her pajamas to open the door. Lucy returned to washing the dishes, lost in her thoughts of home.

"Lucy, your boyfriend's here." Amber dropped onto the couch as if she had just said something normal. Lucy didn't even register that she had broken a glass in the sink.

She stared at the broken glass and turned around quickly, her eyes catching Dylan's at the front door. "I... uh, um, hi." She glared at her sister as she walked past, but Amber just smiled as if she knew some secret she wasn't willing to share. Lucy closed the door behind her, leaving her alone in the hallway with Dylan.

"Merry Christmas Eve." He grinned. "You look cute." He tugged on her scarf, pulling her toward him until his lips pressed against hers. A small sound of surprise escaped her, but he quickly silenced it with a press of his tongue. She had missed him more than she had wanted to admit.

"Merry Christmas Eve." She giggled when her head hit the door and he trapped her against it with his arm. "You seem pretty happy tonight."

He shrugged. "The whole family is here. Dinner was delicious. My brother is a jackass. Oh, and Sam said yes."

"Oh my goodness, that's exciting!"

His lips grazed her forehead as he leaned against her. "Yeah, but that's not why I'm here."

Her fingers slid against his chest, hands fisting into the softness of his T-shirt. She could get used to this relaxed version of Dylan. "Mmm, then what are you here for?" She blinked her lashes at him.

"I wanted to invite you and Amber to Christmas dinner tomorrow...and before you tell me you're busy, I already know that you're not." Lucy blanched at the thought of having dinner with his entire family. It felt like an intrusion. His breath was hot against her ear as he whispered. "I can hear you thinking, Luce."

"I don't want to be a bother. The apartment is already full. And Amber and I would make it even—"

He nipped at her earlobe. "I want you there." She shivered, feeling a sudden need to press her thighs together. "You're not gonna make me beg, are you, Lucy?" Her head slipped down the wall as her legs buckled. Dylan chuckled in her ear. "Is that a yes?"

"Only because you asked so..." she gulped, glancing up to meet his eyes. "Nicely."

He kissed her neck, causing goosebumps to prickle on her arms. "See you tomorrow, Luce." And then he was gone, and Lucy could only sway slightly on her feet, trying to catch her breath.

Lucy felt both overwhelmed and full of joy at being welcomed by the Lancaster and Forrester families at Christmas. She had met Ken already, but now there was an older brother and his girlfriend. Blake's mother and sister were also very interested in her. She had never had so many eyes on her.

Dylan's hand on her knee under the table was the only thing that kept her from wanting to crawl under it and hide.

"So, Lucy, what is it you do?" Jackson had leaned over and nudged her.

"I work at a bookstore."

Dylan cleared his throat beside her. "She manages Amber too."

Lucy snorted and shook her head. "Oh, no, nothing official. I'm not that important."

"I'd never eat if you weren't around. Probably miss all my appointments, too." Amber winked at Dylan, and he raised a glass in her direction.

"She volunteers at the Mission with Blake too." Dylan leaned around her to speak to his brother. "Lucy is pretty much a saint." *What in the Scooby Doo mystery was going on with those two?*

"You can ignore them both. I work at a bookstore. I put books on shelves. That's it. I'm pretty boring, honestly."

Dylan grumbled beside her. "You do more than that."

"I'm going to put my plate in the sink." She stood up, but before she could exit the table, Dylan grabbed her plate from her hand.

"I'll take it."

She sat back down. She didn't know what had gotten into him. "I've never seen my brother act like that before." Jackson snorted. "He's damn near out of his mind for you."

"We're just friends," she corrected, running her fingers along the tip of her water glass.

"Is that so?" She could feel Jackson examining her, and she flushed slightly under his gaze.

"I like your dress, Lucy." She turned toward Jackson's girlfriend, Allison, whom she had met earlier.

"Thanks, I got it for my...Christmas. I got it for Christmas from my parents."

After all the awkwardness, the conversation flowed naturally. Allison was very pleasant to talk with. Before long, she found herself embroiled in a chat with the girls. Sam was simply glowing as Amber and Allison grilled her about her eventual wedding plans. Blake's sister, Kelley, tossed out outlandish ideas. A wedding on a ferry, getting married in the middle of a creek, and even having a dog as the best man. Lucy was having difficulty keeping up with the fast-moving conversations.

She hadn't seen Dylan for an hour and wondered where he might have disappeared to. She wouldn't put it past him to hide out on the roof in the middle of a family event if he was feeling overwhelmed.

Before she could excuse herself to go look for him, Blake tapped her on the shoulder. "Hey, Dylan asked me to give this to you."

She glanced up. Blake had a genuine smile on his face as he held a small piece of paper against her shoulder. "Oh, thanks." She got the feeling he knew what the contents held as he walked away. She unfolded the page in her lap, holding her breath as she saw Dylan's handwriting scribbled inside.

Butterfly Girl,

By now, I'm sure you are feeling overwhelmed by all the activity. I know I was.

Do you trust me?

Water St. & State St. Come find me.

Cartoon Man

Lucy exited the taxi at the cross streets on the note. Dylan was standing at the corner of Battery Park, waiting for her with a smile and a bushel of daisies. "What are you doing here?"

He smiled and reached for her hand. "Wanted to get you alone." He handed her the flowers. "These are for you." He pulled her further into the park. "Come on, I have a surprise for you."

"Where are we going?"

"Do you not understand how surprises work?" He laughed, squeezing her hand. "I haven't found the time to tell you yet, but you look really pretty tonight." His voice was soft, and Lucy got the feeling that he was nervous.

They walked further into the park, each step closer to the water, and Lucy wondered if they were going to stand at the water's edge. Maybe he wanted to see the Statue of Liberty. But then he paused and turned, and Lucy's heart stopped.

There was no way he could have known.

"Happy birthday, Lucy."

She swallowed, staring at the colorful lights dancing in front of her. "Dylan, how did you..."

"Amber told me you used to ride the carousel on Christmas Day and that this was your favorite way to spend your birthday." He stood in front of her, blocking her view of the bright pink and blue glass building. "I know it's not like the one in California, but I thought it was pretty amazing, just like you."

She launched into his arms, pressing her lips against his. It was the most special thing anyone had ever done for her. "Are we going to ride it?"

"That was the plan," he said, taking her hand and walking toward the building lit with pink and blue lights. The bright colors of the iridescent fish glowed brighter the closer they got to them. She had only been to the Seaglass Carousel once, but she never got to ride it.

"I know which one I want to ride," she whispered. "There's a butterflyfish."

"Then, Lucy Patel, let's get you to a butterflyfish."

It was the most magnificent thing she had ever done in her life, riding the Red-Lined Butterflyfish on the Seaglass Carousel on her twenty-sixth birthday.

She held her hands out on either side of her, her head held up to the sky, the biggest smile she had ever worn on her face. Lucy was the happiest she had ever been. When she looked to her right and saw Dylan sitting on a bright pink illuminated Betta fish, laughing and taking pictures of her, she knew that this was a memory she would cherish the rest of her life.

This was her romance novel. The adventures of Dylan Lancaster and Lucy Patel. She didn't know what the epilogue would hold, but she was living the story now, and she knew how she wanted this chapter to end.

Two hours later, she stood in front of her door, her heart pounding in her chest. "Do you want to come in?"

"I don't want to bother Amber."

"Amber's not home. She had a Christmas event tonight." Lucy shrugged, pushing the door open with her butt. "I'm sure she won't mind if you drink one of her beers."

Dylan seemed uncertain but followed her through the door anyway. "Water will be fine."

When she returned to the living room with two glasses in hand, he had removed his jacket. Lucy joined him on the couch. "I have one more gift for you," he said.

"Dylan, you already gave me enough," she tried to protest, but he wouldn't hear anything of it. He dug into his jacket pocket and pulled out another piece of paper.

"It's not a big deal, Luce. Just something I made for you."

She didn't know if it was possible to love someone more at that moment. There was so much insecurity and doubt in his eyes as she took the page from his hand. "Then I will cherish it forever if you made it." She unfolded it and gasped. The entire world had faded away. Staring back at her was her own face. In delicate lines and shades, Dylan had captured her in her garden, surrounded by her butterflies.

"I had to draw some of it by looking up the butterflies online, since most of them had left already, but..."

"I love it, Dylan. This is amazing." Her hand touched the page tenderly. "No one has ever done anything like this for me before. Any of it. Dylan, tonight, the carousel, my birthday...thank you."

"You're special to me, Lucy. You deserve to have a birthday that makes you feel that way." He leaned over and kissed her gently, his lips barely touching hers. "I hope you enjoyed it."

Her heart was beating so fast that she wondered if she could even say what she wanted to say to him. "I did, but..."

He leaned back and stared at her with a frown. "But what?"

"There is one more thing I want for my birthday that you could give me." Biting her lip, she touched his chest and leaned forward, breathing against his lips. "Will you have sex with me?"

She felt his body tense. "What? Lucy, no, we talked about this."

"But you did all that other stuff with me, so why won't you—"

Dylan tucked her hand in his and pushed her back toward her side of the couch. "I told you to wait for someone you are in love with, Lucy. We can't do this." He stood up and grabbed his jacket. Lucy watched him in silence. She couldn't let him leave. Not like this, not without telling him the truth. Once again, it was time for Lucy Patel to be brave.

"That's why you're the only one who can do this." Her voice was timid, and she stared at her hands before looking up. He was staring at her, his face blank and difficult to read. She stood up, closing her eyes before taking a deep breath. "I want it to be with you, Dylan Lancaster, because I love you."

He shook his head. "No, Lucy, you can't." His voice was shaking as he tried to look away. "Please, I don't deserve you. I'm a broken man."

"I don't care." She placed her hand on his chest. "I love every shattered piece of your soul. And even if you never figure out how to put all the pieces back together, I'll still love you just the same. Because I love you, Dylan. I love every single piece of your anxious, angry, beautiful, perfect soul."

There was a beat of silence, and Lucy was afraid he was going to leave, because he just stared at her. Then he blinked, and his hand was in her hair, looking at her like she was a piece of glass that might shatter in his hands. "Say it again."

She smiled. "I love you, Dylan."

He inhaled and nuzzled his face into her neck. "Are you sure you want this?" He kissed her ear. "You need to be sure, Lucy."

She closed her eyes, running her hands through his hair, smiling as he shivered. His hands dug into her waist, clinging to her for dear life. "I want *you*, Dylan. More than books, more than butterflies. I want this. I've never been more sure of anything in my life."

He lifted her hands, kissing her palms. "We need condoms."

Lucy's eyes went wide as she realized the one flaw in her plan, but then she smiled. "Amber." Dylan's eyes narrowed as she turned and rushed toward her sister's room. She dug through the side table beside her bed. Amber always kept a stash in here. She had seen them when she was putting away her things. "Ah ha!" She claimed the box and held it above her head triumphantly. She turned and found Dylan leaning against the doorframe, staring at her. "I found them."

She handed him the box, and he bounced it in his hand before once again meeting her eyes. "Come on." She swallowed nervously and followed him toward her room. Her legs felt like they were full of concrete the moment he opened her bedroom door and closed it behind her. It wasn't like this was unfamiliar territory for them. He'd touched her before, put his fingers inside her, hell, he'd had his mouth on her last time they were alone. But now, standing in front of him in the moonlight of her room, she felt anxious and unprepared. He reached for her, and she flinched.

"Hey, we don't have to do this."

She shook her head and leaned against his chest. "No, I want this. I really want this. I'm just nervous and a little scared."

He bent over, meeting her eyes. "It's just me, just Lucy and Dylan."

"What if..." she buried her face in his chest. "What if I'm not good at it? What if it's not what you're used to?"

He lifted her chin, and her heart stopped. "Lucy, I honestly don't want this to be like anything I've ever done before. For me, my world splits into two things after tonight. Before you, and after. And right now, making sure this is perfect for you is all that matters to me."

"Yeah, but I don't know what to do and—"

He placed a finger over her lips. "We'll do it together, you and me. Trust me, there isn't any way you could do this wrong. You drive me crazy. I've been thinking about this for longer than you can imagine."

"You have?"

He growled, and Lucy swore the temperature in the room rose twenty degrees. He drug her hand down his body, pressing her palm against his groin, which was solid against her hand. "I'm doing everything I can to calm down for you." She stroked him through his pants, and he pulled her hand away. He chuckled breathlessly. "Nope, that is not helping." When she jutted her bottom lip out into a pout, he pulled it between his teeth, sucking it into his mouth.

It was her turn to moan. It happened quickly. Dylan's hand slipped under her dress, pulling it over her body and tossing it somewhere in the room.

The cold air reminded her she was standing in her bra and underwear. She had been intimate with Dylan, but she had never been fully naked in front of him. Knowing that she was two flimsy pieces of clothing away from full frontal nudity terrified her, yet she wanted to own the moment. She needed him to know that she had no doubts about being with him. She stepped back, unclasping her bra and letting it drop to the ground. Dylan sucked in a breath. She closed her eyes and hooked her fingers into her panties and shoved them toward the ground, stepping out of them before straightening up to face him.

Dylan was staring at her like he'd never seen a woman naked before. "God, you're perfect."

"Stop it." She blushed, forcing her arms to stay at her side.

His arms wrapped around her waist, and his mouth nipped at her collarbone. "Lucy, I'm so hard right now, I think I might die. You are the most beautiful woman I've ever seen."

She giggled and pushed his hair from his forehead. "You are either the best liar I've ever met, or really sweet."

He looked like she had just slapped him. "I would never lie to you."

"Alright." It was breathtaking, having a man say these things to her while she stood naked in front of him. "I don't know what to do now," she whispered.

"Lie down on the bed." She gulped, but did as she was told. She reminded herself to breathe while he smirked at her as he yanked the shirt over his head. Lucy could get used to having her own strip show. He unzipped his pants and shoved them to the ground. His boxers did nothing to hide his obvious arousal. When he discarded them, she almost choked on her tongue. She had wrapped her hands around him, had peeked while stroking him, but seeing him now, knowing where he intended to put the enlarged appendage now fully erect between his legs, suddenly she felt weak.

"That's going to fit?"

He smirked and lay down next to her. "It's going to fit, Lucy." He rolled on top of her, brushing her hair away from her face. "Relax, I promise I'll take care of you." The kiss pressed to her forehead relaxed her, easing her into the pillow as he settled over her. "I want to take my time and do it right."

She squirmed. "Can't you just, I don't know, put it in and get it over with?"

He lowered his head and shook with a laugh. "No, Lucy Patel, I will not just put it in and get it over with." His lips flattened against her breast, and Lucy arched into him. Her body felt alive with every touch of his mouth and hands. "When I put it in you, I want you to feel everything."

"Then, what do I..."

His lips found hers, soft and slow. "Shh. I want to savor this." She bit her lip, silencing herself. His hand slid down her body, heat pressed to flesh as his palms skidded roughly between her legs. His fingers slid inside her, a soft moan leaving her mouth. Her head tipped back, allowing Dylan's mouth to fit neatly against her neck. She was vibrating everywhere. His mouth was on her neck, his fingers inside of her, his thumb pressing firmly against her most sensitive spot. She felt herself floating.

Dylan was whispering against her skin, kissing a trail down her body until Lucy cried out, gripping the sheets and arching off the bed.

Dylan's cheek was against her thigh, placing a kiss against the softest spot of her skin. She lifted her head and smiled down at him. "I take it back." His brow raised as he crawled up her body. "I think I love you even more than I thought possible."

He smirked. "Yeah?" He leaned over the bed and grabbed a foil packet from the table. "You're still sure about this? Because if you've changed your mind, that's okay too. We don't have to do anything more than this if that's what you want."

Lucy could feel him hard between her thighs. She reached up and ran her hands through his hair, pulling him against her. "I want you. Make love to me, Dylan."

Chapter Twenty-Three

Dylan

Everything about this moment with Lucy felt different. Each touch, quiet murmurs against flesh, every swipe of his tongue, was like coming home. Like safety.

Lucy loved him. She loved Dylan Lancaster from Titusville, Pennsylvania, and she didn't care about the parts of him he hated. In fact, she loved those parts, too.

Not that sex in the past was lacking—sex was sex. An orgasm wasn't something you ever hated or turned away. But being loved was something entirely different. It transformed even the smallest intimacy into something bigger, more meaningful.

Dylan wasn't nervous about his first time with a woman. The women he was with usually left his bed satisfied. Knowing that Lucy had never been with a man before added a layer, an almost terrifying requirement. He needed to make sure she enjoyed her first time.

The only time he'd been with a virgin was his own first time, and that had been clumsy and unremarkable. It didn't even rank in his own top ten. In fact, he'd rather forget it if he were honest. His nerves were so intense his first time, he had trouble putting on the condom and didn't last long enough to make the cost of the latex worth it.

This night needed to be perfect. He wanted it to be everything she had read about in her books.

She was staring up at him, fluttering her lashes, biting her bottom lip, and trusting him with everything—body, soul, heart. He rolled on a condom, then met her eyes as he settled into the space between her legs. "I don't know if this will hurt or not. We'll take it slow, alright, and you tell me when to stop."

She nodded, her bottom lip snagged between her teeth, her beautiful eyes blinking at him. If she kept that up, he was going to need to close his eyes and start thinking about changing the oil in some beat-up truck before he ruined it for her. He reached down, his fingers slipping through the wetness between her legs. She moaned and pinched her eyes shut. When he finally slid himself inside her, it was a feeling he couldn't describe. She grunted beneath him, and he had to force himself to still. "Are you alright?" he gritted out, his jaw clenched tight.

She shook her head, her eyes wide. "I...oh..." He bent his head, breathing heavily against her shoulder. The sensation to move was almost too much. His eyes pinched shut. "Move, Dylan," she said, running her hand through his hair. "I'm fine."

It was slow, moving his hips forward, biting back the groan he wanted to release into her ear. When his hips met hers, he was panting, his heart racing. He held her head in his hand, kissing just below her ear. "Luce, are you..." He needed to catch his breath. "Are you sure you're alright?"

He kissed her cheek, his mouth pecking each inch of her jaw until it rested against the corner of her mouth. He opened his eyes and found her staring back at him. She nodded, the corner of her lip arching into a smile. The hand in his hair gripped him, pulling him against her mouth. It started slowly, but with each touch of her lips, each swipe of her tongue, the intensity grew until her leg hitched against his own.

Dylan slid out of her slowly and then found a rhythm that had them both moaning softly. He heard his name whispered, and he was sure that at some point she had uttered a curse word, which brought a smile to his face. Sweat was dripping from his forehead. The grip on her hip was firm as his thrusts grew more erratic with each soft murmur of his name. And with her eyes on him, one hand on his shoulder, another on his heart, he cried out her name the moment he felt his climax overtake him. He thrust into her once more, as if finally understanding the meaning of the word home.

When he settled beside her, it was the first time in years that his body and his mind finally felt at peace.

She was staring at the ceiling when he returned from cleaning up. He climbed into bed beside her and traced his fingers across her collarbone. He swallowed before he spoke. "Penny for your thoughts, Lucy."

"I'm just...processing." She turned toward him, touching his cheek. "I mean, I've read a lot of books about this." His heart was racing. "I was terrified it was going to hurt a lot. And I suppose at first it did, but..."

"I feel like I'm back in school and you are grading my book report, and I'm afraid of the grade you're about to give me."

Lucy leaned over and kissed him. "You were amazing, Dylan. It was way better than anything I had ever read before." She lay back on the pillow and smiled at him. "I think when I read it in the books, I was always trying to figure out how it was supposed to work. I understood the basics, of course, but the mechanics of it all confused me. I used to lie on my bed and act it out."

Dylan snorted. "I'm gonna need you to show me that sometime."

"Absolutely not." She slapped his shoulder. "I just never expected to feel so...connected to you. Obviously, in the physical sense, duh. But, in here." She held her hand to his heart, and Dylan cupped a hand over hers. "Is it always like that?"

"No." Dylan touched her cheek. "I've never felt what I felt with anyone the way it felt with you."

She snuggled into his arms, and he rested his chin on the top of her head. "I love hearing that. It makes me feel special."

"You are special, Lucy."

"Yeah, I know you keep saying that, but it's different. I don't know. I don't think you understand. It's different with you. I feel like I can tell you anything. Things I wouldn't tell anyone else." Dylan closed his eyes as her fingers brushed through his hair. When he opened them, she was watching him with a sense of wonder. "I love how you react to me touching your hair."

He chuckled. "If you must know, it drives me ridiculously insane." He tapped her nose with his finger. "So, tell me something you've never told anyone else."

She scrunched her nose and pinched her eyes shut. "I want to own a cat, but I'm not allowed to because Amber is allergic, but...I have one hidden at the bookstore. I'm hoping one day I can take her home."

Dylan's mouth dropped. "Lucy Patel!"

"I know, and I think Jared is on to me." She frowned. "I don't know how much longer I can hide Penelope before she gets thrown out onto the streets."

Dylan kissed her ever so tender, allowing his lips to memorize the contours of her mouth. It was the sort of kiss that said, *"I adore you,"* because he did. Hiding a secret cat was exactly what Lucy would do. Looking at her, lying naked on top of her bright yellow and orange bedsheets, he knew there would be nothing he could ever hide from this woman.

"Can I tell you something?"

"Always...Yes, please." She grinned.

"You know the cartoons I've been drawing?" She nodded, her eyes glowing in the moonlight. "They're based on my family, mostly my siblings. Sam, she had this bunny when she was little, Mr. Jangles, and Jax—we always called him Grumpy Gus, this angry little cat. Sam, she had this dumb nickname for me."

Lucy giggled. "Are you the little bear with the rainbow colors?"

He growled and nodded. "Yeah, that's Dilly Bear. I just...I've been writing some stories about when we were kids. It's the dumbest idea I've ever had. It's never going to go anywhere but—"

"I think it's amazing. Why wouldn't it go somewhere?"

"It's not really that good, I guess. It's just something I do when I'm anxious or missing my family. I'm grasping at straws, you know, cause I can't keep riding my sister's couch forever."

Lucy frowned. "Oh, are you, uh, are you going back to Titusville soon?"

"I haven't decided what I'm going to do." He wrapped his arm around her and pulled her against his chest. "But I also don't want to worry about that right now."

"And what would you like to do instead?" She grinned.

Dylan kissed her lips, smiling against them. "You know what's better than having sex for the first time on your birthday?" She giggled and shook her head. "Having sex for the second time on your birthday."

Dylan rolled over to grab the box of condoms. He was determined to make this the best birthday she had ever had, and with each passing minute, he realized that his home in Pennsylvania was no longer the place he wanted to be.

Home was with Lucy.

Dylan woke up before Lucy the next day. He watched her as she slept under the bright covers, her hand folded under her cheek, her hair sticking up wildly around her, her feet jutting out the bottom of the sheets. She was chaos and beauty, and everything he wanted for the rest of his life.

He wasn't sure how he was going to stay in New York City. It wasn't as if he had a job. He had no way to support himself and nowhere to stay. But he loved Lucy, and he wanted to be here and make it work. But he also knew he didn't want to tell her until he was sure he'd figured out how to do that.

He slipped out of the apartment and headed back to Blake and Sam's for breakfast. As soon as he entered the apartment, he smelled bacon cooking.

"I hope that's the Blake special!" Dylan rounded the corner, only to be met by his brother Jackson.

"Well, look what the cat dragged in."

"Where is everyone?" Dylan asked, tossing his jacket onto the chair. "I expected Blake would have breakfast ready by now."

"Actually, everyone went out for breakfast." He flipped the strip of bacon in the pan. "I elected to stay back, you know, in case the prodigal son showed up."

Dylan grabbed the orange juice out of the refrigerator and poured two glasses. "Guess I should have expected someone would notice my absence."

"Oh, we all had quite the conversation last night." Jax raised an eyebrow. "Do you want to know who placed bets on your joining the circus and which one of us thinks you've already got a family of children you're supporting upstate?"

"I spent the night with Lucy." Dylan sighed, leaning against the counter.

"Yeah, that was my bet." He chuckled. "I like her. She's adorable."

"Go on, say what you really want to say," Dylan said, crossing his arms, trying not to get defensive.

Jax pushed the skillet away from the stove and turned it off. "Just what I said. I like her. Don't get so defensive. I've just never seen your head so in the clouds over a chick before. I suppose it's kind of nice."

"It's different with Lucy. She makes me feel different. When I'm with her, I start thinking crazy thoughts, stuff I never thought I'd consider before. You know. Things like, like..."

"Like not coming home?"

Dylan exhaled and stared at his feet. "Yeah." He looked up and met Jax's eyes. "But that's nuts, right? What would I even do in New York? I can't live here, but what's the point of coming home? I'm a terrible mechanic. Still, how would I even survive in the city?"

"You figure it out, one day at a time. That's what love is."

"Is that how you do it? With Allison."

Jax laughed. "There were so many reasons for things not to work between me and Allison. She and I are from different worlds, yet we make it work. There are sacrifices. I eat a hell of a lot more kale than I want to, which is none! And she gave up heels and the city to

work in grease and the country. But there isn't a day it's not worth it
"

"Yeah, but you own your own business. You can provide for her."

Jax studied him for a moment. "Do you love her? Not just superficial, not just because your dick wants to fuck her?"

"Lucy and I—we...we didn't, we never, I mean, we didn't until last night. I wouldn't have if she hadn't told me she felt the same way." Dylan's jaw clenched.

Jax held his hands up defensively. "It was just a question."

"Yes, I really love her, Jax."

Jax patted his shoulder with a soft smile. "Then make it work, brother."

Chapter Twenty-Four

Lucy

Lucy stretched her arms and yawned, peering through the slits in her eyes. She rolled onto her back and immediately felt an aching soreness between her legs. Absentmindedly, she reached between them and scrunched her nose. The moment she touched herself, her eyes flew open, and she looked over at the other side of her bed. The ruffled bedsheets and the abandoned pillow showed signs of being slept on, but Dylan was gone.

She brushed her hand over the pillow, remembering the night they had shared. It had been so much more than she had expected. Dylan was patient, gentle, and so sexy. She swore at one point she melted into the mattress. He had ruined romance novels for her, or at the very least enhanced them. She no longer had to hump her pillow anymore, trying to imagine the positions.

A grim thought swept over her. What if Dylan went back to Titusville now? She hugged the pillow to her chest, breathing in the scent he had left behind. How was she supposed to go back to *the Lucy who read about love in books* now that she had held it in her arms?

She pushed her hair out of her face and crawled out of bed, searching the floor for a pair of pajamas to put on. When she stumbled out of her room, Amber was already in the bathroom. Lucy waited in the hall for her turn, and when her sister emerged, she stopped in front of her. "Well, hello to you." Amber leaned against the doorway. "I got in pretty late, but it seems like the party was in your room."

Lucy felt her cheeks heat. "Um, I didn't hear you come in last night."

"I'm sure you didn't with all that noise you two were making. But good for you!"

She covered her face with her hands. "Oh God. Please don't make a big deal about it."

"I'd ask you how it was, but..." Her back was to her as she headed to the kitchen. "I think the *'Oh God Dylan, yes'* shrieks were enough to tell me it was pretty damn good."

"Oh my God, was I that loud?" Lucy chased after her.

She made a mental note to add a new rule to her guidebook. *Rule #124: Never have sex within a five-mile radius of other human beings.*

"Enough to wake half the neighbors, I'm sure. I bet his whole family even heard you." Lucy couldn't imagine ever facing his family again. The horror of knowing that anyone heard her having sex was enough to keep her locked in her room for life. "Luce, I'm just joking. I only heard you because I'm in the next room, and frankly, I was jealous as hell. I tried to jump his bones plenty of times, and he turned me down because he's crazy in love with you."

"No, he's not." Lucy laughed. Dylan hadn't actually told her he loved her last night. Sure, *she* said she loved him, and he slept with her because that was part of the requirement he gave her. She knew Dylan liked her a lot and thought she was special. But if he loved her, he would have told her that. *Right?!*

"Lucy, he's in love with you."

"Amber, stop. Dylan isn't in love with me. And that's okay," she said, trying not to let her voice stutter as she said it. "He knows how I feel about him, but he's probably going back home anyway, so I just...I don't want to talk about it."

She turned and rushed into the bathroom, letting her head fall against the door as soon as she closed it behind her.

Lucy hadn't seen Dylan since her birthday. She had to work the day after, since it was always busy at the store after Christmas Day. Dylan was busy with family the next few nights, and Lucy tried to stay busy doing other things. When Blake knocked on her door and asked if she wanted to volunteer, she jumped at the offer.

"I never got the chance to congratulate you privately." Lucy had her hands shoved into her hoodie as they walked toward the Mission. "It's been so busy since Christmas."

"Thanks, Luce. I've never been so happy knowing I'm about to get married and maybe get to have a family." She watched as Blake's eyes seemed to crinkle as he smiled. He seemed genuinely over the moon about the next stage of his life.

"I'm glad. Do you think you and Sam will stay in the apartment?"

Blake shrugged. "I've been talking to Allison. She's a real estate analyst, so she knows a lot about this stuff, and she's trying to help me find a place outside the city. Not right away, but eventually, you know. After the wedding."

"I'm happy for you—and Sam, of course." She would miss Blake most of all. She'd always wanted a brother, and Blake had been the closest she had come. "I'll miss you at the potlucks and stuff."

He frowned. "Hey, you know we'll stay friends, right?"

"Yeah, sure." She smiled, but looked away. That was the sort of thing everyone said when they left and never called again.

Blake chuckled. "With Dylan being practically attached to your hip, it's not like we won't see each other."

"Until he moves back home," she sighed.

They walked silently until they got to the Mission, and Blake yanked the door open. "He hasn't said anything about moving back, has he?"

"Not directly, no." She frowned and stared at him. "Has he mentioned it to you?"

He shook his head. "No. But Dylan isn't exactly big on sharing information."

"Yeah," she sighed. "He's a pain in the ass."

Blake's eyes widened. "Did I just hear you swear for the first time by besmirching my best friend's name?"

Lucy held her hand over her mouth and laughed. "Maybe. But we love him anyway, right?"

Blake's brow lifted, and the hint of a smile grew on his face. Lucy realized she had told him something she hadn't meant to. But this time, Blake didn't seem upset about it. Instead, he laughed. "Yeah, I guess we do."

When they returned that evening from the Mission, she had hoped to find Dylan at the apartment, but found Sam, Kelley, and Allison sitting in the living room laughing about something that had happened earlier in the day instead. Lucy left her coat on, determined to head back to her place, when Sam asked her to join them. She hated to be rude, so she found herself nestled between Dylan's sister and his brother's girlfriend, trying to keep up with the conversation.

"Have they always been that stubborn, or did they just grow into it naturally?" Allison asked Sam.

Sam snorted, tipping back a beer. "Oh heavens, I think both boys came out of our mother refusing their milk bottles and reaching for a beer."

"You act like you aren't marrying one just like him," Kelley said, tossing one of the chair pillows at Sam. "My brother is just as stubborn as Dylan."

"I think all men are just difficult and have problems communicating what they want." Lucy's voice was timid and soft, and everyone turned to face her.

Kelly whistled. "Your mouth to my ears, girl. That's why I date women."

"I think my brother knows exactly what he wants." Sam arched her brow and leaned into her.

"He was putting off some pretty serious mating vibes," Allison chimed in beside her.

Lucy wanted to disappear under the couch. "Dylan and I are—"

"Girl, you don't have to explain it to us," Kelley interrupted. "Trust me, you and Dylan are a breath of fresh air compared to what I had to put up with Sam and Blake. I needed a bucket of ice water with them." Sam shot her a dirty look.

"I think Dylan deserves something good after the year he's had." Allison patted her knee.

"Really, though, Dylan and I are just...well, I don't really know exactly what we are." She frowned.

All three women sighed until Allison spoke. "Ah, welcome to the club of women who love Lancaster men, Lucy. We're a tough breed. You need to be strong enough to handle their stubborn streaks, maintain a sense of humor to deal with their mood swings, and be brave enough to call them out when they're wrong."

"My brothers can be difficult, but I promise you, they are worth it," Sam smiled.

"Speak for yourself. My brother is a pain in the ass. Best of luck on your wedding, Sam." The girls laughed, and Lucy settled onto the couch, letting the girls continue with the conversation. She could see herself being friends with these girls. It was a thought that made her happy. Having friends was something she had wanted her entire life.

Hours later, when Jackson and Blake came crashing through the door with four boxes of pizza and two six-packs of beer, she started getting concerned when Dylan wasn't with them. It had been four days now since she had seen Dylan, and this was feeling more like Dylan avoiding her again rather than him being too busy to see her.

Lucy offered to clean up the living room, picking up blankets and pillows to make room for everyone to sit when she kicked over a stack of books in the corner. When she picked them up, she recognized them immediately as Dylan's sketchbooks. She flipped through the pages, admiring the work he had been doing on his stories for Mr. Jangles, Grumpy Gus, and Dilly Bear. The tales drawn on these pages were more than just the rambling thoughts of some anxiety-driven attack. Dylan failed to grasp how smart, funny, and wonderful they really were.

"Hey there, Sunshine." Jumping, she turned to find Jackson standing behind her. "Sorry, didn't mean to startle you."

She held the sketchbook behind her back. "You didn't—I just, I thought I was alone." She tilted her head. "You haven't seen Dylan, have you?"

"He was out with our dad and Linda tonight, I think."

"Oh, I just haven't seen him for a few days." She tried not to frown, but she could tell she had failed the moment Jackson looked at her.

"Woah, hey there, Sunshine, don't worry. I'm sure he'll be home soon." He sat down on the couch. "You really love the little asshole, don't you?"

Lucy narrowed her eyes and pinched her lips together. "Must you call him names?"

"Woah! I meant no harm." He looked at the spot on the couch beside him. "Sit down, I promise. I don't bite."

Lucy was hesitant to sit, but she had nowhere else to go, so she dropped into the seat, placing the sketchbooks on the floor, back in their hiding space. "I just think you should be nicer to him. Calling him an..." She lowered her voice. "Asshole...isn't conducive to his feeling good about himself."

"Wow, alright then, fair point."

"Your brother loves you, but I think sometimes he feels like he's never going to be as good as you. I disagree with that thought because I already think Dylan is the most creative and amazing person I know. But Dylan looks up to you and Sam, and I think he worries he'll never be smart or successful enough to stack up to you two. And if he's going to go home, I need someone to show him he's enough just being who he is. So I want you to promise me you'll be that person."

Jackson stared at her, his brow furrowed, a stiffness in his jaw. "You know, Lucy, I liked you before, but now..." Lucy gulped. "Now you just might be my most favorite person in the world."

"What's going on in here?"

Lucy's eyes met Dylan's, and she felt her heart speed up. "Hey."

"Lucy and I were just getting to know each other better," Jackson said, patting her knee and standing up from the couch. He walked past his brother, patting him on the shoulder. "Everything good?" Dylan nodded and then they were alone.

"Hey." They stared at each other, and Lucy wasn't sure if she was nervous or angry that he had been avoiding her. She stared at her hands as the couch dipped beside her. "How's work been?"

Small talk? He wanted to discuss work after disappearing for days after taking her virginity and making her feel the happiest she had ever felt in her life.

"Busy..." Her voice trailed off as she stared down at her hands, her heart beating like a drum in her chest.

"Yeah, me too." His foot was bouncing anxiously next to hers on the wooden floor. The silence between them was killing her. As if understanding all of that without speaking, he slid his hand across the couch onto her lap. It was hard not to smile as he took her fingers and laced them between the hollows of his own. "I missed you." Locks of hair hid her face from his as she stared down at their hands.

With a tilt of her head, she peered at him through darkened strands. "Alright, maybe I missed you a teensy little bit." The nervous pounding in her chest slowed as his face lit up, and the anxious bounce of his leg ceased. It was as if they were each other's peace, a calm in the storm. They remained that way until the call for pizza came from the kitchen. It was pizza, after all.

Dylan remained by her side the rest of the evening, holding her hand, touching her back. Although he was always nearby, she sensed a barrier between them. Something she knew he wasn't telling her. It was in the way he smiled at her, or the way he kissed her knuckles when she told him about the new book she was reading. It was the something behind his eyes that said, "Maybe later."

When she said her goodbyes, Blake told her Dylan was on the roof with Jackson. She made the climb up the stairs to find him. When she pushed open the door, there were voices. Lucy knew it was rude to eavesdrop. She wouldn't normally do it, but something had been sitting on her mind all night. Those little hairs on the back of her neck that stood on end when she felt danger. So she stayed behind the door a little longer.

"I think the job's gonna be good for you, Dylan. I mean, you were right. You can't just stay on Sam's couch forever." Her heart sank at the sound of Jackson's voice.

Dylan seemed happy as he spoke. *"Yeah, I start right after the New Year. I think this will be a fresh start for me, and at least it's not oil changes."*

"You hated the garage. This is gonna be nicer." Jackson paused. *"But, uh, you need to tell Lucy."* Lucy put her hand to her mouth, trying not to make a sound.

"I want to, I just..." Dylan's voice trailed off and Lucy felt her heart breaking.

"She cares about you a lot. You don't want to keep her in the dark about it." Lucy nodded. She knew she liked Jackson. *"She already has her suspicions that you're leaving town."*

"I'm not trying to keep her in the dark, but I also don't want to upset her by letting her in on the news until everything is official." Dylan sighed. *"It's been hard not to tell her all of this for the last few days."*

Lucy leaned against the wall. So that was why he hadn't been talking to her. He'd been planning to leave, and he didn't want her to know about it because he didn't want to upset her.

"And what about the sketchbooks?"

"That's all done." Lucy gasped and put her hand over her mouth. She rushed down the stairs and back toward the apartment. She couldn't let Dylan give up all his dreams and talent.

She knocked on the apartment door, and Blake answered. "Hey, Luce, did you find Dylan?"

"Um, yeah, I just left my bag in the living room."

"Oh, sure, everyone is still cleaning up." She rushed past Blake and into the living room. The books were sitting right where she had left them by the couch. Without thinking, she gathered them up and stuffed them into her bag. Draping the bag over her shoulder, she rushed to the door.

"Thanks for the pizza, Blake. See you guys later."

"Bye, Luce."

She walked back to her apartment with a new determination. If Dylan wasn't going to let the world see his talent, she was going to take his talent to the world.

Chapter Twenty-Five

Dylan

"And what about the sketchbooks?" Jax asked with a smile on his face.

"That's all done." Dylan had only told Jax about the sketches a few days ago, and his brother had been over the moon, even proud of him. "I have a meeting with the guy right after New Year's. Can you believe someone might actually make those stupid drawings into a book?"

"Yeah, bro. They are smart, funny, and that Grumpy Gus is kind of sexy."

"He's a cat in a children's book, Jax. He's not sexy." Dylan patted his brother on the shoulder and leaned against the table.

"Agree to disagree."

"Hey, you two. I was wondering where you ran off." The brothers turned to greet their father, who joined them on the roof. "Party's over. I gotta get Linda and the girls back to the hotel."

"Yeah, Dad's been having a sleepover with his old high school sweetheart," Jax announced, and Dylan observed their dad shift on his feet.

His dad chuckled and coughed. "It was the right thing to do. No one expected Kelley to show up with a girlfriend in tow. She needed a place to crash, and my room had two beds. Linda and I are adults. Why don't you two knuckleheads try acting like one for a change?"

"Wow, Dad, thanks for the advice," Jax groaned. "I think my childish ass is gonna go collect my girlfriend and head out so we can play with our Pokémon cards."

Dylan chuckled as his brother stomped off like a pompous ass, leaving him alone with his father. "How you doin', kid?"

"Honestly..." His face lit up like a Roman candle. "I'm nervous but excited. I've kind of felt like throwing up all night, though."

The cold air was visible as his dad exhaled through his nose, a chuckle bouncing from his throat. "I'm proud of you, kid."

"I haven't done anything yet."

"You found something you wanted, and you're going for it. That's what matters," Dylan thought about everything he had accomplished in the last week. Going to the bookstore to talk to Jared was a risk. But Lucy was worth it.

Jared had been a wealth of information to talk to about what to do next. He hadn't expected the topic of his drawings to come up. Jared had mentioned he worked in comic book illustration for a time, and one thing led to another, and before he knew it, he was sharing his idea for the children's book. Jared suggested he speak to the owner of the bookstore, who apparently knew a guy in publishing. It was hard doing it all behind Lucy's back, but he didn't want to get her hopes up in case he couldn't stay in New York.

"I don't even know if anything will come out of the meeting."

"You're still giving it a shot, and that's what matters." His dad paused. "Your mom would be so very proud, kid."

Dylan bit the inside of his cheek, staring off into the distance. "I hope so...I miss her."

"Me too, kid. I think I always will."

Dylan glanced at his dad and raised his brow. "So...what about this woman you were talking about when you were here last?"

He didn't miss the way his dad blinked and bowed his head. "Oh, yeah, you know, love is one of those things."

"One of what things?" Dylan grinned.

"When you find something, you hold on to it with both hands, and you don't let go, kid. Sometimes you don't get second chances in life, so when a good thing comes around, take the chance."

Dylan narrowed his eyes. "That is excellent advice, Dad. But I also notice it does nothing to answer my question about the woman."

"Maybe some other time, kid. Right now, I just want you to focus on yourself."

Dylan left the roof in search of Lucy. Things had been awkward between them, and he knew that was his fault. This entire week he'd been making moves to stay in New York, throwing spaghetti at the wall, hoping something would stick, but he'd left her out of it for fear none of it would work and he'd end up leaving her in the end. He couldn't bear to break her heart.

That was why he went to Jared for help. Jared found him a job at this hole in the wall art gallery near the bookstore with a friend of his. It didn't pay much, but the guy needed someone who was interested in art, who was also strong enough to help carry in some of the artwork on the weekend and help set up the shows. Dylan thought it was a perfect fit and jumped at the opportunity.

Jared also offered him a place to stay for a few months until he could get his feet under him. He had a spare room no one was using, and it wasn't far from the bookstore and the gallery, so it would mean he could see Lucy after work.

He hoped it would be the best New Year's Eve surprise ever. He planned to decorate the roof and invite Lucy to join him. Then all he had to do was tell her how much she meant to him, and yeah...That's how romance novels work, right?

When Blake told him she had already gone to her apartment, he rushed to her door and knocked. Amber answered the door and groaned. "Great. Are you two going to keep me up again?"

Dylan smirked. "I brought you a present." He tossed her a box of unopened condoms. "To replace the ones we took from your room."

"Whatever, just keep it down in there."

He smirked and left her standing at the door. "Night, Amber." He made his way to Lucy's room, his heart fluttering the closer he got. His life had changed so much since coming to New York City. Since Lucy. He knocked on the door, and he heard her rustling behind it.

"Go away, Am. I'm not in the mood for Top Model tonight."

He peeked his head in the door and frowned. "What about annoying guys from Titusville?"

She screeched and held the covers over her face. "Dylan, what are you doing here?"

"I felt bad for not seeing you this week, thought I'd stop by and make it up to you." He grinned and leaned against the door frame. "Unless you want me to go."

"No!" He chuckled at her eagerness. Slipping in the door, he shut it behind him.

"Amber says we have to be quiet."

Lucy hid under the covers. "Oh God, I'm never leaving my room again." Dylan ducked beneath the blankets and lay next to her, running his fingers along her jaw.

"I like it when you're loud, but we can just lie here if that makes you more comfortable."

She frowned and rolled onto her side, her hands fisting into his shirt. Her eyes swept up his chest until they reached the spot under his chin. "Dylan, you'd tell me if something was wrong, wouldn't you?"

He swallowed, wondering where the question was coming from. "Of course." He lifted her chin until her eyes met his, glassy and wide. "Why do you ask?"

"No reason, I just, if you changed your mind about me, or—"

He kissed her, hoping to eliminate her worries. "When Blake told me to come to New York to get a new perspective, I'll be honest. I thought this whole thing was BS. I came to get away from home, thought maybe I'd clear my head a bit, but I never thought I'd get anything out of it. But then I met you." He pressed his lips to hers. "And in an instant..." He kissed her jaw. "My whole life changed." He nibbled on her earlobe. "Where there used to be only darkness, you came in and these little rays of sunshine filtered through." His tongue tasted the salt on her skin. "You're my sunshine, Lucy. And now my world is full of color."

She moaned, arching her back against the mattress as his hand slid into the place that made her say his name in ways that kept him up at night. When he held her, their bodies soaked in sweat, his hips pressed tightly against hers, whispering her name softly against her ear, he knew that this was going to be where he wanted to be forever. Home.

When she climbed on top of him, his dad's voice echoed in his ear.

"When you find something, you hold on to it with both hands, and you don't let go, kid."

And he did. He gripped her hips with both hands, and he didn't let go. He watched her in awe above him, his eyes focused on hers.

Her hands moved lazily across her breasts and down her body. She pulled his hands with hers up to her chest.

That night with Lucy wasn't about sex; it was about something deeper. Dylan left everything in his past behind him. None of it mattered anymore. All that mattered was his future with Lucy. When a stray tear trailed down her cheek that night, he thought she must have felt it, too.

Waking up on the sofa in his sister's apartment the next day, he popped in his earbuds and let the sounds of Noah Kahn's "No Confidence" wash over him. Today was the start of the first day of his new life in New York. There was no more thinking about the past. He was only going to look forward. He grabbed his markers and his coat, ready for some new ideas for his book before his meeting with Mr. Earnblock. However, when he went to collect his sketchbook beside the couch, it was gone.

In fact, not a single sketchbook was where he left it.

"Uh, Sam, have you seen my books? I left them by the couch." He yanked his earbuds from his ears as the panic set in.

"No, they were there the other night. I haven't touched them."

Dylan stared at the space next to the couch, his heart beating out of his chest. All his drawings, everything he had worked on for years, were missing.

Chapter Twenty-Six

Lucy

Lucy usually loved New Year's Eve. But this year, she despised it. Absolutely dreaded it. Dylan was going to take her to the roof and tell her he was moving back to Titusville. She wondered whether she could refuse to go. Maybe if she refused to hear his goodbye, it wouldn't happen.

At the New Year's Eve party, Lucy ate her weight in cookies to drown out her feelings. When they passed around the glasses of champagne, she took one from Kelley and downed it before anyone noticed. The bubbles tickled her nose as she tried to swallow the liquid discreetly.

A pair of arms slid around her waist. "Lucy, you were adorable last time you drank, right until you yelled at me, but I really need you sober tonight." Dylan's voice rumbled in her ear. She leaned against him, trying to memorize the way his body felt wrapped in hers.

"Come on, Dylan, it's New Year's." Faking enthusiasm wasn't hard for her. She'd done it for years at Amber's events. "Live a little." She squeezed his hand and pulled away from him, grabbing another glass and tipping it back, feeling the warm well of tears behind her eyelids.

Dylan's hand was on her shoulder, pulling her toward the door. "Come on, let's get out of here."

"What? No, I want to stay."

"I just need to talk to you first." She wanted to scream, to fall on the floor, kicking her feet, and beg him to stay. He had her by the hand, pulling her toward the stairs, and she was coming up with every reason to delay. "Lucy, what is wrong with you? I just want to talk to you away from the party."

"Can't it wait until later?"

Dylan shook his head and laughed. "Lucy, seriously, can we just be alone for a minute?"

As soon as they reached the roof, she dropped his hand. "I don't want to do this." Dylan flipped a switch and the entire roof lit up with twinkling lights.

"Luce, what is going on with you?"

She stared at the lights, not understanding why he would make everything so beautiful, only to stab her in the heart with the dirty reality they faced. "I don't want to talk about it, Dylan. Can't we just go back downstairs and pretend that everything is fine for one more night?"

"Come here." He reached for her, pulling her closer to him, but she yanked her hand away.

"No!"

"Lucy..."

"If you're just going to break my heart, Dylan, get it over with. Don't dress it up in whatever this is, thinking it will hurt less." She hugged herself tighter, wrapping her arms around her jacket.

"Break your heart? Lucy, I don't understand."

"I know about the job. That you're leaving me, going back to Titusville. I heard you talking to Jackson."

Dylan stared at her wide-eyed and mouth open like a fish out of water. "Lucy, that's—"

"No! Just stop before you say anything else. I also know you are planning on giving up your talent, too. And I want you to know that I won't let you do that."

"I am so confused," he whispered to himself.

"If you think I'm going to let you throw away your talent or your sketches—"

Dylan's eyes lit up. "Wait, do you have my sketchbooks?"

Lucy stepped back. "You aren't getting them back, Dylan. I won't let you—" Dylan started laughing, his hands on his knees as he bent over. She glared at him, anger settling in her stomach. "Are you laughing at me?"

He was wheezing, shaking his head as he looked up at her. "No, no, I'm sorry, I'm not laughing at you, it's just...Wow. I really am one of those dudes from your romance novels, because I have totally messed up the communication here."

Lucy just stared as he walked closer to her and pulled her toward the table. "Lucy, I'm not going back to Titusville."

"What? But I heard you; you were talking about getting a job, and Jackson was..."

"Jared got me a job at his friend's gallery around the corner. It's nothing special. I'm working the register, sweeping the floors, and helping set up the shows on the weekend."

She blinked. "Jared, I don't understand."

"I didn't want to disappoint you if it didn't work out, so I asked Jared for help. He helped me find a job, even offered me a place to live until I'm on my feet."

She felt as if she were drowning in a swirl of turbulence. Nothing was making sense. "You're...wait, you're moving in with Jared?"

"Just until I can afford my own place. I don't know how long he'll want to put up with me, honestly."

His hand was on hers, rubbing circles on top of her palm, and she stared down at it in confusion. "Why? I'm so confused, Dylan."

"Lucy, look at me." His voice was calm and firm, and she pinched her eyes closed, trying to convince herself of every reason she shouldn't look at him. Maybe it was a trick. Perhaps everything he was saying was an illusion, a lie. Why would Dylan stay in New York? She wanted it to be true with all her heart. She knew the reason she wanted him to stay, but her heart was so scared of why he was staying. "Lucy, please."

She bit her lip, the uneven breaths sending pains through her chest, but she lifted her head and turned her eyes in his direction. When she blinked, he was staring back at her, with a soft smile on his face. "Dylan, I'm terrified of what you're about to say..." she whispered.

"Don't be. You have nothing to fear from me, Luce." His palm touched her cheek.

"I'm afraid of losing you." She choked out the words, his palm held firm to the side of her face.

He knelt between her legs, bringing his face closer to hers. "Lucy Patel, ever since I met you, there has been something pulling us together. This connection is so strong even I couldn't fight it. You are my entire world. Just the thought of leaving you—well, that didn't work for me." He chuckled. "I have spent years thinking I was a failure, feeling like I would never be good enough for anyone. But all it took was one look from you and I wanted to be better." He leaned over and kissed her lips. "You make me feel like I'm Superman. Like I can do anything, be anyone."

"You can be Dylan."

"That's the thing, though. I don't want to do any of it without you. It's you and me, Lucy." He smiled, and Lucy felt her heartbeat slow. "Do you understand now? New York isn't about New York. None of this is possible without you. Because I love you."

Her heart stopped. "You...what?" She wanted to believe it, but she needed to hear it again, because it was everything she had wished to hear from him for so long.

He stood up, pulling her to her feet and wrapping his arms around her waist. "I love you, Lucy Patel. My beautiful Butterfly Girl, who has stolen my heart. I love you."

She nuzzled her cheek into his chest and squeezed. "Oh, Dylan, I love you too. I thought I lost you. I was so scared."

"Shh." His hand was in her hair, softly brushing his fingers through each strand. "I'm not going anywhere."

Looking up, she caught his eyes in the twinkling lights glowing against the night sky. "Does this mean I get to send you on more adventures now?"

He scrunched his nose and hummed. "That depends."

"On what?"

"Will my girlfriend be going with me?" His forehead touched hers, and she thought she liked the sound of that very much.

"I think I can make that happen," she said, kissing his jaw.

Dylan groaned the moment her hands slid into his hair. A gesture she realized she could do freely anytime she wanted now. He kissed her ear and moaned. "Perhaps I might have a few X-rated adventures of my own that I'd like to suggest."

"Oh, well, that seems, quite..." her knees gave out the moment his tongue hit that spot that she loved so much. My God, the things this man could do to her.

"But, uh, Lucy. I do actually need my sketchbooks back. I have a meeting with Mr. Earnblock this week." Lucy stopped moving, yanking her head from Dylan's face.

"You what?"

"Jared set it up for me. He wants to talk about the children's book."

She blinked once, wondering if she had misheard him, but he was still smiling, and she knew she had understood him just fine. A smile grew on her face. "Dylan, that's—oh my God." She tackled him and they tumbled to the ground. She hovered over him, staring at him through wet lashes. "I'm so proud of you."

"I haven't done anything yet. It's just a meeting."

"You took a risk, all on your own."

He squinted his eyes and smiled. "I suppose I did."

She licked her lips and swept her eyes down his body, biting on the tip of her finger. "I should reward you for doing that. Care to teach me something new?" She ran her hands down his chest until they rested on the edge of his pants. His eyes went wide. She tugged on the button, popping it free. She slid her body down his legs until her face was even with his zipper. "Shall we get him out?" She tapped the growing bulge in his pants with her finger.

"Here? Right now? What if someone comes..." Dylan looked around the roof with wide eyes.

"Don't you want to teach me, Dylan?"

Her bottom lip jutted out, and she could feel the moment he gave up the willpower to resist her. Dylan ran his fingers over her mouth, his eyes lost in the way her lips opened and her tongue slid out to lick his finger. He groaned once before unzipping his pants and pushing them over his hips. "Fuck, it's cold."

She slid her hands over him. "Let me warm you up."

He moaned as he rested on his elbows, staring down at her. "Fuck, Luce."

"Language, Dylan." She gripped him in her hand and stroked up and down his shaft until her fingers touched the tip, enjoying the way his eyes glazed over. "Do I just..." She looked up with a sweet smile and opened her lips. "Put my mouth on him?" The moment she took him in her mouth, Dylan let out a string of curse words and his hand rested on the back of her head. It was crazy having that kind of control over a man.

She slid her mouth further, just enough that it caused her to choke, and Dylan's grip on her hair tightened.

"Son of a fucking bitch!"

The uninvited voice caused them both to flinch. Lucy fell to her side, and Dylan rushed to pull up his pants as Blake stood in the doorway, white-faced and mouth agape. Dylan stumbled to his feet. "We were uh, um..."

Blake and Dylan stared at each other before Blake finally spoke. "It's settled. Now we're even. I don't want to talk about this ever again."

Rule #129: Only give blowjobs behind locked doors.

Epilogue

Dylan

*E*ight months later...

"Can you go see if Sam has my tie? I can't find it any-where." Blake's room looked like a tornado had gone through it by the time Dylan entered. There was clothing everywhere—on the floor, tossed on the bed, stacked on top of the boxes they had in the corner, ready to go to the new house.

"What have you done in here, dude?"

Blake growled at him, and Dylan was sure he was behaving worse than a lion let out of its cage at the zoo. "Do I look like I know what I'm doing right now?"

"You didn't need to do show and tell. You already have an outfit for today." Dylan chuckled.

"It's hot in this monkey suit." He tugged at the neck of his dress shirt. Dylan lifted a few items of clothing off the bed and located the missing tie.

"I think you're looking for this." He wrapped the green tie around Blake's neck and straightened it. "Everything good?"

"How's Sam?"

"She looks beautiful. I don't think I've ever seen her in a dress, and I have to say my dad is a blubbering mess because it was Mom's dress." Blake's hand ticked nervously at his side. "I'm not sure white suits her, not with that potty mouth of hers and the way you two whores go at it."

Blake's hand hit the back of his head, and Dylan tightened the tie tighter than necessary. "Tell me how that works out for you when you propose to Lucy."

"Don't talk about Lucy like that." He grinned. "You know she's the angel of my life."

"So, when is the big day? I know you've been carrying that ring around for a month now." Dylan stared at his friend.

"How did you..."

"You left your jacket on the counter when we were doing the walkthrough of the apartment last week."

"Fuck, I need to be more careful." Dylan stepped back, admiring his amazing skill. The tie was lopsided, but at least it was on. "You might want your mom to fix that."

"So?"

Dylan grinned. "I'm waiting until we're settled in here, after the book launches." He could hardly believe that in another month, they would move into Blake and Sam's apartment and he would become a published author.

"Good for you. You deserve it. Lucy, the book, all of it. I'm just really happy for you, Dylan."

"Don't go getting sappy on me now. It's almost go time, and I swore to Sam I'd keep you from crying until I got you to the altar."

Blake's hands were on both of his shoulders, and his forehead pressed against his. "Brothers for life, man."

Dylan softly whispered. "Yeah, brothers for life."

There wasn't a dry eye left on the rooftop during the wedding. A rare occurrence for a Lancaster event. But Sam wasn't a Lancaster anymore; she was Samantha Forrester. And this Sam cried. A lot. By the time he got to dance with his sister, he figured she would be fresh out of tears. But as the lights twinkled that night on the rooftop, her cheeks wet with tears, he had guessed wrong. "Since when did this family cry so much?"

Sam's head fell back with a light laugh. "I think it's a good change."

"Yeah, maybe."

"You certainly looked happy tonight." She tussled his hair. "Love looks good on you."

"Yeah, who would have thought, huh?"

"You and Lucy are going to be so happy at our place. And before you know it, it's going to be the two of you up here." Dylan looked down, hiding the giant smirk on his face before looking around the roof to find Lucy sitting next to his father, chatting excitedly.

"Is that what you think?"

"I'm not blind, Dilly Bear."

"Speaking of not being blind, can we talk about Allison?" He leaned toward her ear. "Is it just me, or is she swapping out her alcohol tonight?"

"Oh my God, I was going to ask you the same thing, but then I thought for sure Jax would have said something if it were true." Sam turned discreetly and then spun back toward him. "She just gave her beer to Jax and drank water instead."

"So, we agree. She's definitely pregnant."

Sam gestured as Jax got up and walked toward the bar. "You want to interrogate a sibling with me?"

"Now you're speaking my language."

Together they danced toward the bar, spinning along the outer edges of the dance floor until they "accidentally" tripped into Jackson. "Well, look who we found, Sam. It's our oldest brother, Jackson."

"Imagine running into you over here at the bar." Sam wrapped an arm around Jax's shoulder, who looked positively spooked by their sudden interest in him. "How ya doing, bro?"

"What do you two want?" He eyed them both suspiciously.

"Why do we need to want anything? Can't we just miss you?" Dylan asked.

"No, not when you're together. What gives?"

"We were just observing that Allison appears really thirsty for water tonight?" Sam leaned against her brother and smiled.

Jax groaned. "Can you two losers be less observant for once?"

"So, it's true?" Sam asked, her voice rising three tones.

"Would you hush? Allison didn't want to tell anyone. We were trying to be respectful of your wedding."

Sam wrapped her arms around his neck, squealing in delight. "I'm so happy for you."

"We only found out a few months ago," Jax said, a smile playing on his lips as he glanced at Allison. "Nobody knows." Allison watched, a puzzled expression on her face, trying to decipher the exchange between him and his siblings.

"We'll keep it quiet, but congrats, bro. I'm happy for you." Dylan couldn't believe his brother was going to be a dad. The fact that anyone let him procreate was a miracle.

Later that evening, as they sat around the table, exhausted from all the dancing, Allison held tightly to the bouquet she had caught earlier that evening. "Now you'll be the next one to get married," Lucy said with a cheerful laugh.

Jax smiled at the redhead seated next to him and rubbed her leg. And Dylan was sure it wouldn't be long before there was news of a baby and another wedding to attend.

"Is anyone else seeing this?" Dylan followed Blake's stare onto the makeshift dance floor as he watched his mother swaying with his father. They were huddled close together, his hands low on her waist. "Do they look especially close to anyone else?"

Blake's observance wasn't wrong. His father's hands were intimately close to Linda's backside. "Um, that is..."

Sam and Jax exchanged glances. "Are they, uh..." Sam's mouth was open as Blake leaned closer to the table.

"What are you all gawking at?" Kelley approached the table, with Gretchen attached to her arm.

"Is Mom a little close to Ken?" Blake asked his sister, who turned and looked at the dance floor.

Kelley snorted and turned back to the table. "Of course she is. They've been dating since Christmas, at least."

"What?" everyone at the table shouted at once.

"Did they tell you that?" Dylan asked, blinking in shock.

"No, but I assumed everyone figured that out when we came to visit at Christmas." Kelley looked around the table at the reactions. "Didn't you guys notice them sneaking off together, or holding hands when no one was watching them?" When no one reacted, she just shook her head. "Am I the only one who pays any attention around here?"

Kelley left the table, and every sat in silence.

"Holy shit," Jax said suddenly. "You two just got married, and now your parents are dating."

"Shut the hell up, Jax," Blake growled. Sam simply ran her fingers through his hair and smiled.

Dylan chuckled as Blake sat quietly staring at his mother dancing happily on the floor. All Dylan could think about was his conversation with his dad that night on the roof eight months ago.

"When you find something, you hold on to it with both hands, and you don't let go, kid. Sometimes you don't get second chances in life, so when a good thing comes around, take the chance."

Maybe he should have known he was talking about Linda. It made sense; they had been there for each other over the years, after his mom and Bobby died.

When his dad looked up and caught his eye, Dylan smiled, reached over and took Lucy's hand in his and clenched it. His dad was right. Life was about taking chances, and if Linda was his dad's second chance, then so be it.

"You alright?" Lucy breathed into his ear.

He turned and faced her. "Yeah, let's get out of here."

She grinned from ear to ear, and Dylan couldn't wait to get her home and show her over and over again just how much he loved her.

Two months later...

The leaves were turning orange as they drove down I-8 and made the turn into Titusville. It had been a year since Dylan had been home. Lucy squeezed his thigh from the seat beside him. Dylan usually hated driving, but he made an exception when Blake let him borrow his Mustang, and Lucy looked damn beautiful sitting in the passenger seat.

They were making the drive to Titusville to pick up the last of his belongings as Lucy and he finished moving into the apartment. Living with Lucy was a dream come true.

Their apartment was a colorful, happy place, surrounded by drawings of Lucy and her butterflies. Oh, and their cat, Penelope, because Dylan made sure Lucy got her cat. So yeah, he was a cat dad now. That was a thing.

On days when he felt tired, he would come home and find Lucy standing in front of the stove, making macaroni and cheese or baking a pizza in nothing but an apron with bright red letters that said, "I read past my bedtime." Penelope purred happily at her feet.

Life with Lucy wasn't always perfect. Sometimes he would come home tired or moody and take it out on her. And she would remind him he was being an asshole, only she would use the word "a-hole," because Lucy still didn't swear unless he was rocking his hips into her, his hands on her breasts, and his mouth against her ear, telling her how beautiful she was.

But life didn't need to be perfect, because it was theirs, and that's all that mattered.

Lucy hummed beside him, and he glanced over as she turned the page in the book. "What part are you reading?"

"Grumpy Gus and Dilly Bear are fighting." She turned to the next page and smiled. "Dilly Bear is still my favorite."

"Of course he is." His book, *Mr. Jangles & the Oil Creek Adventure,* was set to release next week and Lucy made sure he brought down an advanced copy for Jax and Allison, so they had one for the baby, even though "Baby Girl Lancaster" wasn't due to arrive for another four months. But Lucy was pretty insistent, and whatever Lucy wanted, Lucy got.

Packing up his tiny apartment over his dad's garage didn't take long. Lucy seemed obsessed with anything that had to do with "Old Dylan." Every picture, every drawing. She wanted to save it all. Dylan wanted to see it all burn. But he let her take back whatever she wanted. Maybe one day it would matter.

They stopped at Linda's Diner for lunch. Lucy could hardly believe she was getting to eat at a place the Forresters owned. Stepping inside felt strange.

The eighties music still played on the speakers, but it felt different without Blake, Kelley, or Linda behind the counter. "Take a seat anywhere you—" His eyes landed on the one person he hoped to avoid. "Holy shit, Dylan Lancaster."

He tensed. "Hey, Donna. I didn't realize you worked here still."

She led them to a booth in the corner, and Dylan slid in as Donna stood next to him, blocking Lucy from sitting down. "You, uh, mind letting her in?" He gestured behind her, and Donna turned and smiled tersely.

"Oh, sorry, didn't see you there."

Lucy was staring at her, and Dylan could see the look on her face, the way she had tortured herself over Donna ever since she heard her name. Lucy took a seat across from him, and he smiled at her. "This is Lucy, my girlfriend. Lucy, this is Donna."

Donna stared at Lucy. "Oh, wow." Dylan cleared his throat, and Donna turned back to him. "Um, I'm just shocked you settled down."

Dylan shrugged. "Yeah, well, a lot has changed."

"Right, I mean, it's crazy, Linda leaving this place to travel the world with your dad. That's crazy, especially after Blake and Sam married. How scandalous."

Lucy's eyes widened. "I think it's really sweet, actually."

Dylan pushed her foot under the table and grinned. "That's because you're full of sunshine and happiness."

"Hush, I am not."

"She really is." Dylan looked back at Donna. "So, what have you been up to?"

Donna flipped her hair. "Well, um, I have another million followers on Insta. I'm sure you know that, though."

Dylan shrugged. "Not really. I don't have time for that kind of thing, been busy with the move and the gallery."

"And the book," Lucy said so proudly it made his heart soar.

"Book?" Donna stared at him.

"Dylan wrote a children's book." Lucy smiled, her voice so strong he almost laughed out loud.

Donna snorted. "That's hilarious." Then she looked at him and frowned. "Wait, she's serious?" He nodded. "Holy shit, what? A children's book—that's so, so, so not like you."

"Well, maybe you don't know Dylan anymore." Lucy shrugged and stared down at the menu.

Dylan picked up his menu and smiled. "Change is good, Donna. Change is good."

Dylan parked the car next to the gate and turned off the engine. "Are you sure you want me to come?"

"Yes, Lucy. I want you to come."

Dylan looked out over the steering wheel and exhaled deeply. It had been a year since he had been here. He stepped out of the car and met Lucy by the gate, taking her hand and walking toward the familiar bench under the tree.

"It's pretty up here."

"Yeah, she always liked it up here. We used to camp farther up the road when we were kids."

He reached the stone and brushed his hand across the granite, wiping away the leaves. There was a picture lying next to the stone. He recognized it as a photo of their family taken around the table on Christmas. A friendly reminder that Jax and Allison had visited here. "Hey, Mom, I brought a visitor." Lucy glanced at him and smiled. "Mom, this is Lucy. I met her in New York." Lucy sat down on the bench, and he brushed her hair out of her face. "I told you I'd come back when I was better. Well, I'm back, and Lucy is a big reason for that."

Lucy giggled. "I don't know what I'm supposed to do."

He sat down and took her hand. "It's okay, Luce. You don't have to do anything. Just being here is what I need."

She squeezed his hand and looked at his mother's stone. "Hi, Mrs. Lancaster. I'm sorry I never got to meet you, but I hope you know I really love your son and I'll take good care of him."

Dylan felt a tear on his cheek and reached up to wipe it away before he wrapped his arm around her back, pulling her against him to press his lips to the top of her head.

"Thanks for being here," he whispered.

They sat there for a while, sharing stories with his mom about the last few months. There was laughter and a few tears, but in the end, he mostly felt love.

"Come on, let's go home," he said after a while.

He stood up, and she lifted on her toes to kiss him gently. "I'll meet you in the car." Dylan nodded and watched as she walked silently back to the Mustang, leaving him alone with his mom.

"I know. She's the best, right?" He reached into his bag and pulled out a copy of his book, flipping to the front page as he looked around the empty cemetery.

"I brought this for you." He read softly from the front page, his voice cracking. "To the mom a son will miss forever. The father who raised him right. The brother who never let him forget who he was. The sister who stood by his side. The best friend who was there through it all. And the Butterfly Girl who stole my heart. I love because I am loved."

He set the book down in front of the stone and pressed his hand against the hard granite. "I love you, Mom. I gotta go now. But I think you know that we're all gonna be okay."

He stepped away from the stone and looked up at the sky, wiping the tears from his eyes. As he walked toward the car, he felt the ring in his pocket. His future was just beginning.

And behind him, the dragonfly fluttered away into the clear blue sky.

I love you, Hypothetically
Coming in 2026

I t all started the night before the *big lie*.

My best friend Holly was salivating over some hunky Hemsworth looking man standing at the bar while I was busy trying to lock down a tall, lanky version of Will Wheaton. Awkward, safe, and carrying on a conversation about something I had little interest in.

"Ash nazg durbatulûk."

Moisture pooled on my cheek, and I immediately brushed a hand against my face with my napkin. "Bless you."

His little scoff was an immediate trigger, letting me know I must not have been following the conversation for longer than I thought. "No, it's from the book. Ash nazg durbatulûk." He repeated, as if this would somehow make the words magically turn to English in my ears. "It's what's inscribed on the ring." Will, or Ashton at least I was pretty sure his actual name was Ashton, furrowed his brow before he leaned closer to me and whispered. "One ring to rule them all."

I snorted in the most unattracted way possible, nostrils flaring and the sound of a dying cat exited my mouth. Not that it mattered. The chance of Ashton and me enjoying a mutual orgasm tonight was getting slimmer the longer this conversation continued. "That about sums up marriage," I said.

Ashton wasn't a fan of my humor, apparently, because he simply stared down into his beer and shrugged. "No, Tolkien isn't talking about marriage. In the books—"

I should have controlled the heavy sigh that escaped my mouth, but I was always the girl in the corner with the resting bitch face or the first person at a party who vomited her emotions.

Last year we went to Holly's work friend's Christmas party, and everyone did that normal thing where they lied about how good the food was or how happy they were to hang out with people outside of work. It was going great until I blurted out, "Hey Stacy, I think you might want to throw away the cheese because it smells like ass and I think it's molding." How was I supposed to know there was something called marbling?

"Sorry, I think my friend needs me," I said, and I'm pretty sure Ashton breathed a sigh of relief the moment I left the table to pull Holly away from Mr. Hemsworth.

"I was just about to close the deal, Pip," Holly said through gritted teeth. Her fake smile was for Mr. Hemsworth, who didn't care. He was already moving on to the sexy redhead in a miniskirt.

I didn't give Holly another chance to argue before I had her halfway to the restroom. "I'm sorry, but I'm calling in a Sarah McLaclan."

Holly's head tipped back, her fingers pinching her nose. "You can't need rescuing that bad, not tonight, Pip! Did you see how hot Steve was? I think he could bench press me with one arm."

"My date is speaking to me in some form of Elvish," I groaned. "Dear God, why?"

I crossed my arms defensively across my chest. "I might have asked him the question."

Holly's eyes narrowed before she grabbed my shirt. "You didn't."

"In my defense, I was just checking to see if he fit my description."

"He's tall, with a sort of Napolean Dynamite aura to him. Looks like he just left a Star Trek convention, couldn't lift a dumbbell if you asked him to, and I think he asked the waitress if his beer had gluten in it. He checks every safety box you could ever want. Why would you ask him *the* question?"

"The Napolean Dynamite comment is offensive. Besides, I think he looks like Will Wheaton. He's kind of cute." Holly glared at me, and I knew she had a point.

But I had rules about men. Rules that I had put in place when I moved to California that were meant to keep me safe.

Rule number one: never date a man who's hotter than Ryan Gosling

No one needs to wake up in the morning to a man who looks like he just rolled off the cover of GQ Magazine. I had a hard enough time managing my own expectations about my looks. I didn't have time to stroke his ego too. Besides, there was nothing wrong with waking up next to a man who looked like he could be a science professor. Being smart was an attractive quality!

Rule number two: never date a man who puts *fitness above everything else.*

I worked at a men's health magazine, so I dealt constantly with men and their egos about fitness and muscles. If a man wanted to spend all day sweating in a room with other men, that was his decision. I just assumed there were better ways he could spend his time.

Rule number three: never date a man who doesn't get along with your cat.

This rule needed no explanation. The men I met were usually dog people. Meanwhile, I had a cat named Ellie. She was adorable to look at and also the meanest cat you would ever meet. So, most likely, I was never getting married as long as she was alive.

But most important of all was Rule number four. Rule number four was the one that usually destroyed all relationships I attempted.

Rule number four: never date a man who didn't like the Notebook.

Yes, it was cliche, and yes, it was asking a lot out of a man, but if you can't be happy watching Ryan Gosling and Rachel McAdams kiss in the rain and then sob under the covers when she lost her memory and they died holding hands, then you just weren't the man for me.

Holly cleared her throat. "And how did he answer the question?"

I closed my eyes and sighed. "He had not seen the Notebook, but he did tell me all about his favorite movie series of all time, The Lord of the Rings."

"Ah yes, I like that one. Orlando Bloom is hot as hell. Pointy ears are sexy."

"He spat on me while he was speaking in some other language about a ring. I'm calling in my rescue, *please*." I pouted, pushing my lip out and blinking my eyes at her. It was a dirty trick, but it always worked.

"Fine, but you owe me. Steve was really hot," she whined, pinching her lips together, staring back into the bar as Steve made a move on another chick in high heels.

"He's not worth it. The hot ones never are," I said.

She growled and dragged me toward the back door. "You need to grow up and date men worth your time, have a real relationship for once, Pip."

I shriveled my nose, stepping over the garbage pile in the alleyway as we made our way toward the street. "Ugh, no. If I wanted a relationship, I'd invent one."

"That's very mature of you." Holly glanced down at her phone as she ordered our Uber and shook her head. "When was the last time you had an actual date with a man you were interested in?"

I rolled my eyes as I mentally went through my dating deck in my head. "I went out with that guy on Saturday."

"One-night stands don't count."

I groaned. That cleared half my deck. "It's not like I was going to two-night stand the guy. He wasn't interesting. Plus, he failed to mention he likes to watch wrestling."

"One of these days, Pip, you are going to have to ditch your rules and stop running from commitment." Holly flagged down the approaching vehicle, and we slid into the backseat.

"That's not what I'm doing, you know!" I crumpled down into the seat and sighed. "Dating is scary these days. It's not like it was for my parents. The love of your life doesn't just fall out of the sky into your backyard."

I wish I could say I was exaggerating, but my parents actually began that way. My father had been working a nine-to-five job for most of his twenties when a gorgeous nineteen-year-old erratically drifted from the nearby skydiving school into his backyard. My mother was the breath of fresh air and lack of responsibilities he didn't know he was missing. The rest, as they say, was history.

"Pip, I've known you for five years now. You're terrified of letting anyone get to know you that is actually worthy of doing so. You're gorgeous, funny, and smart. Try being real for a change."

I stared out the window and frowned. "I don't need real. Right now, I'd settle for whatever will get you off my back."

And that, ladies and gentlemen, is called foreshadowing.

The morning of the *big lie* started like any other morning, with Ellie screeching on my chest, her butt in my face. Usually this worked as an effective alarm clock, only this morning, Ellie started her morning ritual fifteen minutes later than normal, which meant I was going to be late for work.

By the time I got on the freeway, I was already half an hour late, and I knew the only thing that would keep my tardiness from getting called out was a stop at Randy's Donuts. My boss, Mr. Boseman, enjoyed an occasional donut, but he couldn't resist the blueberry iced cake donut from Randy's.

It was a bit out of my way on my drive from my apartment in North Hollywood to my office in Burbank, but the reward was going to be worth the hassle. More than anything, I really didn't want to see the satisfaction on my coworker, Dan Wilder's face when I walked into the meeting late.

Dan had been extra annoying lately, always providing an extra jab or salacious comment about my articles. I worked for a men's health magazine, and while I was neither a man nor an avid believer in health and exercise, I was good at my job. My witty articles, though few and far between, had been popular among our readers.

But more than anything, I wanted the coveted marketing position that had been sitting open for the last two weeks. *(RIP Sean Murphy, we miss your humor.)* Oh, he wasn't dead, but Mr. Boseman didn't allow anyone to say his name around the office anymore, so he may as well be dead to us since Men's Weekly Magazine "stole" him last month for twice his salary.

Anyway, the position hadn't been posted yet, but word around the office was that Mr. Boseman would be announcing the posting soon.

I walked into the conference room with my head held high and a full box of Randy's Donuts. Of course, Mr. Boseman was delighted and thanked me for being ahead of the game and knowing that everyone would be exhausted from the long weekend and needed a pick me up. Dan was fuming, but it seemed to keep his big mouth shut for the rest of the day, which was the icing on the donut for m e.

My drive home went about as expected for someone living in the city. Traffic was horrendous, too many people went about applying the use of their car horn when there was nothing useful about it at all, but by the time I pulled up to my apartment, I couldn't help but feel happy about living another beautiful day in sunny L.A.

I collected my mail as I always did: junk as usual. No one ever sent me mail that came under my actual name. It was always "Resident" or addressed to Anderson Cooper. Who I am positive is not the silver fox who gets drunk every New Year's Eve on television. But nothing ever came addressed to Piper West.

Before I left the annex, I peered around the corner and peeked into the box next to mine. The corner of the magazine was sticking out just as it always did. I tugged and yanked it free, shuffling through the pages until I found the recipes in the back. This month's edition of Food & Wine had a recipe for Honey Walnut Shrimp. That appeared way too complicated for my nominal cooking skills. I thumbed through the pages until I located the drinks. There was a recipe for a Rusty Nail that looked promising, and I had all the ingredients. I carefully tore out the page and closed the magazine. Glancing around, I shoved the magazine back into the box and headed toward the elevator.

The door to the atrium opened, and I heard voices just as the elevator doors were closing. I peered through the slit in the door and glimpsed blonde hair right as the metal doors slammed closed. I stared down at my recipe, excited about my prospects of a good drink to go with my dinner of boxed macaroni and cheese.

The moment the door to my apartment opened, Ellie was at my feet, nipping at my ankles. "Hello to you too, my demon span angel." She shrilled angrily at me, her angelic face in deep contrast to the fact she was trying to claw her way up my denim pants with fiery eyes. "Mommy will feed you in a moment." I shrugged her off and decided I should feed her first or else I would never get around to my dinner without claw marks and bandages.

I had barely sat the food on the counter when the noise in the hallway alerted me to my neighbor's arrival home. Josh Burke. Tall, dark, and unavailable in 3D. I was sure that Josh had broken all my rules. He was hotter than any man I had ever laid eyes on. And he was always coming home from the gym.

I rushed toward my front door and tipped up on my toes to stare through the peephole. Josh was standing outside his apartment door talking to his girlfriend. (Name unknown). He had his keys in his hand and his back to me. It appeared they had just come home from the gym (again). I pressed my ear to the door to listen, like I always did when he came home.

"Well, you didn't tell me you were working late again." The un-known hot blonde was speaking in a tone that I didn't appreciate her using toward Josh.

"I'm sorry; it was a last-minute request from Mr. Lucas." Josh seemed very apologetic. I sighed and then covered my mouth be-cause I really was standing very close to the door.

"There is always a last-minute request from Mr. Lucas, babe. Grow some balls." The unladylike gasp that cleared my throat must have been louder than I realized because, to my horror, Josh turned toward my door. I scrambled away from it as if it had suddenly caught fire.

Ellie stared at me from the counter. "Well, that was just rude." I shrugged, walking toward my bedroom to change into my pajamas and settle into my boring evening alone.

By the time my water was boiling, my cocktail stirred in my glass, and the sounds of Avril Lavigne blared from my stereo, I had decided that Josh's girlfriend was no good for him. Obviously, she didn't appreciate him, or she wouldn't speak to him like that. By the time I was sitting down to eat my macaroni, I had decided that she must be a yoga instructor named Bridgette who forced Josh to come to the studio every day to do hot yoga and only allowed him to eat vegetables and quinoa.

When I started my second Rusty Nail, my phone rang. My mother's name came up on my screen, and I groaned. "You answer it, Ellie. I can imagine your life is more interesting to her."

When Ellie only purred, I sighed and answered the phone. "Hello, Mama."

"Pip, darling, how are you?"

It always started this way, the niceties. How was your day? Are you getting enough sun? But it never ended there...

"I'm great Mama, where's Dad?"

"Philly, it's Pip. She's asking about you." My mother's shrill voice screamed through the other end. I could hear a screen door opening and could imagine the enormous fields of my parents' farm in Colorado.

"You didn't have to call him in," I said softly, knowing it wouldn't matter. My mother was like that. She did whatever she wanted. She was always a free spirit.

"Is she on now?" My father's voice wafted through the line, and I smiled. I do miss them now and then.

"Hi, Dad."

"Pippy, are you getting enough sun?"

"Yes, Dad. I get plenty; it's California." I chuckled and then held my breath, waiting for the questions to come, because they always did.

"How's the job, dear?" *One.* "Are you looking for anything else?" *Two.* "What about prospects?" *Three.*

I inhaled deeply. "Mama, the job is fine. I'm doing great. I'm happy doing what I do."

"Yes, but you are better than those silly columns you write. They barely make it in the magazine; half the time they only end up online, and I can't find them anywhere. You know I don't do the internet, Pip." I shook my head and shriveled my nose. "I worry about you, Pip. I'd feel better if you had someone out there with you."

"I have Holly."

"Holly doesn't count. You two got lost crossing the street." My dad's stern voice is a reminder of the one time in college that Holly and I did get lost coming home from a party. We were drunk, but

I didn't want to tell my dad that. But of course, that is the only memory of my best friend that he ever brought up.

"I hope you guys bother Pax about this stuff, too." My wayward brother, Paxton. He was more of a gypsy than anyone in the family. He roamed across the U.S. like money didn't exist. "Speaking of Pax, where is he now?"

"Your brother is in Montana, but we aren't talking about him. We are talking about you. When are you going to settle down with a good man who deserves you? I worry about you, Pip!"

Now, maybe it was my mother's voice and the way she whined the last four words, or maybe it was the fact that I mixed those Rusty Nail's a little strong, but the next thing that came out of my mouth started the *big lie.*

"You don't have to worry about me anymore, Mama."

She shrieked, causing me to jump, dropping my phone, confused slightly at what excited her so much. "Oh my God, you're dating? What's his name?"

"What?" I juggled the phone, staring at Ellie, who simply meowed and walked away.

"I'm so happy for you, Pip. You have no idea how worried I've been and knowing that you have someone now. It just feels like such a relief." My mother was nearly in tears, and I was retracing my steps to where it all went wrong.

"Mom—"

"Pippy, we are so happy for you." My dad sounded so pleased. Worse yet, he sounded proud of me. "Now tell me the young man's name and how you two lovebirds met."

And so, this is how it all began...

"Well, his name is Josh, and he lives across the hall from me."

I'm absolutely not crying while I type this. Maybe just a little. I can't believe it's over. When I created the Lancasters in my head, it was supposed to be a one and done book. Dylan, Jax, and the rest of the family outside of Sam and Blake were supposed to be side characters with little backstory. My daughter refused to allow that to become reality and rallied for the other siblings to get their day in the sun.

After book one, I had so much I wanted to do with Jackson that I dove right into book two, and Jax's story quickly became my favorite.

I will admit I put poor Dylan through the ringer in book two and started to question what the hell I was doing to him. By the time it came to write Butterfly, I just knew I needed something special for Dylan. He had earned his Lucy.

Lucy's inspiration came while watching Dash & Lily, and maybe deep down from a part of myself. Though as my family and my friend, Cara, have told me, "Girl, I hate to break this to you, but all your female characters are you, in some way." I guess, as an author, we all have to come to grips with that at some point in our writing careers. Authors write what they know. And suddenly, all these little quirks and behaviors slide onto the page.

Dylan and Lucy's journey slowly became my favorite story to tell. It was heartwarming and bittersweet to build Dylan back up and send him on his way.

I want to thank everyone for coming along on this journey with me as we dealt with grief, love, second chances, and facing our demons.

I wouldn't have been able to do any of this without the support of my family. Gary, Eric, and Felicia: Thank you for always being there at the dinner table to bounce ideas off of, even when I know you guys were so tired of listening to me talk about these fictional people as if they were about to sit down to dinner with us.

Felicia & Gary, I appreciate you listening to every single chapter, for being my editors, my beta readers, my therapist, and for distracting me with F1 and trips to Goodwill when you got tired of it.

Faith and Bek: Thanks for being the first ones eager to support me all the way from Missouri. Hyping my book and always being my #1 fans. And no, Faith, I'm still not ready to write the prequel for what happened with Bobby, Ken, Mary, and Linda in high school, or as you have already named it, "Housefly."

Thanks to my parents and sister, Lori, for all the support growing up and buying my books, even though I wanted to cover them in sticky notes so you wouldn't read the dirty parts!

Cara: Thanks for all your support every single day. If I didn't have you to tell my darkest thoughts to, I would go insane. I appreciate having somewhere to bounce all my awful ideas, trash talk when I have writer's block, and have somewhere to go when I'm feeling like I'm having a bad day and don't know why I started this journey in the first place.

Team Goforth at work: Thank you guys for always supporting me in every endeavor I do and for being the great hype you've been for my books and dragging it all over campus when you went to the onsite, when it's totally NSFW!

And thank you to the company I work at for getting me started with the Quest. I couldn't have gotten these books off the ground without my passion project, and I appreciate that I work somewhere that believes in the people who work there.

Saying goodbye to Titusville, the Lancasters, the Forresters, and everyone in these stories was hard for me to do. I can't say they won't pop up as an Easter egg one day, but for now, the Dragonfly has flown away.

May she rest easy.

1. How did the Lancaster series explore themes such as love, trust, communication, family, identity, or sexuality?

2. Dylan finally found his happy ending with loveable sunshine Lucy. How did you feel about the main couple's chemistry and compatibility? Did you root for them or not?

3. Dylan's arc in all three books was the most emotional of all the Lancasters. How did the book make you feel? Did it evoke any emotions? Make you laugh, cry, or cringe?

4. Across the Lancaster series, who was your favorite character and why?

5. We met a few other characters in Titusville and New York, for example, Donna, Casey, Mrs. Hattie, Jamila, and Amber. How did the secondary characters impact or influence the main character(s) or story along the way?

6. What do you think happens to the characters after the novel concludes?

7. The books explored small town Titusville, PA, and the big city of New York, NY. Which do you prefer? City life or country life?

8. A lot of discussion went on behind the scenes about putting Linda and Ken together at the end of the book. How did that twist make you feel? Did you see it coming? Was it the right call?

9. I had a specific cast of characters in mind when I wrote the Lancaster series, but who would you cast in the roles for the main characters? (You can check out my Pinterest page @stacygoforthauthor to see who I cast on my book aesthetic boards for each novel.)

10. The series spanned a few different tropes: brothers best friend, enemies to lovers, grumpy sunshine, injury, but what is your favorite romance trope?

About the author

Stacy Goforth was born on the east coast but spent most of her young life moving from state to state and overseas with her parents. After settling in Arizona as a young adult, she found an addiction to sunshine and the ease of never needing to set her clock back again too good to be true and settled down. Now, 20-plus years later, she has grown a life with her husband, four children, one grandchild, two dogs, and two cats.

After spending the last 14 years writing fanfiction for shows like Glee, Once Upon a Time, and Bridgerton, she created The Lancasters, with Dragonfly, A Lancaster Novel, the first book in the series. To hear more about her thoughts, writing process, and book ideas, you can join her on the following social media sites:

Instagram *@stacygoforthauthor*

Tumblr: *https://stacygoforthauthor.tumblr.com/*

Facebook: *@stacygoforthauthor*

Website: *https://stacygoforthauthor.com/*

Sign up for this author's newsletter to get exclusive access to Digital Art. Joining also gets you access to other exclusive content like bonus chapters from the books, new POV chapters, and other artwork. Join by following the QR code.

Also by

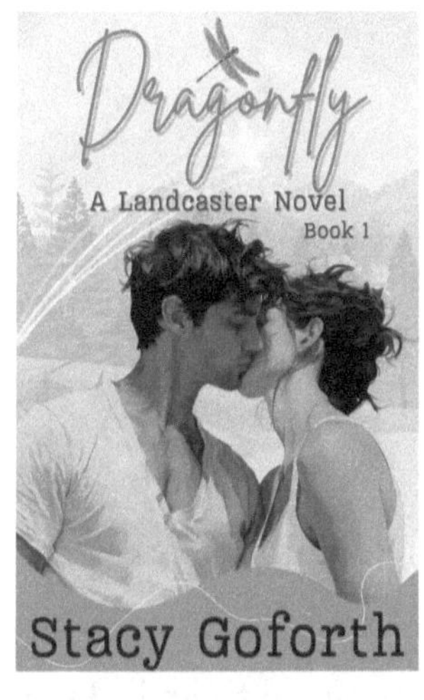

Dragonfly: *A Lancaster Novel*

Book 1

By: Stacy Goforth

Samantha Lancaster never thought she'd see Blake Forrester again. He was her high school crush, her unrequited first love, and her older brother's best friend. But when she returns to her hometown to help her brother recover from a motorcycle accident, she's suddenly thrust back into the world of know-it-all blonde bullies and awkward sexual tension. And to make matters worse, she can't seem to stop sticking her foot in her mouth.

Blake Forrester and Dylan Lancaster lived by a strict bro-code. But with Sam back in town, Blake can't stop thinking about her. He knows he shouldn't break the code, but the temptation is too strong. And with each passing day, the bro-code seems to become more and more complicated. Will Blake be able to resist his feelings for Sam and stay loyal to his best friend, or will the pull between them be too strong to deny?

For fans of forbidden romance and small town drama, "Dragonfly" is a must-read. With relatable characters and a steamy love story, you won't be able to put this book down.

Available on Paperback and eBook on Amazon and booksellers online.

https://books2read.com/stacygoforthauthor

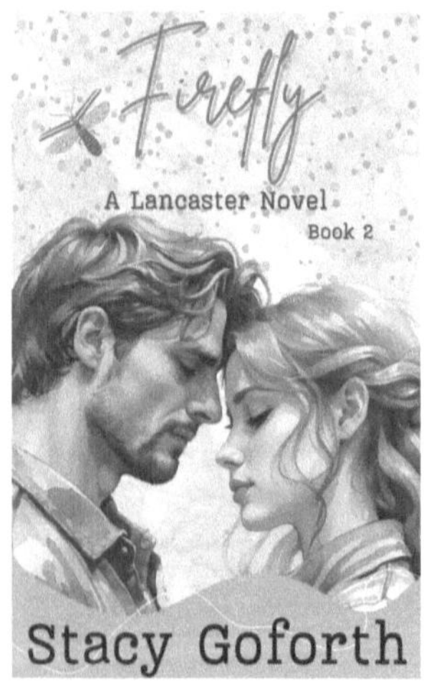

Firefly: *A Lancaster Novel*

Book 2

By: Stacy Goforth

Jackson Lancaster, a brooding and hardworking mechanic, is still recovering from a terrible motorcycle accident. But he had no time for self-pity, not when there were cars to fix and a livelihood to maintain at Lancaster's Auto shop.

So when his father sends help in the form of a fiery redhead named Allison Hanover, Jax is less than thrilled. He's a loner, a hard worker, and he certainly doesn't need some city slicker poking her nose into his business.

Allison Hanover had clawed her way to the top of the male-dominated world of real estate, but her success came at a price. When she's sent to help Jax with his finances, she's less than thrilled. Yet, as she gets to know the prickly and guarded Jax, she begins to see past his tough exterior and finds herself drawn to the man behind the scars.

As tensions rise and sparks fly between Jax and Allison, they both must confront their pasts and their fears in order to find love in the present. But as secrets are revealed and outside forces threaten their budding relationship, will Jax and Allison be able to overcome the obstacles in their way?

For fans of small town romance and enemies-to-lovers stories, "Firefly" is a heartwarming and steamy tale of two people from different worlds finding unexpected love in the most unlikely of places. Don't miss out on this touching and captivating read.

Available on Paperback and eBook on Amazon and booksellers online.

https://books2read.com/stacygoforthauthor

This book contains the following content that may be disturbing to some readers: Mention of death of a parent due to an illness (Cancer), alcohol use, sexual content, thoughts of suicide, and swearing.